The Millstone Crusade

Joshua Fields

Published by Joshua Fields, 2022.

ISBN 978-0-9915352-7-9

Table of Contents

1 – Mustard Seeds

"... but whoever causes one of these little ones who believe in Me to stumble, it would be better for him to have a heavy millstone hung around his neck, and to be drowned in the depth of the sea." The Gospel of Matthew 18:6.

Father Ray watched in astonishment as fifteen-year-old Judas Trent's fist flashed forward and crashed into the squat, muscular boy's chin. The sudden strike sent the stunned youth to the blacktop.

"Not today, Judas," muttered Father Ray. Dashing past them in a burst of speed, Judas evaded the late swings of the two other boys and then spun around to face them as they charged. Their comrade moved very little.

"Nigger lover!" yelled the shortest of his assailants, both of whom were older than Judas. Sidestepping the advance of the red-haired, freckled-faced teenager, Judas accelerated forward, placed a hand on his chest and wrapped his leg around his shin. A hard shove caused the boy to immediately fall backward and careen into the pavement. The third teenager, who was taller than his companions, turned to pursue Judas but stumbled over his friend and fell to the ground next to him.

Judas veered towards the line of cars in the Summerfield High School parking lot. Deftly grabbing a long, metal pipe from the back of a pickup truck, he returned to defend his ward.

"We're gonna kill you," snarled the tall boy, a handsome, dark-haired teenager with squared-shoulders and a broad chin. His companions stood behind him and scowled. Undaunted by the hyperbolic threat, Judas spun the pipe like a bo staff and readied for the next wave of attacks. His body remained inert but his eyes flickered with blue flames.

"Then do it," Judas said hauntingly, the blue flames burning low and becoming embers. A heightened awareness arose within Judas at that very moment and, unlike before, it allowed him to perceive every living thing around him. He acutely felt the boys' life forces from the beating of their hearts to the coursing of their blood to the electrical impulses in their brains. Sensing the overwhelming hostility emanating from the tall boy, he

1

concentrated on him and thought of blotting out his spiritual signature. The boy abruptly lost consciousness and fell to the ground.

"*All right*. That's enough."

The deep, raised voice of Father Ray boomed and rolled over the parking lot. Judas's remaining assailants froze and looked to him with frightened faces while the tall boy stirred and sat up as if awaking from a coma.

"What the hell's going on here, boys?" asked Father Ray, his voice returning to its normal volume and tone. A brown-haired man of average height and weight, he wore the traditional, black garb of a priest with a white clerical collar.

"These three still think it's the 1960s, Father," answered Judas, his angered attention loosely attached to his opponents as he pondered his newfound ability. Behind him, a black teenager sat on the ground and used his shirt sleeve to wipe away the blood from his nose. Twirling the pipe again but feeling as if he did not need it, Judas sneered, "So I'm going to teach them what decade it is."

"He, he attacked us with the pipe," insisted the redheaded boy anxiously as he and his companions fearfully scowled at Judas. Returning their vitriolic expressions without trepidation, he slammed the pipe to the ground twice. The resultant clangs caused them to start, each boy taking several steps backward. The tall boy did so by reverse crab-walking.

"I said *enough*!" barked Father Ray, his intimidating voice returning. He studied the tall boy and asked, "Are you okay?"

"Y-y-yeah," stuttered Ethan Barnes as he cautiously rose to his feet and dusted himself off. He kept his eyes glued to Judas.

"Good," replied Father Ray. Gesturing towards the black boy, he instructed the three white teenagers, "Gentlemen, don't just stand there. Help your classmate up."

All eyes save those of Judas darted to the priest but the boys faltered and averted their gazes under the brilliance of his sharp eyes. The youths hesitated, each one wondering if Father Ray simply toyed with them for his amusement.

"Let's go, gentlemen. Chop-chop," Father Ray ordered them with two claps of his hands. Slowly at first but then with increasing speed, the triumvirate moved past Judas while giving him a wide berth. Father Ray folded his arms and supervised them as they carefully lifted Mike Jarrett from the ground and he, with wide, uncertain eyes, accepted their assistance. Nodding in approval, Father Ray added, "Take him to the office and get him patched up. And remember: 'Truly I say to you, to the extent you did it to one of these brothers of mine, even the least of them, you did it to Me.'" (Matthew 25:40).

"Okay, Father," said Ethan to the puzzled looks of his companions. Judas seethed.

"And boys," called out Father Ray, "I want you to stay with him until he's all set."

"Yes, Father," said Ethan while Mike Jarrett and the other two boys looked at Father Ray as if he were insane. They paused, pondered his strange command and then, urged forward by Ethan, walked off in silence. The priest watched them depart into the building and then turned his attention to Judas.

"Guys like that don't take verbal instruction well," grumbled Judas, the teenager furious with Mike's attackers and disapproving of Father Ray's methods. He felt an elusive disappointment in the thirtysomething priest and it angered him. Refusing to look at Father Ray, Judas restlessly tapped the pipe on the ground and said with ire, "They needed a different type of teaching. Now they won't get it."

"Perhaps, but you could've killed one of those boys with that pipe," Father Ray commented, his words constituting more of a warning than a charge of wrongdoing.

"I could've killed them without the pipe," Judas stated coldly. He took the abrupt revelation of his new power in stride and without any fear. Father Ray's expression became grave.

"Judas, Judas, Judas," said Father Ray while shaking his head disapprovingly. Studying Judas as he stood with the improvised weapon in his right hand, the cleric added, "They suspended you for two days, ya' know."

"Yeah," replied Judas impatiently, "I know."

"'But I say to you, do not resist an evil person; but whoever slaps you on your right cheek, turn the other to him also,'" Father Ray recited with a shrewd look of discernment. (Matthew 5:39). He held out his open hand.

"What if it's not my cheek?" asked Judas pointedly and without delay. He turned to Father Ray with a somber mien and prepared for a rebuke. He instead received a wise smile.

"That, young man, is for you to figure out," Father Ray replied. Grasping the pipe, he held it until Judas released it and added, "But in the meantime, no more using weapons against your classmates. Understood?"

Sensing the Holy Spirit working within Judas, Father Ray tapped the pipe on the ground. The troubled teen reluctantly obeyed his command with simmering anger and nodded his head in the affirmative.

"And Judas," Father Ray said.

"Yeah," grumbled Judas.

"Let's keep the other thing quiet for now, huh?" Father Ray suggested. Judas again nodded his head though without any anger. Father Ray pointed in the direction of his truck and said, "C'mon. Let's get you home."

******

The clear night sky sparkled with thousands of stars and a multitude of frogs boisterously sang their springtime tunes. Sitting on one of the wide steps leading to the doors of St. Arnulf Catholic Church, Father Ray gripped Judas's metal pipe and occasionally tapped it on the stone.

"Another beautiful night in *Mon*-roe County," Father Ray said quietly, the priest ruing the lack of pizza delivery in his rural parish. He patiently waited for the Wednesday evening Women's Bible Study group to wind down so he could lock up, head to the rectory and smoke his evening cigar. Reckoning that two vehicles remained in the parking lot, he exhaled and said, "Two to go."

Father Ray pondered Ethan Barnes's strange fainting episode. He lifted the pipe and swung it downward several times without striking the ground.

"Man, that was odd," Father Ray whispered, "that kid just dropping like that."

An engine whined and then sputtered to life, the noise chasing thoughts of Judas and Ethan from his mind. One of its squeaky belts drowned out the frogs.

"That'll be old Mrs. Kuras," Father Ray remarked with a smirk and a chuckle. He recognized the familiar sounds of her old Ford Crown Victoria as it trundled out of the parking lot. Its headlights soon flooded the hayfield across the street and Mrs. Kuras and Father Ray exchanged waves as he said happily, "That just leaves Vickie and Ursula and then Father Ray can go meet with Brother Jack."

Vickie Taylor, at forty-five-years-old, was one of St. Arnulf's youngest adult parishioners and a ball of faith and energy. Conservative in all aspects of manner and dress, the bespectacled brunette constantly urged Father Ray to shepherd his flock more actively. He knew that she would spend at least twenty minutes meticulously cleaning up after the meeting so he engaged in more stargazing and quiet thoughts. His mind turned to Vickie's niece, Ursula Baumé, whom she adopted after her mother's death.

"Speaking of odd," Father Ray said aloud as he shook his head. Mousey in personality and build, the cute, fourteen-year-old wore glasses like her aunt. She rarely spoke and often avoided eye contact. Sympathizing with Ursula's plight, Father Ray sighed and said, "I guess losing your only remaining parent'll do that to a kid."

A chilling scream interrupted the silent prayer that Father Ray said for the child. He leapt down the church stairs and charged towards the parking lot with Judas's pipe in hand. Rounding the corner of the building, he saw a dark figure wielding a knife. A body lay crumpled beside the front, driver-side tire of Vickie's blue Chevrolet Traverse.

"Oh, shit," Father Ray whispered amid competing surges of adrenaline and trepidation. Paralyzed as his gaze fell on Ursula, he watched the whimpering teen cower against the grill of her aunt's car. Her attacker taunted her by slicing at the air with a long knife. Unentangling himself from webs of fear, Father Ray charged towards them and bellowed, "Hey!"

His intervention came too late. The man haphazardly sliced Ursula across her right cheek and, with a second swipe, from her nose down to her chin. Her crying ceased as she fell to the ground and the man whirled around to meet his adversary.

Father Ray swung the pipe with all his might and, with a sickening crack, he connected with the side of the attacker's head. The man immediately toppled over backwards and lay motionless on the cement. Father Ray implored his Master for help with a single utterance.

"*God.*"

Pulling free of his suit jacket, Father Ray folded it and applied it to Ursula's face to stanch the bleeding. He glanced over his shoulder, confirmed the man's incapacitation and fumbled in his pocket for his mobile phone. A bloody cough from Vickie distracted him, Ursula's aunt bleeding from a stab wound in her stomach.

"Vickie? *Vickie,*" Father Ray beckoned hoarsely. Ursula stirred and attempted to speak.

"Auwnt Vic-kwie," called out Ursula despite her bloody wounds. She attempted to crawl past Father Ray but he held her fast.

"Easy kid, don't talk," Father Ray replied. He located his phone, swiped the screen and quickly accessed his dialer. Punching in 9-1-1 and the speaker button, he set the phone down on the ground and implored Ursula, "Hold this on your face."

"*Auwnt Vic-kwie,*" demanded Ursula in a commanding tone that send a chill down Father Ray's spine. His phone rang twice while she used her right hand to hold his jacket to her bleeding face and crawled towards her aunt.

"9-1-1, what's your emergency?" asked the 9-1-1 operator. Stupefied by the youngster's composure, Father Ray gaped at Ursula. She placed her left hand on Vickie's knife wound and bowed her head to pray.

"What're you doing?" Father Ray inquired though, despite the absence of glowing light or another supernatural sign, he knew what Ursula attempted.

"Sir, what's your emergency?" queried the 9-1-1 operator again. Failing to heed Father Ray or the operator, Ursula continued to pray.

"There's . . . there's been a knife attack at St. Arnulf in Summerfield Township," Father Ray answered harshly despite his heavy breathing, "and we need an ambulance and a Sheriff, yesterday!"

"Is the attacker still there?" asked the operator. Glancing at the motionless assailant, Father Ray confirmed his incapacity.

"Yeah, but he's taking a little nap," Father Ray said as he collected himself. Uncertain as to whether he should interrupt Ursula's efforts, the priest continued, "Two people have serious knife wounds. *We need that ambulance.*"

Ursula lifted her head with difficulty and exhaled. Tugging up her aunt's blouse, she revealed the blood-stained yet unblemished skin in the area where she was stabbed. The operator continued speaking but Father Ray ignored her.

"*1508*," he uttered cryptically with wide eyes. A second chill not only rippled down his spine but wracked his entire body. Vickie began to stir. Father Ray, astounded by Ursula's gift, quickly removed his jacket from her face and pressed her right hand to her lacerations. Her horrific wounds bled profusely as she wavered on the edge of lucidity.

"Now it's your turn, kid," Father Ray begged Ursula desperately. He implored her, "C'mon, do it. *Ya' gotta do it.*"

"Let no one seek his own good, but that of his neighbor," said Ursula in a strong, clear voice despite her disfiguring injury. (1 Corinthians 10:24). She gazed at Father Ray with blue eyes set beneath prominent eyebrows before swaying and losing consciousness.

"Ursula!" called Father Ray as a recovering Vickie screamed and reached out to her niece. Wrapping her face in his jacket and applying pressure to it once again, he yelled at the phone, " We need that ambulance!"

"Sir, what's happening?" asked the 9-1-1 operator with growing concern. A distraught and frightened Vickie bawled and pawed at her niece while Father Ray engulfed Ursula in his arms.

"Send the damn ambulance!" Father Ray ordered. Locking eyes with his panicking parishioner, he said in a calm, deep voice, "Vickie, get a blanket. We gotta keep her warm."

Vickie paused but, after regaining her senses, nodded her head and scampered off with tears streaming down her cheeks. Rocking Ursula back and forth like an infant, Father Ray prayed and listened intently for sirens.

"I know you're gonna spare her," he said earnestly to God. Sensing the strength of life within her despite her injuries, he asked, "*But for what?*"

******

A scattered herd of thunderstorms roamed across the area, their passage bringing periodic downpours and chain lightning that illuminated the entire sky. Flashes rippled overhead, their white light exploding like colorless fireworks, and thunder boomed all around them.

Tamara Parker tapped her metallic-blue cane on the floor. Her thick, natural hair tumbled over her shoulders, its rich, blonde tresses seemingly tinted with orange. Short for an eighth grader, she wore no makeup on her pale skin and sported dark circles under her blackish-brown eyes. Her cute, rounded nose was prominent and overshadowed only by her uniquely hued hair

"It'll be a sparse crowd tonight," conceded Tammy's mother as she alternated between watching the road and watching the storms. The rain lessened as they neared St. Arnulf amid nature's light show. Her mother added with a glance and a grin, "Seniors don't do bad weather."

"It's a sparse crowd *every* night," Tammy replied with a dubious expression. She then returned her gaze to the rain-soaked countryside. Far ahead on the left, she noticed an orangish flash of lightning. Tammy straightened up.

"That was weird," said Tammy, the teenager puzzled by the bolt's strange hue. The flash, however, did not fade away but steadily grew into a scintillating glow on the thick clouds. Tilting her head as she examined it, she inquired, "What's that over there?"

The rain slackened to a drizzle as the vehicle sped forward and the glow on the clouds increased in size. The light flickered but remained constant.

"It almost looks like something's on fire over there," remarked Tammy's mother, her concern growing with each word she spoke. She inhaled as if to say more but caught her breath and remained mute. Depressing the accelerator, she grasped the steering wheel with white knuckles and stared forward. The rain ceased.

"Oh, shit, it's the church," Tammy said. Despite her vision being obscured by a thick tree line, she detected glimpses of a large fire beyond it.

"Tammy!" scolded her mother. She drove quickly past the tree line and, across the hayfields, they saw St. Arnulf burning. Tammy's mother shrieked, "Oh, no!"

She hung a harrowing right turn onto Cornette Street, the abruptness and speed of her turn causing the tires to slide. Regaining control of the vehicle, she drove past the church and swung into the parking spaces in front of the rectory. A quick stop threw both passengers forward against their seatbelts.

Tammy noticed Father Ray standing motionless in the parking lot between the church and the rectory. Deftly unfastening her seatbelt, she disembarked and hobbled to the priest. Her mother exited from the vehicle as well but froze when her eyes fell on the immensity of the raging fire.

"A quarter mile that way, it's raining," Father Ray said as Tammy halted next to him and he pointed his thumb over his shoulder. He smoked his evening cigar, the priest occasionally studying its burning end. Gesturing in frustration, Father Ray complained bitterly, "That storm drifted right by us, just a few hundred yards away. Ya' know, the rain just might've helped. Of course, the fact that there's an apartment building fire in progress and a ten-car pileup on 23 did *not* help."

"Sorry, Father," Tammy said with a disheartened look. Insinuating herself underneath Father Ray's right arm, she wrapped her left arm around his torso and clung to him.

"Well, there are two ways to look at this," Father Ray said to Tammy while watching flames engulf the church. A stained-glass window shattered and tongues of fire extended out of it to lick the side of the building. Father Ray expounded in a somber-yet-noble tone, "We can remember the legend of our patron saint, St. Arnulf, who, as a raging fire threatened the French town of Metz, stood before the flames and declared, 'If God wants me to be consumed, I am in His hands.' He then performed the sign of the cross and the fire immediately receded."

Tammy glanced at the eerie silhouette of Father Ray against the backdrop of the stormy sky. Irked by his inaction, she detached from him, performed the sign of the cross and stepped forward to challenge the fire. Father Ray, however, grasped her by the arm and yanked her back. Tammy struggled against him but he held her firmly and, as part of the building collapsed, she reversed course and clung to him again. Her mother clambered back into her car and, fishing out her mobile phone, frantically called 9-1-1.

"Or, in the alternative, we can remember the immortal words of Janine Melnitz from *Ghostbusters*," replied Father Ray with an expression of resignation. He paused for effect as the steeple of the church gave way and then said, "'Yeah, it's a sign, all right: *Going out of business*.'"

Tammy disapproved of Father Ray's apparent faithlessness in the face of adversity. She unentangled herself from him and stepped away.

"Aren't priests supposed to have faith?" Tammy scolded him. Giving her a sidelong glance and a smirk, he closed the distance between them.

"Let me give you a little priestly advice, my dear," Father Ray said, the cleric amused by Tammy's rebuke. Lowering himself to her level and gazing on her gravely, he gripped her shoulders and continued, "Always remember this verse. One, because it's a little dose of reality for *all* Christians. Two, because if you accept it as truth, which it is, it'll strengthen you in times like these."

Father Ray paused as he listened to the thunderclaps rumble and viewed the brilliant displays of lightning dance in the East. Standing up, he released Tammy's shoulders and looked back to her. Her calamitous surroundings faded and she saw only Father Ray's emotionless face.

"'If anyone wishes to come after Me,'" Father Ray said grimly as he puffed on his cigar, "'he must deny himself, and take up his cross daily and follow Me.'" (Luke 9:23).

He pointed to the burning church with his right hand. Tammy watched the thin trail of smoke rise from his cigar and then turned her attention to the flames.

"My cross," Father Ray said. Taking his left index finger and pointing at her permanently injured foot, he nodded at her and said, "*Your cross*."

******

Father Ray sat on the open tailgate of his truck, the priest eating an egg McMuffin and drinking McDonald's coffee while observing the aftermath of the fire. The burned-out husk of the Church of St. Arnulf loomed silently in the thick morning fog that covered the area in grayness and moisture. He looked skyward.

"You couldn't burn down the rectory, too?" Father Ray complained after sipping from his coffee. He bit into his sandwich, chewed and swallowed before adding, "That place was more of a dump than the church."

"And there's nothing more pathetic than a priest without a church," said a distinctive female voice. Father Ray, despite being surprised by his mysterious visitor, failed to physically react to her presence. He was simply too exhausted and too defeated for extraneous movement.

"To the contrary," Father Ray answered with a sigh. Taking another bite of his McMuffin, he said through his food, "A priest without *a congregation* comes to mind. Ya' know, the whole shepherd without any sheep thing."

"I don't think that's a thing," replied the voice. Father Ray looked over his left shoulder and saw a woman – a tall, willowy and alluring woman - who oozed charm, exuberance and, more than anything else, unwavering confidence. Her emerald eyes and brilliant smile would have entranced and overwhelmed even the most unabashed chauvinist. Given that Father Ray was no chauvinist, she momentarily ensnared him with her feminine wiles. She seemed like a vibrant flower standing alone in a field of lifeless, gray vegetation.

"You the insurance adjuster?" Father Ray inquired before tearing his gaze away from his attractive guest. He tossed the remainder of his sandwich down on the flattened McDonald's bag, brushed off his hands and took a quick swig of coffee. Hopping off the tailgate, Father Ray threw a hasty finger towards the rectory and said, "I got everything you need inside."

Clad in a black blazer, expensive jeans and a bright-red, low-cut blouse, the woman sauntered up to him. Her rapt attention made Father Ray feel slimy.

"No, I'm not," answered the woman as she clacked forward on red pumps. Arriving in front of Father Ray, she said playfully, "*I'm even better.*"

Father Ray avoided her gaze by turning his own to the corpse of the old church. The destruction pierced his heart like the spear that pierced Jesus's side.

"Ya' ever think that maybe, just maybe, you're in the wrong line of work?" Father Ray inquired as he stared emotionlessly at the ruins of St. Arnulf. The words he spoke to Tammy the night before replayed in his mind: "*. . . it's a sign, all right: Going out of business.*"

"Not at all," answered Aubrey without hesitation, "but I didn't just get punched in the balls like you did."

"Eh, I guess I can't complain," Father Ray continued while ignoring the woman's comment, "The Archdiocese'll probably just move me to another parish with more people, more responsibility . . . *more problems*. And the cosmic tumblers tumble . . . ."

Glancing to the woman and then beyond her, he noticed a black Jaguar F-type convertible parked on the east side of Cornette Street. The woman indulged in Father Ray's confused countenance while folding her arms and waiting for his mind to process her.

"Insurance adjustors don't drive Jags and wear jeans – stylish as they may be," Father Ray said as he examined the woman suspiciously, "so who the hell *are* you?"

"Aubrey Stillerson," replied Aubrey with a muted smirk and a suggestive gaze. She held out her hand but Father Ray hesitated to take it.

"And how may I help you this fine morning, Ms. Stillerson?" Father Ray asked as he relented and cautiously shook her hand. Her grip was unexpectedly strong.

"*Aubrey*," insisted the woman. Father Ray released her hand at which point Aubrey's smirk became a sly grin and she said, "I'm the woman who's going to build you a new church, Father."

Father Ray's expression became harshly incredulous but, when Aubrey showed no signs of cracking, his countenance softened and he laughed. He patted the side of his truck.

"This truck's gettin' pretty old," Father Ray said with a chuckle. Placing his hands on his hips, he nodded to her vehicle and asked, "Can I have the Jag, too?"

"Whatever you want, Father Ray," asked Aubrey in a tone of earnestness, the blonde delighting in her continued besting of Father Ray. His mirth faded when she mentioned his name and, placing his left hand on his truck, he leaned against it.

"Look, *Aubrey*, whatever you're up to here, I'm not interested," Father Ray stated. He returned to his seat on the tailgate and resumed his meal, expounding, "I haven't slept in over twenty-four hours and my church just burned down, so, if ya' don't mind, I'd like to finish my breakfast in peace."

Aubrey sneered and paused to ponder her next move. Several seconds later, she marched up to Father Ray, took his half-eaten sandwich from his hand and chucked it into the parking lot.

"Hey! I wasn't done with that," Father Ray growled as he grabbed his coffee and held it away from her. Aubrey planted a hand on either side of Father Ray and leaned into his personal space. He moved away from her but found little room for retreat.

"My Daddy left me a helluva lotta money through good, old-fashioned oil, and I made a helluva lot more by being a market genius . . . and maybe a taking few *shortcuts* here and there," explained Aubrey pridefully. Capturing Father Ray's attention and holding it hostage with her gravitas, she continued, "By some odd twist of fate – or, maybe more to your liking, the will of God – I just happened to be in metro Detroit this week, and I saw you on the local news last night, talking about all those poor seniors who lost their beloved church. And seeing those baby blues of yours made me want to buy you a new one . . . and even replace that dump of rectory if you want."

Father Ray squirmed under Aubrey's assault of his senses as even her perfume proved enticing. Extricating himself from between her arms, he slid onto his feet and stepped back from her.

"How 'bout we start with you buying me breakfast?" Father Ray asked warily, the priest wishing to further size-up the enigmatic Aubrey Stillerson and her too-good-to-be-true offer. Despite the centripetal force of her overwhelming presence, he sensed an elusive centrifugal force within her and it worried him. He pointed and said, "Especially given that you just threw mine away."

"Who's the blonde?" asked Tammy as she approached along the driver side of the truck. Defying Aubrey's look of irritation, she stopped next to Father Ray and surveyed her with suspicion.

"*Tammy*," Father Ray admonished her. Tammy snuck underneath his right arm and wrapped her own arm around his waist, the move appearing, at least to the tired cleric, to be protective in nature. She continued to examine Aubrey and, as she did, her countenance hardened and her eyes narrowed. Father Ray gestured towards Aubrey and said, "Uh, this is Ms. Stillerson. She saw our little disaster on the news last night and offered to help us rebuild St. Arnulf."

Aubrey bent over and placed her hands on her knees to bring herself to Tammy's level. She grinned haughtily.

"I've got a *lot* of money, little girl, so Father Ray can build a really big church," Aubrey informed her as she patted her on the head like a dog. Tammy pulled away from her hand and scowled.

"'It is easier for a camel to go through the eye of a needle than for a rich person to enter the kingdom of God,'" Tammy recited tersely while making no effort to conceal her dislike for Aubrey. (Mark 10:25). Father Ray cringed.

"Then why would anyone want to go there?" replied Aubrey brusquely. An awkward silence arose as Aubrey and Tammy traded glowers, the teen surprising Father Ray with her hostility. A rooster crowed in the distance.

"Well, that was ominous now, wasn't it?" thought Father Ray. Plagued by the recent convergence of powerful people and their destinies on his very doorstep, he faked a smile and asked, "So, Ms. Stillerson, how about that breakfast?"

2 – Sister Mystery

Father Ray poured himself another drink, slumped into his chair and set his glass on the desk with a "thunk". Exhaling in exhaustion, he closed and then rubbed his eyes.

"A mass, Last Rites, a wedding and a funeral all in one day," Father Ray sighed. The unexpected illness of a fellow priest thrust him into service on what he had hoped would be an easy Saturday. The construction of the new church also proceeded at a breakneck pace behind Aubrey's monetary might and business acumen, the project consuming much of his time and requiring frequent travel to the site. He retrieved his glass and griped, "Father Walt schedules too damn much."

"Hello, Reynald," inquired Sister Palladia in an Australian accent. Father Ray jumped when he looked up and identified the visitor standing in his office doorway. She looked much as he remembered her.

"Holy Hell, are you trying to give me a heart attack?!" Father Ray exclaimed. His surprise subsided as he studied his guest, his startled state becoming one of utter defeat. Sliding further down in his chair, he exhaled and said, "*Not you*. Not today."

"I see your feelings about me have changed," commented Sister Palladia with an offended grin. Noticing the cigar and the glass of whiskey on Father Ray's desk, she let her smile fade and added with disapprobation, "As has your view on the material pleasures of this world."

Sister Palladia wore the full garb of a nun with its white habit but her robes were maroon. A leather necklace hung prominently from her neck, the adornment bearing a small, wooden shield charm. The shield contained a large cross in its center which divided it into four quadrants, each one of which contained a smaller, carved cross.

"It's a long flight from Asia just to come here and break my balls about the booze and the cigars," grumbled Father Ray. He wished he had stayed at Divine Grace's rectory for the night as Father Walt suggested. A concerned Sister Palladia narrowed her eyes and examined Father Ray.

"The years hang heavily on you, Reynald," stated Sister Palladia sadly. She took a few deliberate steps into his office and, with an expression of pity on her face, added, "They've dulled your heart and your spirit."

"May I help you, Sister Palladia?" Father Ray snapped before gulping from his glass. Realizing that her concern only worsened his mood, Sister Palladia returned to the door and closed it. He sneered and uttered with disdain for his moniker, "And, by the way, it's *Father Ray*. Nobody calls me *Reynald* anymore well, except, ah, *never mind*. Not even my own mother called me *Reynald* so no one else needs to."

"My apologies, Father Ray," said Sister Palladia politely as she returned her attention to him. Father Ray lifted his drink to his lips and indulged in it. Folding her hands in front of her, Sister Palladia walked to his desk and advised, "I'm here to discuss Ursula Baumé."

Father Ray's attempt to drink his whiskey failed and he choked on it. Setting the cocktail on his desk, he slapped the front of his chest and coughed.

"Excuse me?" Father Ray replied while sitting up straight in his chair and continuing to cough. Retrieving his glass and gulping from it, he made a sour face and asked in a strained voice, "You're here to do what?"

Sister Palladia observed Father Ray closely. He met her gaze with the beginnings of a suspicious glare but swiftly transformed it into a puzzled look.

"I've come to speak to you about Ursula," said Sister Palladia, her comely face hardened with resolve. Her words sank into Father Ray's mind and he wondered if his labors to conceal his young charge's gift had failed. Sister Palladia seated herself and queried, "She's one of your parishioners, is she not?"

"Why aren't you in the Ukraine with the Sisters of the Holy Whatever?" Father Ray asked. Sister Palladia stifled a smirk and raised her eyebrows.

"Holy Family of Nazareth. But how would you know that?" inquired Sister Palladia, her expression causing Father Ray considerable consternation. He recovered quickly.

"So, what do you want with Ursula?" Father Ray inquired while forcing a disinterested mien. He smoked his cigar and awaited her answer.

"Well, as I'm sure you know, the number of Catholic religious sisters in America has plummeted since the 1960s," answered Sister Palladia, "and the dioceses around the country are looking for ways to encourage more young women to consider the vocation. The Archdiocese of Detroit is piloting a program where nuns with special skills or knowledge teach courses to high school students in attempt to expose them to the religious life without the pressure of open recruitment. It helps them see that we're real people who live fulfilling lives in Christ."

"Don't you need a Michigan teaching certificate to teach in high schools?" asked Father Ray as he exhaled cigar smoke.

"We can teach under an expert substitute permit," replied Sister Palladia. She grimaced as the smoke wafted over her.

"And, with your background, you easily got one to teach your beloved French to high school students," Father Ray interjected while waving the smoke away from Sister Palladia. Extinguishing the cigar in his desk ashtray, he grinned and asked, "Tricking 'em into Church service, huh? Always schemin'."

"I seek to bring them into the service, and the love, of God," countered Sister Palladia, the nun taking umbrage with Father Ray's characterization of her efforts. She stood up, her height and the shadows of the office giving her an intimidating aura as she said sharply, "Serving God is the noblest of pursuits. Service to oneself is fruitless. Some need to learn that fact . . . and others need to remember it."

"I serve God *and* myself, sweetheart," said Father Ray. His comment, as intended, stoked Sister Palladia's anger.

"You know what Christ said about serving two masters," countered Sister Palladia with blistering disapproval. Father Ray, prickled by her accusation, picked up his cigar and re-lit it with a match.

"And He was right," Father Ray replied after a pause. He haughtily exhaled a plume of cigar smoke that obscured his face and said in a haunting tone, "I love God and hate myself."

Sister Palladia's countenance darkened as she perceived the conflict in Father Ray's soul. She squelched her anger and composed herself.

"I'm sorry, Reynald," apologized Sister Palladia. She again folded her hands in front of her and said, "I thought maybe time would have healed old wounds but I see coming here only reopened them."

"Well that's arrogant," Father Ray growled. Sister Palladia's lips showed the slightest of quivers before she nodded at Father Ray.

"Goodbye, Reynald. I, as always, will pray for you," stated Sister Palladia. She headed for the door.

"Ya' tore me open, twisted me all up inside and then bailed," Father Ray jabbed as Sister Palladia's hand caressed the door handle. He asked, "What's God think of that?"

"I followed His will," said Sister Palladia while squeezing the door handle. Her stomach churned and she wished to comfort Father Ray. Judging the possible escalation of hostilities imprudent, however, she quickly exited as a suspicious Father Ray watched her depart.

******

Tucked away behind a high iron fence and encircled by a thicket of tall evergreens, an imposing statue of The Virgin Mary stood like a holy sentinel watching over those who sat beneath her. The twenty-foot-high, metal statue held out her arms as if a general imploring her troops to fight bravely in the face of overwhelming odds.

Her wise, beautiful face and feminine hands retained the comforting curves of humanness but her flowing robes were of a sharp, angular design. A heart rested upon her breast and a vertical, three-quarter ring formed a halo over her head. The Virgin's sandaled feet stood upon a circular dais of gray stone, the platform in turn encompassed by a basin containing small, gurgling fountains.

Sitting beneath the cherished and closely guarded feature of the new parish, Ursula prayed silently on a wrought iron bench. Several equidistant and identical benches surrounded the statue, each one placed on the outer edge of the wide cobblestone walkway that formed a ring around the basin.

"So much faith for one so young," thought Father Ray. He paused on the cobblestone path leading from the gate to the circular walkway to observe Ursula. A deep, horrid scar ran from her right jaw, underneath her cheekbone and to the bottom right corner of her nose before plummeting across her lips and down to her chin. Father Ray said to himself, "Although she doesn't seem so young anymore."

Ursula was no longer the mousy child he met months earlier. Becoming classically attractive and long-limbed since their first meeting, her brown hair was now flowing and wavy and her pelvis broadened with the curves of womanhood. Emotionally she remained in her shell but even now Father Ray perceived cracks in its façade.

"I'm not sure how I feel about that statue," commented Father Ray as he thrust his hands into his pockets. Appraising the metal behemoth, he said, "It's got a little bit of a golden calf feel to it, but it is beautiful."

"How can it be wrong to honor one who found favor with God," Ursula countered while raising her brown eyes to Mary's face, "and gave birth to Jesus?"

"'Little children, guard yourselves from idols,'" quoted Father Ray though he knew Ursula understood the difference between honor and worship. (1 John 5:21). He sat down next to her, crossed his legs and threw his right arm over the back of the bench, inquiring, "Startin' high school here soon, huh?"

Ursula lowered her gaze to the ground, the teenager abruptly going cold and silent. The breeze died just as suddenly and the sun disappeared behind a puffy, white cloud. Neither Father Ray nor Ursula said a word for twenty seconds. The priest realized she no longer wore her glasses.

"Say it," instructed Father Ray gently. His fondness for Ursula grew each time he saw her and witnessed her spiritual development.

"'If anyone wishes to come after Me,'" Ursula began in a sickly tone before her voice strengthened, "'he must deny himself, and take up his cross daily and follow Me.'" (Luke 9:23).

"You know how it works, Ursula, difficult as it may be to endure at times," said Father Ray while placing his hand on her shoulder. She indulged in his comforting touch and shook her head in the affirmative while warding off tears. Deeming the moment opportune, he said, "I understand you were visited by a friend of mine recently."

"What?" Ursula asked. The wells of her tears dried up and she looked to him with a wrinkled nose. The sun reappeared.

"Sister Palladia," answered Father Ray, the sound of her name in his head stoking his inner turmoil. He realized that his grip on Ursula's shoulder tightened in anticipation so he returned it to the back of the bench.

"Oh, yeah. *Her*," Ursula said, her irritation with Sister Palladia causing her to gloss over the connection between the nun and Father Ray. Incredulousness on her maimed face, she complained, "She wants me to take her French class. She's been bugging me for weeks. Aunt Vicki finally told her to knock it off."

"She didn't happen to say *why* she wants you to take her French class, did she?" asked Father Ray as he sat up with his gaze riveted to Ursula's face. He rested his elbows on his knees and clasped his hands in front of him.

"Something about me having a French heritage. I don't know. She researched it or something," Ursula said bitterly. She shrugged and sighed, saying, "She said French is in my blood."

Father Ray stood up, walked to the fountain and stared into the burbling water. Sister Palladia possessed a peculiar passion for French language, history and culture and traced her genealogy to a particular region in France, the name of which slipped his mind. Her apparent reasoning for targeting Ursula seemed plausible and yet, to him, it provided an unsatisfying answer. He felt Ursula's eyes on him.

"Father?" Ursula asked with uncertainty. Rising to her feet, she moved next to him and peeked upward at his troubled face. Father Ray turned towards her with blurry, hazy eyes that resembled staticky television screens.

"Did Sister Palladia talk to you about anything else? Anything at all?" pressed Father Ray. Deep in contemplation, he saw the outside world as a collection of blurry images.

"No, I don't think so. She just really pressured me to take that stupid class," Ursula replied with a subtle shake of her head. She sifted her own words, shifted her weight to her right foot and then said, "Well, maybe it wasn't pressure. She seems nice, I guess. She was just really intense about it. Father, what's wrong?"

Father Ray glanced into the basin again, the gears of his mind spinning as he weighed Sister Palladia's possible motives. He exhaled and decided to reveal his suspicions to Ursula.

"I think she might be here because of your . . . *gift*," said Father Ray after a pregnant pause. He returned his hands to his pants pockets and lightly kicked the side of the basin, continuing, "I'm not sure about that, but . . . well, let's just say I have my reasons."

"But no one knows about it except you and me, right?" Ursula queried. Despite maintaining her end of the bargain, guilt crept into her consciousness. Her worry swiftly mutated into distress and she said, "I haven't told anyone, Father, I swear I haven't."

"Relax, Urse, I know," responded Father Ray. She trembled as he encouraged her, "All we have to do is stick to the plan, okay? That's easy."

Ursula turned her back to Father Ray. The debate that raged in her mind for months finally escaped her lips.

"Maybe it's time we *did* tell someone else," Ursula suggested sheepishly. She tried to rotate her body to face Father Ray but her feet refused. Bracing for his response, she held her breath.

"Ursula, you have a generous heart but you promised me you'd hold out for now," said Father Ray, his voice interspersed with frustration and sympathy. Pacing and gesturing, he delivered a monologue: "Remember what happened when people found out Jesus could heal the sick? They mobbed him, coming from miles around to bring their sick so he could heal them. And that was before cell phones, social media and airplanes. Think about how many would seek you out *today* if you reveal your gift. It wouldn't be thousands, kid, it'd be *millions*. You're a viral YouTube video away from being inundated by a tidal wave of desperate people, and desperate people are dangerous, especially in those numbers."

Father Ray's demeanor darkened. Ursula shivered; despite her trust in him, his gloom-and-doom predictions frightened her.

"And not all of them would arrive with good intentions," Father Ray added with a haunting mien. Ursula's spirit warred with her discretion and, deeming an argument with Father Ray futile, she relented and turned to face him.

"So what do we do about Sister Palladia?" Ursula asked. She acutely felt the weight of her gift.

"You take the class," said Father Ray bluntly.

"What?" Ursula queried, the teenager puzzled by Father Ray's request.

"You take the class, Urse," repeated Father Ray. He glanced up at the Blessed Mother's face, smiled deviously and said, "Because, if you do, we might just be able to force her to show a few cards earlier than she wants to, and, even if we can't, she'll eventually approach you regarding whatever the hell she's up to. You've just got to be ready for it when she does."

"How do I do that?" Ursula whined. She felt slimy.

"I have a few ideas," answered Father Ray.

******

Father Ray shoveled a forkful of pancakes into his mouth and indulged in the warm, sweet taste. His focus on his mobile phone caused the clinking of plates and glasses and the din of numerous conversations to fade. Scrolling through the day's college football schedule, he sipped his coffee and selected the games he wished to watch in between his unusually sparse priestly duties.

"Good morning, Father Ray," Sister Palladia greeted him, the nun appearing as if she stepped out of a heavy fog. Father Ray jerked up his head to view her and, realizing who stood before him, he rolled his eyes.

"How the hell did you know I'd be here?" inquired Father Ray sharply while returning to his pancakes and the screen of his phone. Sister Palladia's knowledge of his activities prickled him but he did not want to show it.

"I'm having you surveilled twenty-four hours a day," Sister Palladia answered matter-of-factly but with the slightest of smirks. She slid into the booth opposite Father Ray.

"Sure, have a seat," Father Ray grumbled with a feigned gesture of welcome. Pointing at his chest and referencing his casual clothes, he said, "Ya' know, I'm dressed like a civilian this morning for a reason."

"Vickie called me last night. Ursula agreed to take my class," said Sister Palladia with gratitude and a gracious smile. Touching Father Ray's arm and gazing deeply into his eyes, she gushed, "*Thank you.*"

"Don't get all mushy on me, princess," Father Ray rebuked her. Enduring the contact for but a second before pulling back his arm, he wrapped his hands around his coffee cup and stated, "I did you a favor and now I expect one in return."

"Is that so?" Sister Palladia said as her grin disappeared. She offered Father Ray a dubious expression, withdrew her hand and sat up straight. Sipping from his coffee, he eyed her with irritation.

"Yeah, that's so," said Father Ray while setting down his cup. He tapped his phone several times to clear the screen and pushed it aside. Father Ray and Sister Palladia engaged in an optical battle for several seconds.

"Can I get ya' anything, dear?" interrupted an older, haggard waitress holding a large, circular tray. Dirty plates, cups and silverware were heaped upon it.

"Just coffee, please," Sister Palladia replied while faking a grin, albeit a weak one.

"You got it, honey," said the waitress cheerfully. Making light of her burden, she motored towards the kitchen while dodging misplaced chairs and wandering patrons.

"I heard you're teaching a class at Summerfield High, too," said Father Ray while leaning back and folding his arms.

"That's correct," Sister Palladia answered with several nods, the puzzlement on her face amusing Father Ray. He managed, however, to maintain a straight face.

"Well, I've got ya' a student for it," Father Ray stated smugly. Anticipating a lengthy response, he took advantage of the opportunity to finish his pancakes.

"I would love to help you, Father, but the class is full," advised Sister Palladia firmly. Placing her hands in her lap, she stated, "Plus I've hand-selected the students for my classes based on their French ancestry, their academic ability and their maturity. I need motivated students without behavioral issues, students who will immerse themselves in the material, embrace their heritage and develop a lifelong love of French like I have."

"That was a great speech," said Father Ray with cutting sarcasm. Engaging in puffery to persuade Sister Palladia, he said sternly, "But I really had to lean on Ursula to get 'er to take your class, and I don't like doing that, so, now, you owe me one."

Father Ray pushed his empty, syrupy plate aside. Leaning across the table menacingly, he glowered at Sister Palladia.

"I'm trusting you that her presence in this class is solely for *her* benefit," Father Ray said, his protectiveness of Ursula striking Sister Palladia like a volley of arrows. Guilt seeped through the cracks in her composure.

"Of course it is," Sister Palladia snapped while shrugging off Father Ray's emotional offensive and sealing the breaches in her poise. The waitress returned with a pot of coffee, deftly flipped over a coffee cup and filled it.

"There ya' go, sweetheart," said the waitress as she filled Father Ray's cup and scooped up his plate.

"Thank you," Sister Palladia said. She forced a smile until the waitress departed and then scolded Father Ray, "You're getting quite surly in your old age, *Reynald*."

"Oh, that hurts," mocked Father Ray, the priest confident of Sister Palladia's ulterior motive. Deeming it wise to play her game, he shifted course back to Judas, explaining, "As you probably already know, I'm the administrator of a small residential home for boys outside Petersburg, and I've been mentoring one of them for a while now. He almost failed his Spanish class last year which, for him, is ridiculous because he's smart. Incredibly smart. But stubborn. Mind-numbingly stubborn. And he hates foreign language classes."

Sister Palladia's demeanor softened. She sensed the Holy Spirit at work.

"And that's where you come in," continued Father Ray with a pointed finger. He glanced up at a passing patron and then stated ardently, "He needs a strong hand to guide him. Plus, your devotion to all things French will help. Ya' know, the genuineness and all that. I think it'll really resonate with him."

"I'll talk to him today . . . if it's possible," Sister Palladia vowed as the tension between them disappeared. She snagged a packet of Equal and ripped it open, advising, "School starts next week."

"No, not today," interjected Father Ray with a wave of his index finger. Sister Palladia poured the Equal packet in her coffee and stirred it as he expounded, "I know how the kid's mind works. You'll have to give him a couple weeks first. He's had all summer to forget how much he hates Spanish."

"Understood," Sister Palladia said with an easy smile. Her eyes twinkled as she felt Father Ray's love for his young mentee and saw a glimpse of the man she knew long ago. She drank her coffee and asked, "So do you think he'll enjoy French?"

"No," replied Father Ray blithely, "he'll just hate it less. And I'd keep my name out of it. It'll just make him resist even more. But I've got a name you *can* use."

"A name?" Sister Palladia asked, the nun intrigued by Father Ray's cryptic response. She set her cup on the table and held it with both hands.

"The only name you'll need," answered Father Ray with a crafty smile and a nod, "*Courtney Melendez.*"

******

The Summerfield High School auditorium buzzed with student activity as the teenagers filled its seats. Judas ditched his homeroom class and sat with his friend, Mike Jarrett, in a dark corner of the theater-like hall. His eyes locked on a laughing Courtney Melendez when she entered the auditorium with a group of chattering friends.

"Hey, Judas," taunted Mike, the fourteen-old-year-old offering Judas a mischievous grin, "there she is."

Courtney often visited Judas in his dreams, the pretty fifteen-year-old always approaching him in a crowd of nameless people with a blank look on her face. She would glance at him without changing her expression but, as she passed and exited his peripheral vision, he could not bring himself to turn around. His unshakeable bravery in defending the downtrodden did not translate into self-confidence with girls; he never mustered the courage to speak to Courtney in reality or in his dreams.

"Where's Steve?" Judas asked tersely in a failed attempt to change the subject and his focus. Stephen Carruth was Judas's closest friend and loyal wingman.

"Faking sick," answered Mike while scanning the crowd. Laying his head on the back of his seat, he eased into it and closed his eyes, explaining, "Monday Night Football flu."

Judas felt as if he were being pulled apart by the competing compulsions to be both next to Courtney and as far away from her as possible. Pale and round-faced with the slender build of a teenager, she was a mainstay in the world of popularity at Summerfield High. Two unique features set Courtney apart from all other girls in Judas's mind: lengthy hair of the richest black and blue, shimmering eyes that appeared alien in their size and intensity. Few could withstand her gaze for long.

"*There she is*," Judas thought with a glance at Courtney. He caught her waving to her boyfriend, Dillon Buck. The tall, yellow-haired seventeen-year-old nodded to her with conceit and, to Judas's dismay, she blew him a playful kiss. Nauseated and furious, he sneered and thought, "Now *I* feel sick."

"Let it go, man," interjected Mike with an elbow to Judas's ribs, the precise strike causing Judas a sharp pain in his side. Instead of a wince it garnered a glare to which Mike replied, "You could have Cara Gauthier right now if you wanted. She's pretty hot and *crae-crae* about you."

Judas's glare intensified. Responding with an incredulous shake of the head, Mike threw a thumb over his shoulder.

"She's sitting right over there," advised Mike, "staring at you the same way you're staring at Courtney."

"It's *not* the same," Judas admonished Mike with a return elbow. His head swiveled from side-to-side to see if anyone heard Mike's reference to his beloved Courtney and, as he did, he caught Cara staring at him. She immediately blushed and averted her gaze, her response stoking Judas's guilt.

"Whatever, dude," said Mike apathetically. Principal Olivia Messina approached the podium, her actions prompting a hush over the crowd. The aging, heavy-set principal's reputation for running a tight ship and devising brilliantly devious punishments for wrongdoing was legendary. Few dared challenge her.

"Good morning, students," said Principal Messina as her plump-yet-powerful hands grabbed the edges of the podium and surveyed her charges through thin-framed glasses. She paused and shot daggers at the few remaining students who risked her wrath by talking. Silence ensued and Principal Messina continued, "As you know, our county, our state and our country have a serious problem with human trafficking and, whether you know it or not, you are *all* at risk of becoming a victim."

"Blunt as hell," Judas thought. He experienced his share of conflict with Principal Messina but admired her quest for order and organization nonetheless.

"It's for that reason that we welcome Assistant Attorney General Melissa Thrasher who's come to speak to you about human trafficking and help you protect yourselves from it," announced Principal Messina with a pointed expression. A woman rose from her seat on stage to a round of weak applause. She was tall and skinny with short, dirty-blonde hair and donned a run-of-the-mill pantsuit. Pulling off her spectacles and waving them at the audience, Principal Messina instructed, "So, you know the drill: Minds open, mouths shut. Ms. Thrasher."

"Thank you, Principal Messina. Good morning," said Ms. Thrasher as she stepped into the bright spotlight and revealed her freckled visage. She folded her hands in front of her stomach and stated, "Before we get started today, I want to show you two pictures."

Raising a small device, she clicked it and brought up the image of a teenage girl on the auditorium's screen. The first picture revealed a cute, smiling high-schooler with pale-blonde hair and deep-blue eyes. Wearing a strapless dress comprised of red swirls of varying shades, she clung to the side of a handsome, tuxedo-clad classmate.

"This is Emily Fritz," said Ms. Thrasher while glancing at the screen. She grinned softly and looked to the audience, saying, "She lived not far from here in Lambertville and attended Bedford High School. She was sixteen when this picture was taken at her Homecoming dance. Her friends say she was sweet, and kind, and always happy. Emily loved animals and wanted to go to Michigan State after graduation to become a veterinarian."

An anger stirred deep within Judas's spirit as he anticipated the next picture. His countenance became cold and grim and he tightened his hands into fists. Ms. Thrasher pointed the device at the screen and clicked it again.

"This is Emily Fritz three months later," said Ms. Thrasher as a sickening and horrifying image of Emily appeared. Death clung to her: her skin was pallid, her face was dirty and her hair was unkempt. The auditorium became soundless save for the humming of the lights as Ms. Thrasher explained grimly, "Emily was abducted shortly after the Homecoming dance by human traffickers operating in Southeast Michigan. When local police found her on an anonymous tip, she was dead of a drug overdose. The traffickers hooked her on heroin, forced her into prostitution and moved her from house-to-house in Detroit. Unfortunately, her kidnappers vacated the house just hours before the raid. They left Emily there, wearing only an old, stained t-shirt and lying on a dirty, broken cot."

Ms. Thrasher surveyed a sea of stunned teenage faces and let the gravity of Emily's story sink into their minds. Her eyes soon fell upon Judas. She tilted her head with curiosity as she noticed the determined expression on his face and felt the heat of his rage. Uncomfortable under the weight of his stare, Ms. Thrasher clicked the device again and a list of statistics popped up on the screen.

"Principal Messina was correct in saying that you, *all of you*, are at risk," warned Ms. Thrasher with another quick look at Judas. Walking back and forth along the edge of the stage, she expounded, "Forty percent of human trafficking cases involve the sexual exploitation of a child and, believe it or not, most of you are still considered children. But being eighteen doesn't help you, either, nor does being male. Between 2012 and 2016, over sixty percent of the cases reported to the National Human Trafficking Hotline involved adults and about twenty percent involved men. And it's not just sex and prostitution. Many cases involved forced labor."

Ms. Thrasher clicked through several disturbing images of rescued victims of human trafficking, their faces blurred to hide their identities. Judas seethed at the iniquity visited upon the innocent and drifted into a trance.

"'Because of the devastation of the afflicted, because of the groaning of the needy,'" he said to himself without knowing the source of the words, "'Now I will arise,' says the Lord; 'I will set him in the safety for which he longs.'" (Psalm 12:5).

Sensing that someone watched him, Judas exited his reverie. A single face stood out in the field of heads.

"You okay?" mouthed Courtney, the object of his affection seemingly concerned by his intensity. Paralyzed by her attention and her penetrating eyes, Judas hesitated. He finally offered her a few affirmative nods. She responded with a warm smile and turned back to Ms. Thrasher. The moment was over.

"*Damn it*," thought Judas. Ruing his failure and unbearably ashamed, he availed himself of the rapt attention of his teachers and snuck out of the auditorium. Slipping out the nearest door, he chastised himself, "*Idiot.*"

******

Passing a recessed doorway at the end of a line of lockers, Judas sensed a presence within it. His fight reflex activated and he whirled around with fists up.

"Now where would you be headed, Mr. Trent?" inquired a strong female voice in an Australian accent. It belonged to an unfamiliar-yet-attractive woman leaning against one of the doorway's block walls. Her arms were folded and she studied Judas with wise, middling-brown eyes. Judas lowered his fists.

"Who're you?" Judas demanded while relaxing his body into a nonthreatening position. The woman, who stood six-feet tall with an athletic build, concealed a commanding aura like a floodlight beneath a heavy curtain. It seemed as if she expected Judas to appear at that very moment so, with a look of befuddlement, he asked, "Were you waiting for me?"

"Why don't we start with why you're wandering the halls during an assembly, and a very important assembly at that?" asked the woman with raised brows. Her tresses were dark-brown and lengthy and her skin was flesh-toned and flawless. She wore brown slacks and a maroon blouse along with a leather necklace and shield charm. The woman pressed him, "You wouldn't happen to have a hall pass, would you?"

"No," Judas admitted with a slow shake of his head. He noticed the woman's charm and a glimmer of recognition flashed in his blue eyes. The woman walked up to Judas with a wry smile.

"I'm Sister Palladia," stated the woman with an extended hand. An elusive tension arose between teacher and student as if two great powers vied for control but Sister Palladia showed no signs of hostility towards Judas. Realizing that he had no intention of shaking her hand, she gestured towards the doorway and explained, "I'm teaching French courses this semester at some of the area high schools."

"That's great," muttered Judas with burgeoning annoyance over his detainment. All the sisters he knew donned their religious garb every day, that fact prompting him to ask with growing suspicion, "How come you're not dressed like a nun?"

"My order doesn't require me to wear the whole getup all the time, and, of course, it's much more comfortable to dress like a teacher," answered an amused Sister Palladia. Judas's thoughts turned to Courtney and his despair returned.

"Look, I know I'm not supposed to be out here," Judas admitted, the teenager caring very little about his impending punishment. The embarrassment of his failure with Courtney caused his cheeks to burn and, with no desire to return to the assembly, he conceded, "So just write me up and I'll go back in."

"You've had a few of write-ups already," replied Sister Palladia with a knowing look, her revelation stunning Judas. Sensing his surprise, she continued, "You're pushing a suspension and it's not even October yet."

"I don't care," Judas snapped, his frustration with Sister Palladia igniting into anger and overwhelming his surprise. She absorbed his bitterness without emotion.

"I understand you're not enjoying your Spanish classes," ventured Sister Palladia, "and that you nearly failed your intro class last year."

"So *that's* what this is," Judas said incredulously with a roll of his eyes. His emotions stirred by Courtney and the mysterious nun's agenda, he chastised her, "You're just tryin' to fill seats. Isn't that a little manipulative for a nun?"

"I'm offering a mutually beneficial alternative," said Sister Palladia calmly. She walked to the hallway window and placed her hand on the sill, saying, "You avoid a suspension and it counts for credit just like Spanish. What do you have to lose?"

"They're two languages I don't want to learn, except I'll be behind if I switch now," Judas argued with a demonstrative gesture of doubt. He shrugged and said "That's what I have to lose."

"Courtney Melendez," said Sister Palladia, her words hitting Judas like a sledgehammer. His embarrassment spiked and he wavered, his disquiet prompting her to return to him. Pitying Judas due to his unrequited love, she assured him "Don't worry, Judas, it's not common knowledge."

Judas scowled but Sister Palladia remained reserved and unoffended. She folded her arms.

"Courtney's a good student and she's doing well in the class," Sister Palladia explained, "so she'd be very helpful in getting you caught up."

Judas's entire body tingled as he contemplated a semester of closeness with Courtney. He hated Sister Palladia's manipulation of his heart strings but the potential reward was worth it.

"Fine, I'll transfer," Judas grumbled. Bristling at his capitulation, he met Sister Palladia's gaze and said, "You've got yourself a French student . . . *Sister.*"

3 – The Match That Started The Fire

"Dillon, I mean it," snapped Courtney as she struggled against Dillon. He blocked her path like an offensive lineman, his efforts keeping her at bay as she attempted to move forward. His friend and crony, Kyle McMaster, accosted her cousin, Brock, amid a throng of spectating students in the high school parking lot. He cowered from his attacker as Courtney protested, "You're gonna hurt him."

"Take it easy," Dillon said while suppressing his laughter. He wrapped Courtney in his muscular arms and assured her, "He'll be fine. He just needs to learn when he can and when he can't hang out with you."

"Stop it!" demanded Courtney as Kyle shoved her cousin to the ground. Outmatched and overwhelmed, the spindly freshman simply curled into the fetal position and covered his head with his hands.

The encircling crowd murmured and backed away as Judas walked through it. Kyle, sensing the change in its mood, spun around and faced him. Dark-haired and swart with a ripped physique, the teenager smirked and haughtily sized Judas up.

"*You're* the kid who's kicking everyone's ass?" asked Kyle, his tone one of dismissive amusement. A few nervous chuckles rippled through the audience of high school students. Undaunted, Judas continued a direct trajectory towards Kyle as he scoffed, "Guess it was all bullshit."

Kyle's conceit was answered with a swift, hard right to the solar plexus, Judas's strike knocking the wind from his lungs and sending him to the pavement. The entire crowd observed in shocked silence and even Brock peeked out an eye to see where Kyle lay gasping for breath.

"You and I got a problem, Judas," growled Dillon with contempt after he reclaimed his senses. Releasing Courtney and walking to Judas as Kyle gingerly stood up, he said, "You've been spending a lot of time with my girlfriend. That stops today."

"Kyle, don't!" pleaded Courtney to no avail. Judas focused on her briefly and, to his surprise, she looked at him with both desperation and curiosity. It sparked the heightened level of consciousness he achieved whenever he defended the weak and powerless yet, spurred by Courtney's emotion, he achieved it to a greater degree than normal.

"'The exercise of justice is joy for the righteous,'" Judas said in a powerful voice, "'But is terror to the workers of iniquity.'" (Proverbs 21:15).

"What the hell does that mean?" snarled Kyle as he and Dillon balled their fists. Judas, however, moved like he possessed foreknowledge of Kyle's and Dillon's every move and planned his reactions in advance.

Kyle acted first, the young man swinging an errant fist that Judas ducked. The miss caused him to spin around and allowed Judas to kick the back of his knee.

"*Dillon!*" protested Courtney as Kyle plummeted to the ground. Ignoring his girlfriend, Dillion lunged at Judas but was met with a strike to the nose. It instantly broke and bled profusely. A truncated shout followed as Dillion fell over backward and hit his head on the bumper of a nearby car.

Returning his attention to Kyle, Judas delivered a measured stomp to his throat to immobilized him. The battered teen grabbed his neck and choked.

"Oh my god," said an astonished Courtney, her voice climbing above the ambient noise as the dumbfounded crowd slowly dispersed. Judas returned to Brock, who sat up to watch the altercation, and helped him to his feet. Stirring and groaning, a bloodied Dillon pulled himself up on the car bumper while Kyle rolled onto his stomach and lifted himself onto his elbows and knees. Courtney noticed them and called, "*Judas.*"

Judas met Courtney's gaze and then followed it to Dillon and Kyle as they attempted to stand. He scowled and stifled the pair's pained movements by concentrating on their life forces. The young men dropped to the ground.

"Holy shit," uttered Courtney, the only spectator to witness the bizarre occurrence. Frightened by Judas's supernatural power, she hurried up to Brock. Taking him from Judas, Courtney wrapped an arm around her cousin's torso and quickly ushered him away.

"Sorry about your boyfriend," Judas apologized to Courtney as she looked at him with uncertainty. Her eyes paralyzed him but, unlike most others, he withstood her gaze. Plagued by regret, Judas rued his poor judgment and thought, "Beat up her boyfriend and scare her to death. Nice, Judas."

"It's okay," replied Courtney, the girl letting her haunting eyes linger on Judas for a moment. Turning to Brock, she said, "C'mon. I'll drive you home."

Standing alone with an unconscious Dillon and Kyle, Judas watched Courtney escort Brock from the scene. The remainder of the throng melted into the sea of parked vehicles as Mr. Bennington approached.

"*Judas!*" he screamed.

******

A fuming Judas slumped onto the couch in the common room of Saint John Berchmans Home for Boys, the Catholic-run facility named for the patron saint of altar servers. Located near Petersburg, Michigan, the group foster home housed twelve male teenagers between the ages of thirteen and eighteen. The building was empty as the staff and the rest of the residents ventured out for movie night.

"I don't like it any more than you do," grumbled Sister Genevieve, the fifty-year-old nun's intimidating aura not entirely due to her size. The imposing blonde, who donned a light-gray skirt-suit and a modest, white blouse, stood six-feet tall with a solid build. Her austere, light-gray habit seemed too small for her head and her black veil flapped as she paced behind the couch. Glowering at Judas, she said, "I would've enjoyed going to the movies tonight with everyone else but instead I'm stuck here babysitting *you* because *you* can't control yourself in public. You broke that young man's nose, Judas."

Boiling with rage, Judas stared at the television. His intense focus on the screen caused the images to blur and all he saw was movement and the changing of scenes. Every word the nun spoke grated on his ears.

"Getting into fights at school, on outings, in the church parking lot, everywhere you go," scolded Sister Genevieve. Stopping and pointing a crooked finger at Judas, she ranted, "And don't you dare tell me you're 'defending the innocent'. *You're only fifteen-years-old* yet you run around like some crazed vigilante or bully-busting superhero. You're lucky you live in this day and age, young man. When I was fifteen, the sisters could still deliver appropriate physical punishment, though even then the world was becoming soft when it came to disciplining children. Take me back to the days of rulers and belts and I'd beat that violence out of you."

"Did she really just say that?" Judas thought. Displaying incredible restraint for a hot-blooded teenager, he remained still and silent just as Father Ray coached him. His former tactic of debating the morality of his actions with Sister Genevieve always failed miserably and lead to harsher punishments; therefore, his spiritual guide urged self-control. Father Ray allowed Judas full venting privileges after each encounter and promised to help him seek emancipation if he behaved himself.

"Who's this?" asked Sister Genevieve as headlights pulled into the driveway. She dutifully marched into the large foyer, flipped on the porch lights and peered out the front door's high, square window.

"Who cares," Judas mumbled. He had no desire to see the movie yet loathed his confinement to the house, especially with Sister Genevieve skulking throughout its corridors. Judas's mind centered on Courtney and how much she probably hated him. He also considered his revelation of his gift to her and muttered, "Father Ray's gonna kill me if she drops that info."

"Whoever it is they're certainly taking their time," complained Sister Genevieve with her hands on her hips. The car gradually rolled into a parking space but its driver remained inside the vehicle for several minutes with the headlights on and the engine running. Opening the front door and stepping onto the wrap-around, stone porch, the nun warned Judas, "Stay put, young man."

Judas, of course, disobeyed her command and moved to the front window as soon as Sister Genevieve shut the front door. Pulling aside the heavy curtain, he observed a shadowy figure emerge from the car and travel the sidewalk towards the porch. Entering the halo of illumination emitted by the lights, the driver revealed her identity.

"Courtney?" Judas whispered. Her unexpected appearance both terrified and exhilarated him and he hid himself behind the curtain.

"Good evening, young lady," said Sister Genevieve while studying Courtney with a raised eyebrow. She walked to the edge of the porch and inquired, "How may I help you?"

"Uhhh . . . I'm Courtney and I, uh, go to school with Judas. We're in the same French class," explained Courtney. The sixteen-year-old was intimidated by the towering nun who, because she stood on higher ground, seemed that much taller. Hesitant to place a foot on the first porch step, Courtney shivered and added in a wavering voice, "Is he, uh, home?"

Judas's body trembled, his heart thumped and his hands shook. He contemplated the reasons why Courtney would visit him, his guesses ranging from the wish to express gratitude on her cousin's behalf to the more-likely desire to excoriate him for pummeling her boyfriend.

"Yes, yes he is," answered Sister Genevieve, "though, unfortunately, my dear, we do not allow our boys to have visitors after eight o'clock. And Judas is also what you teenagers call grounded."

Judas's nervous excitement over Courtney's visit swiftly turned to suppressed rage. Sister Genevieve's interference raised his ire even though he feared speaking with the object of his affection. The nun, however, remained even keeled and her earlier anger evaporated.

"Oh," replied Courtney guiltily, her countenance dimming as she averted her eyes. A knowing expression washed across Sister Genevieve's face as she waited for the girl to consider her next move. Conflicted and uncertain, Courtney squirmed and said, "I didn't know that. I'll . . . I'll come back later. I'm sorry."

"You wouldn't happen to be the young lady whose boyfriend Judas assaulted today, would you?" queried Sister Genevieve shrewdly with a raised chin. Her question shocked Judas to his core, the normally courageous teenager anxiously hanging on every word of the conversation. He was about to discover how Courtney felt about him and the suspense gnawed at his insides.

"Well . . . yes and no," said Courtney uneasily. She paused and shifted her weight to her left foot before continuing, "He's not my boyfriend anymore."

"I see," replied Sister Genevieve. She sensed Courtney's infatuation with Judas although he could not. The teen steeled her will and asked, "Sister, can I tell you something?"

"Of course," answered Sister Genevieve. Judas grasped the curtain in his left hand and squeezed it tightly.

"Please don't punish Judas too hard," begged Courtney, the slightest hints of tears coming to her eyes. Feeling protective of him as he had of her cousin, she said with emotion, "My boyfriend – my *ex*-boyfriend – was being a jerk and they could've hurt my cousin, 'cuz he's so much smaller than they are, and I know Judas should've like, gotten a teacher or something, but . . . he stood up to them when no one else would. That's gotta count for something, right?"

Recognizing the genesis of young love, Sister Genevieve permitted herself a warm half-grin. She returned to the front door, opened it and stuck her head inside.

"Judas? Come here, please," called out Sister Genevieve. Waving Courtney onward, she said, "You, too."

Courtney complied with Sister Genevieve's request as Judas scrambled back to the couch to make it appear if he sat there the entire time. Pausing to compose himself with deep breaths, he then walked towards the front door and into the foyer, repeating in his mind, "You can do this. You can do this. You can do this."

"What's up, Sister?" Judas said in the best voice of nonchalance he could muster. He exited the house to the stunning radiance of Courtney's eyes and froze where he stood.

"You have a visitor," advised Sister Genevieve while gesturing towards Courtney. Judas inwardly panicked and searched his mind for the perfect words of greeting. Perceiving his disquiet, Sister Genevieve said, "Since Miss . . . what is your name, dear?"

"Sorry," apologized Courtney, "it's Courtney Melendez, Sister."

"Since Miss Melendez wasn't aware of our visiting hours, I don't think it will do any harm to make an exception just this once," said Sister Genevieve. She offered Courtney a muted smile but, after looking to Judas, her face became stern and she advised, "Twenty minutes, young man. You can sit on the porch swing but make sure to let Miss Melendez know about our 'shoulder rule' here at St. John Berchmans."

Staring stupidly at Sister Genevieve, Judas waited several seconds to react. She nodded at and gently pushed him towards the swing.

"Yes, ma'am," he answered. Turning his gaze to Courtney, he smiled awkwardly and indulged the flippant thought, "The nun's being nice and the beautiful, popular girl came to see *me*. This isn't gonna end well. It just can't."

******

"What's the 'shoulder rule'?" asked Courtney as she and Judas stood alone on the porch. He rolled his eyes and exhaled in annoyance.

"When we're with girls, and we're not under *direct adult supervision*, we have to sit far enough away from you that we can reach out and touch the side of your shoulder with the tips of our fingers . . . that's as close as we can get," Judas expounded bitterly. The teenagers were free of Sister Genevieve's oversight and felt more at ease though still nervous as they spoke. Courtney walked past Judas and accidentally bumped into him.

"Oh, sorry," said Courtney as she swiftly sat down on the far-right end of the bench. She smiled, stretched out her arm with her open palm facing downward and asked playfully, "This about right?"

"Uh, I think that's cheating," Judas replied with a smirk. He took two cautious steps towards the bench and said, "My arm's longer than yours."

"I didn't think you were a rule-follower," commented Courtney as she leaned and stretched her arm further outward. Judas seated himself at the far-left end of the bench and just out of her reach. He yearned for her touch and yet simultaneously feared it. Courtney surrendered and dropped her arm.

"Look, I'm sorry about Dillon," Judas blurted as the moment overwhelmed him. He wanted to move closer to her but knew Sister Genevieve lurked in the house.

"Don't be," countered Courtney. Her ire rising, she complained, "He was being a jerk – he *is* a jerk – and he deserved what he got."

Courtney shifted uneasily and slowly sat up straight as her anger dissipated. Judas knew what she was thinking and the issue of his gift wiped away the anxiety he felt in her presence. A grave expression on his face, he slid next to her.

"You saw what I did today, didn't you?" Judas inquired as he saw the apprehension in her eyes. Pressing her lips together and subtly cowering from him, Courtney nodded her head.

"Yeah," she said, the word the only one she could muster.

"You don't have to be afraid," Judas said sympathetically. Courtney's body gradually relaxed as he delivered an impassioned monologue, "I have . . . *a gift*. I don't know why *I* have it, but I know what I'm supposed to do with it. I have to protect those who can't protect themselves, and fight for those who can't fight. I could've left Dillon and Kyle alone, Courtney, but what if they wanted to keep fighting? I would've had to hurt them even more, or they could've hurt Brock . . . *or you*. I wasn't going to let them do that."

Judas trailed off and his eyes glazed over. Sister Genevieve's warning knock on the window wrested him from his reverie.

"Okay, okay," replied Judas as he waved her off. Moving to the porch's stone wall, he placed his fingertips upon it, gazed out into the nighttime stillness and felt the growing chill of the oncoming cold front. Courtney huddled into her hoodie and observed him with admiration and adoration scintillating in her eyes.

"'The exercise of justice is joy for the righteous, But is terror to the workers of iniquity,'" Judas recited, the words seeping from his brain and into his spirit. (Proverbs 21:15). Courtney watched him in wonder as he lingered in a brief trance. Returning to the present, he shook his head in the negative and said gravely, "Nobody can know about it."

"I swear, I won't tell anyone," pledged Courtney without the slightest trace of reluctance. The desire to stand by Judas's side as he fulfilled his destiny burgeoned within her.

"Thanks," Judas stated before the two teenagers smiled at one another. Riding a wave of confidence, Judas decided to take a risk and inquired, "Ya' wanna go out this weekend? I might be able to con Sister G into it."

"Well, I kinda just broke up with Dillon like an hour ago," said Courtney with an apologetic mien. Each beat of Judas's heart became painful and his body tingled with embarrassment. Courtney fidgeted and said, "It's just a little soon. Homecoming's this weekend, too, and I'm, like, going with a group of my friends instead of him."

"Sorry, I'm sorry," Judas replied with a reddening face, the teenager mortified by his failure. Abandoned by his courage and his confidence, he took a step back and said, "Way too soon. My bad."

Courtney's eyes flashed to the front window. Failing to detect Sister Genevieve's presence, she jumped to her feet, insinuated herself into Judas's arms and kissed him. He returned her affection for several seconds before she ended the kiss.

"Just give me a little while. It won't be long, I promise," whispered Courtney into Judas's ear. She kissed his cheek and, with her body tingling, she said in a normal voice, "See ya' Monday."

Detaching from his body, she scurried across the porch, down the front steps and to her car. Courtney hesitated after opening the door, waved sheepishly at Judas and then disappeared into the vehicle. He watched it depart with unfettered anticipation.

"Be forewarned, young man," said Sister Genevieve, the nun standing in the doorway. Turning his attention to her, he felt uneasy as she advised, "That one will be hard to hold on to."

******

"Hey, Mom," Courtney said into her phone. Parked at a brightly lit gas station, she locked the doors of her father's Jeep Wrangler. She stuck a wad of bills into her purse and countered, "No, Mom, I'm not driving. I just stopped for gas."

Courtney rummaged through her purse and listened to her mother's instructions. She abruptly widened her eyes in irritation

"Because I had a few other things to do first. I popped into Martie's to pick up the shoes she's letting me borrow," Courtney explained while retrieving her mascara, "and then I stopped at that Judas's house to say thanks for helping Brock."

The mention of Judas caused Courtney's heart to flutter but it deflated as her mother admonished her for deviating from her itinerary. Scowling in annoyance, she set the phone on the seat next to her and touched up her mascara until her mother finished.

"It's fine, Mom," Courtney assured her as she put away her mascara and reapplied her lipstick. Examining her face in the rearview mirror and pressing her lips together, she let her mother continue for ten seconds and then explained, "It was just a couple of quick stops and, as soon as you stop biting my head off, I'm going right to Stephanie's and I promise I won't leave her house. I won't even go outside, okay?"

Courtney inserted the key into the ignition and the engine rumbled to life. She decided to throw in the towel and let her mother continue her tirade for another minute while her mind wandered back to Judas.

"Yes, Mom. No more stops and straight to Steph's. I promise," Courtney said, the sixteen-year-old trying to veil her agitation. She listened to her mother's final words and said, "I gotta go. Love you, too."

Courtney ended the call and tossed her phone into the passenger seat before shifting the car into drive. She accelerated forward, rolled slowly up to the road and, satisfied that it was devoid of traffic, turned onto it.

"I'm sixteen, not six," Courtney griped as she sped off. She knew her mother loved her but, in her young mind, the constant oversight was unnecessary and frustrating. She glanced in the rearview mirror and added, "I can't wait to turn eighteen."

The drive to Stephanie's was lengthy and dark as her friend lived in the country amid farms and woodlands. The only light came from the occasional oncoming vehicle or her own headlights. Fifteen minutes into her journey, she turned onto a stretch of dirt road. Another car followed but it drove slowly and soon lagged far behind her.

"Pretty night," Courtney thought as she looked up through her windshield and examined the star-dotted sky. A deer suddenly leapt in front of Courtney though, to her, it seemed as if it simply appeared there. She screamed and swerved, the Jeep missing the animal by inches. Her overcompensation and a massive pothole caused her to veer back across the road and careen into a shallow drainage ditch. The force of the crash threw Courtney's body forward but her seatbelt caught her and hurled her back into her seat.

"No! Not in the Jeep!" Courtney cried as she burst into simultaneously angry and frightened tears and lashed out at the steering wheel. Turning her attention to her seatbelt, she pushed the release button though, in her panic, she failed to unlatch it. She yanked on it and mewled, "Come *on*!"

Thinking of her mobile phone, she forsook the seatbelt and searched the seat next to her. The car that traveled behind Courtney accelerated to the point of her accident and slid to a halt. Its headlights rolled over her and alerted her to its presence.

"Oh, thank God," Courtney whimpered with a sigh of relief, the arrival of a good Samaritan calming her nerves. Composing herself, she carefully shifted the car into park and removed the keys from the ignition. The engine died as Courtney repeated to herself, "You're okay. You're okay."

A tall, well-built man with stringy, jet-black hair and a matching, manicured beard exited the car and scrambled into the ditch. His tanned skin was leathered with age and he wore a jacket, old black jeans and a gold chain that hung from his neck. The man put his face up to Courtney's window.

"You all right?" shouted the man, his gruffness startling her. He made no immediate effort to aid Courtney.

"*Yes*. Please just get me outta here," she pleaded while tapping the window with her left palm several times. The man manipulated the door handle as she again worked over the seatbelt's locking mechanism.

"Unlock the door!" shouted the man when it failed to open. Courtney yanked on the seatbelt in frustration.

"Okay, geez," Courtney muttered. She hesitated with sudden dizziness but managed to grant the man access to the vehicle by clicking her key fob. The man threw open the door as she pulled on the seatbelt and said, "Thank you. I can't get this stupid seatbelt . . . ."

Taking advantage of Courtney's inattention, the man lunged into the car and shoved a soft, white cloth in her face. She attempted to avoid it but a strange scent overwhelmed her and her world went dark.

******

"What are you doing out of your bedroom at this hour, young man?" Sister Genevieve chastised Judas as she descended the stairs and marched to the front door. All the other residents at Berchmans slept soundly and the house was still. Sweeping into the foyer, the nun said, "This seems to be the night for unexpected visitors."

Judas laid on the living room couch in a sleepy daze. The teenager was awakened by knocking at the front door and the conversation between Randall Davis, the night staffer at the home, and the Monroe County deputy sheriff who stood on the porch. They had barely dispensed with the normal pleasantries before Sister Genevieve intervened.

"I'll handle this, Randall, thank you," Sister Genevieve said. He relented and retreated as she moved in front of him and asked, "How may I help you this evening, deputy?"

Randall disappeared. Judas sat up.

"Does a Judas Trent live here?" inquired the Deputy Sheriff, the question causing Courtney's angelic face to appear in Judas's mind. The image, however, did not bring him joy but instead a painful awareness of her peril.

"Why, yes. Yes, he does," Sister Genevieve replied with rising ire. Standing at the door in her matronly bathrobe, she paused and glanced at Judas, querying, "What has he done now?"

Judas leapt to his feet and marched to the door with a commanding aura raging like a river before him. The deputy stepped back and subtly placed his hand on his firearm as Judas nudged his way past Sister Genevieve.

"It's Courtney, isn't it?" Judas demanded. Fires of determination burned in his eyes

"Courtney Melendez, yeah," advised the deputy slowly. A look of suspicion on his face, he inquired, "But how did you know that?"

"What happened?" Judas demanded while stepping onto the porch and closer to the deputy. His larger-than-life presence intimidated the deputy and he faltered before his advance.

"Calm down, kid," replied the deputy with a shaky voice and a tight grip on his pistol. He reluctantly closed the distance between he and Judas but the teenager stood his ground. Sister Genevieve grasped Judas by the arm and pulled him back. He resisted.

"Judas, control yourself," Sister Genevieve directed him while continuing to pull on his arm.

"Tell me what happened to her," Judas ordered the deputy, who, as if under the young man's authority, submitted to his directive. Sister Genevieve released his arm and observed her young charge with awe.

"We think she was abducted a few hours ago," said the deputy. He bowed his head and released his weapon but kept his eyes on Judas.

"How horrible," commented Sister Genevieve with a sad, disgusted scowl. The nun grasped her chin, silently prayed for Courtney and then uttered forlornly, "Poor child."

Judas's anger simmered. His mind, however, entered another level of cognitive processing, the young man remembering the human trafficking assembly and sifting through the news and rumors he heard of such operations in Monroe and Lenawee Counties. Plans of action developed as his face hardened and he realized a simple truth: the sporadic defense of bullied teenagers was no longer enough.

"I'm so sorry, Judas," said Sister Genevieve as she placed a reassuring hand on his forearm. She felt a cold veneer beneath which raged a tempest of spiritual energy.

"'The exercise of justice is joy for the righteous,'" Judas said in a strong tone, "'But is terror to the workers of iniquity.'" (Proverbs 21:15).

"What did you say?" asked a stunned Sister Genevieve. Standing slack-jawed with her hands at her sides, she watched as Judas, at least to her, transformed into a holy warrior of the Crusades born into the present and cloaked in the righteousness of God. The deputy followed suit. The nun said hoarsely, "*Judas*!"

Judas registered the sound of her voice but failed to process her words. He remembered Courtney's face and, yearning with all his heart to rescue her, he let her image burn into his brain, the mark a binding signature on a contract to save her.

"Good night, Sister," Judas said. Turning away from her, he walked through the living room and ascended the stairs. Sister Genevieve watched him depart while repeating the Bible verse in her mind so she could later search for it.

"'*The exercise of justice is joy for the righteous, But is terror to the workers of iniquity.*'"

4 – Never. Again.

Ursula rested the side of her head on the window of Aunt Vickie's car but quickly pulled it back upon seeing her reflection. Nearly six months after the attack, the sight of her wound still nauseated and embarrassed her.

"Why?" Ursula asked in the faintest of whispers. It seemed to her at first that she addressed the world as it whizzed past but, upon further reflection, she realized that she spoke to God. She whispered a little louder, "Why did it happen to *me*?"

"What was that, Urse?" asked Aunt Vickie with a quick glance. Ursula flawlessly feigned ignorance.

"I didn't say anything," Ursula replied as she leaned her head into the glass again. Aunt Vickie let her eyes linger on her niece and then returned them to the road.

"Excited to see the church?" inquired Aunt Vickie with eagerness in her voice. She gripped the steering wheel and leaned forward as if the new house of worship pulled her towards it.

"It's just a building, isn't it?" Ursula asked while pulling out her phone. Fiddling with it and opening up Facebook, she added with disinterest, "Why didn't they just build it where the old church was?"

"It's a whole lot bigger than our beloved little breadbox was," answered Aunt Vickie. Stretching out her arms and pushing herself against the back of her seat, she said, "Don't tell anyone, but I heard Miss Stillerson talking to Father Ray about it last week, and she built it bigger than he thought. He was actually a little upset about it."

"Please tell me she's not gonna be there today," Ursula said, her words garnering a glare from Aunt Vickie. Demonstratively sighing and sulking, she said, "I *don't* like her, and most of the other parishioners don't, either."

"Now, Ursula," scolded Aunt Vickie while throwing her a look of disappointment. Ursula averted her gaze as she said, "Her personality may leave something to be desired but *she's building us a new church*. All of our seniors can keep going to mass in their own community. It's a wonderful thing, a gift from God."

Arriving at the church, Aunt Vicki clicked on her turn signal and decelerated. The sun shone brightly in the blue autumn sky and a warm breeze blew from the southwest.

"Gifts aren't always a blessing," muttered Ursula. The parish campus and its church, named St. Saturnin on the insistence of the Archdiocese of Detroit, were built by the financial juggernaut of Aubrey Stillerson. The building resembled a miniaturized cathedral of a bustling European metropolis. Designed in the Gothic revival style utilized in the eighteenth and nineteenth centuries, it boasted high, pointed arches and large, stained-glass windows. Soot-colored stone of varying shades comprised the shell of the building while the door and window frames were constructed of beige stone.

The church was built in the shape of a cross with two small wings jutting from its bottom and possessed seven towers with high, pointed spires. Three sets of two identical towers marked the bottom and sides of the cross and demarcated the main entrances. The seventh tower, which was larger and housed the church's bells, rose from the intersection of the cross. Lancet windows decorated each of the towers.

"There's Father Ray," announced Aunt Vickie as she saw the priest gathered with the parish council in the parking lot. Entering the grounds, she parked and climbed out of the car. Ursula failed to stir so Aunt Vickie stuck her head inside and asked pointedly, "Coming?"

"Yeah, just let me finish this text," Ursula said in an annoyed tone as she typed away on her phone. Aunt Vickie closed her door and walked hurriedly towards the group. Ursula hit "SEND" and pocketed her phone, saying, "Like I have a life or something."

Disembarking from the vehicle, Ursula shielded her eyes with her hand. The sound of a dog barking arose behind her and, after surveying the immensity of the church site, she rotated around. A bull-headed Rottweiler charged directly towards her. Ursula screamed.

"Urse!" Father Ray called out in desperation. He was too far away to intervene as the snarling Rottweiler swiftly closed on Ursula. The memory of the knife attack flaring in his mind, he sprinted towards her. She screamed again and he shouted, "Urse!"

The slobbering Rottweiler arrived at the vehicle, lunged at Ursula and snapped its jaws. Jumping backward and pressing herself into Aunt Vickie's car, she managed to evade the dog's bite; however, it reset itself and lunged again. The attack caused Ursula to emit a high-pitched shriek but the Rottweiler never reached her: a metallic-blue cane thwacked it on the back of its massive head with a sickening crack.

"Go on, get outta here!" shouted Tammy as she raised her cane and hit the dog again, this time delivering a perfect strike to its nose. The contact briefly stunned it and it staggered sideways. Regaining its senses after a third hit, the Rottweiler yelped and fled.

"Stupid hillbillies in this county," griped an undaunted Tammy as she watched the dog run away. Flipping her cane around, she grasped its handle and set the proper end on the ground. Tammy scowled and continued, "They always let their maniac dogs run free. *Backwoods idiots.*"

******

Ursula squirmed in Aunt Vickie's arms while a group of seniors fawned over her or praised Tammy's quick action in warding off the Rottweiler. Feeling the prickly attention of the parishioners as if they all touched her scar, she yearned to escape and inched towards the Traverse.

"Nice work, kid," Father Ray lauded Tammy while patting her on the shoulder. He discreetly moved her towards Ursula.

"It's all in the cane, Padre," said Tammy with a hint of haughtiness. She resisted his physical guidance and twirled the cane around, her skill with it reminding Father Ray of Judas's abilities with the metal pipe. Her words, however, reminded him of someone else.

"You've been hanging around Aubrey too much," Father Ray grumbled with a dubious mien. He turned his efforts towards his parishioners and said in a raised voice, "Why don't we move inside folks? There's a lot to see and quite a few decisions left to make."

"Okay, okay, *stop*," Ursula complained as she extricated herself from Aunt Vickie. Fortunately for the fourteen-year-old, Father Ray redirected the crowd's energies towards their continued tour of the property. The parishioners slowly meandered back towards the church, the group followed reluctantly by Aunt Vickie who turned back to look at Ursula several times.

"I'm fine. *Go,*" Ursula insisted with a dismissive wave. Father Ray lingered near her and wrapped his arm around Tammy's shoulders.

"Ursula, this is Tammy Parker," Father Ray said. Tammy shrugged off Father's Ray's arm and tottered up to her.

"Thanks," Ursula said feebly, her gratitude reflected in her facial expression. Tammy examined her scar with great interest, the move causing Ursula to blush and recoil.

"So you're one of us," offered Tammy. Father Ray winced. Tapping her disfigured foot with her cane, she added bluntly, "Mine was a car accident in middle school. Lost part of my foot. My mother wants me to get a prosthetic but I'm not doing it. I like the way I am."

Ursula caught herself beginning to smile at Tammy's pride in her injury. The teenager displayed no shame and, though acknowledging Ursula's scar, she did not act uncomfortably around her as most others did.

"Ya' don't meet too many people with part of their foot missing, do ya'?" said Tammy. She studied Ursula's face with interest and inquired boisterously, "So how'd you get your scar?"

"C'mon, Tammy," Father Ray rebuked her. Ursula placed her hand on Father Ray's lapel.

"It's okay, Father," interjected Ursula. Despite the dimming of her demeanor, she felt more confidence than she felt in months as she explained, "Aunt Vickie and I were attacked at the old church last year. The guy . . . he cut my face."

"So *you're* that girl? That's a *way* better story than mine," said an impressed Tammy. Stewing over her lack of decorum, Father Ray exhaled through his nostrils.

"Father Ray saved me," Ursula continued while gazing fondly on her spiritual mentor.

"Nice work, Padre," said Tammy as she mimicked Father Ray's earlier praise. She patted him on the back.

"All right, enough of that," Father Ray interrupted, the cleric uncomfortable with the praise and worried that Ursula might accidentally reveal her gift. He nodded at the Traverse and suggested firmly, "Why don't you two just wait in the car?"

"We're good," countered Tammy. Pushing him away, she said, "Go back to your old people."

"Now that's just disrespectful," Father Ray gently corrected Tammy. She relented.

"Mis disculpas, Padre," said Tammy, words to which Father Ray responded with a harsh glance and a shake of his head. She and Ursula stood in silence as he departed and, once he walked out of earshot, Tammy whirled around to face her.

"Can you keep a secret?" Tammy asked with a sly smirk.

"Uh, sure," answered Ursula, her curiosity piqued by Tammy's query. Her smirk grew into a satisfied grin and she lifted her cane.

"See this," Tammy said as she tapped a cylindrical, metal attachment on her cane just below the handle. Ursula nodded in the affirmative. Examining it closely, Tammy continued, "It looks like it's part of the cane, right? But it's not. My dad altered it for me. Ya' know, for self-defense."

Dexterously disassembling the cane, Tammy detached the cylindrical part and proudly held it out to Ursula. She hesitated to touch it.

"Go ahead," urged Tammy. Tossing the cylinder in the air and catching it, she said, "Feel how heavy it is."

Ursula took the cylinder and weighed it in her hand. The metal felt unusually cool and heavy.

"Wow," Ursula said, the teenager uncertain of how to respond.

"Wanna come over tonight?" queried Tammy expectantly. Ursula experienced a rush of anxiousness but Tammy's unquenchable and welcoming spirit brushed it aside.

"Yeah," Ursula answered with smile. Wallowing in Tammy's unconditional acceptance, she added, "Yeah, I do."

******

The early days of October warmed significantly and provided ample sunshine, the sun bathing the Catholic High School of Saint Judith in its light and warmth. Dozens of high schoolers meandered around an empty parking lot during their brief free period.

Sitting behind a tree facing away from the crowds, Ursula prayed for blessings of strength and perseverance. Her first year at the school began horribly as the fourteen-year-old became a target of her more vicious peers. Keeping a low profile proved wise and the large maple tree provided her with consistent concealment throughout the week.

Tammy hobbled up to Ursula with the assistance of her ever-present cane. She sighed dramatically.

"What're you doing way over here?" asked Tammy as she picked her way with difficulty through a maze of tree roots. Both girls wore knee-length navy skirts and white, collared blouses with short-sleeves though Tammy defied the heat by wearing a thin, navy sweater. Halting in front of Ursula, she complained, "It took me forever to find you."

"I thought Sister Fiona had you in detention all week," Ursula replied, the teenager comforted by her best friend's unexpected visit. The pair of social pariahs connected over their permanent disfigurements and their friendship grew ever since their first dramatic meeting.

"Mom got me off the hook," explained Tammy. She smiled with satisfaction and added, "She can be a real bitch when she wants to."

"Aw, look, the cripple club is having its weekly meeting," sneered Delia DeNardin, the perfectly pretty ringleader of a popular clique and the driving force behind its aggressively-spiteful nature. Ursula's heart sank at the sound of Delia's voice. Followed by four of her minions, the blonde seventeen-year-old strolled up to Ursula and Tammy and added snidely, "They should chain both of you monsters to this tree and leave you out here to die."

A chorus of hateful laughs arose from the group. Ursula hugged herself, absorbed the verbal assault and bit her lip to stifle her urge to cry.

"Why don't you get lost?" growled Tammy as she attempted to step forward. A tree root and her suspect balance, however, caused her to plummet to the ground. She winced in pain and squeaked, her misfortune generating another round of laughter from Delia and her companions.

"Tammy!" cried Ursula. She jumped up, retrieved the cane and rushed to her beloved friend.

"Oh, no!" cried Delia with mock despair. Folding her arms smugly, she said, "Did the footless freak fall down?"

"Leave them alone," demanded a towering black girl as she appeared behind the throng of teens. The girl, who awed Ursula with her gorgeous visage and warm brown eyes, appeared to be Ursula's age despite her height. Her skin was also a rich brown and her lengthy hair was coal black.

The crowd of girls whirled around in unison to face Ursula's defender. Their faces went pale and lifeless when they saw the imposing, five-foot-eleven-inch freshman looming over them.

"You do this and you're one of *them*, Charlotte," warned Delia snidely yet with fear in her high-pitched voice. Ursula watched the scene unfold in wonder and realized she no longer felt afraid.

"Good," said Charlotte in menacing fashion, "because I'm tired of you petty skanks."

Charlotte lunged at the group of girls with a glower and they flinched in unison. Sitting up with an amused grin on her face, Tammy watched Charlotte's rescue with delight.

"Don't you dare!" shouted a distressed Delia as she and her friends scattered and fled. Charlotte observed them flee for a few seconds and then stepped over a large, exposed tree root towards Tammy.

"You okay?" asked Charlotte as she lifted Tammy and held her upright. Ursula rose with her and, once Tammy was steady, she handed her the cane and proceeded to brush dust off her skirt.

"Yeah, it happens all the time," conceded Tammy matter-of-factly as she held her cane in one hand and brushed herself off with the other. She looked to Charlotte while beaming and offered her hand in her characteristic heedless manner. She announced happily, "I'm Tammy."

"I know," replied Charlotte with a muted grin. She shook Tammy's hand and said guiltily, "They talk about you a lot."

"You were awesome," said Tammy. Ursula lingered behind her and observed Charlotte cautiously. Both girls sized up Charlotte but only Tammy spoke, praising her, "I bet you can really kick some stuck-up girl ass."

"Why did you help us?" Ursula asked. She retained a small measure of hope that Charlotte's actions were sincere; however, her experience with the vindictiveness of Delia made her suspicious.

"Delia's just evil, and I *don't* wanna be one of her attack dogs," answered Charlotte. She and Ursula watched each other with great uncertainty, each girl hoping for the best but fearing the worst from a potential friendship. Charlotte spoke first, saying, "And besides, I was tired of them picking on you. It's not right."

Neither Ursula nor Charlotte spoke for ten seconds. Tammy's eyes darted between them before she finally shook her head.

"The bell's gonna ring in like thirty seconds," interjected Tammy as she began her trek back to class. Carefully choosing the safest route back to the parking lot, she implored them, "C'mon, you guys. We're gonna be late."

Judging Charlotte to be sincere, Ursula allowed a soft smile to spread across her face. Her new friend returned it and, walking shoulder-to-shoulder, they followed Tammy towards the school.

******

Timidly following Charlotte into her house, Ursula examined her surroundings. Modest in size but homey and pleasant, Charlotte's abode was meticulously neat and well-organized. A small foyer with a closet led into a quaint living room beyond which was a small dining room with a polished, wooden table and matching chairs.

"There's my baby girl!" a stout black woman bellowed as she entered the dining room from the kitchen and approached Ursula and Charlotte. The boisterous, black-haired woman shared Charlotte's skin tone and eyes but that was the extent of their similarities. Temporarily ignoring Ursula, she lovingly embraced her child but, after several seconds, turned her attention to her guest and said while beaming, "And what's your name, young lady?"

"Ursula, Ma'am," answered Ursula politely. She felt overwhelmed by the older woman's positive presence yet at the same time found it joyful and comforting.

"Call me Fanny, Ursula," Fanny insisted as she firmly took Ursula's hands in her own and patted them. Squirming under the penetrating gaze of Charlotte's enigmatic mother, she felt as if her spirit was being judged along with her disfigured countenance. Fanny, however, alleviated her nervousness with a wink and released her hands, saying, "I'm way too young to be called Ma'am."

"This is who I've been telling you about, Momma," chimed in Charlotte as she slung her bookbag to the floor. Grasping Ursula's bookbag, she tugged on it and said, "I'll get that for you, Urse."

"I thought there were two little white girls you were runnin' around with?" Fanny inquired.

"Tammy had a Spanish Club meeting after school," answered Charlotte as Ursula surrendered her bookbag to her.

"Your parents know you're here?" Fanny asked shrewdly with a stern look and a tilt of her head. Charlotte dropped Ursula's book bag next to hers.

"Yeah, I texted my Aunt on the way here, Ma'am," advised Ursula though, after a quick furrowing of Fanny's brow, she said, "I mean Fanny. I live with my Aunt Vickie."

Fanny's strict expression instantly faded and was replaced by her characteristic smile. Ursula returned it, albeit with less enthusiasm.

"What happened to your face, child?" Fanny asked as she non-judgmentally examined Ursula's face by running a gentle finger along her scar. Ursula started and became self-conscious.

"*Momma!*" scolded Charlotte with a gesture of frustration, the girl mortified by her mother's forthrightness. She turned herself away from Fanny in shame and groaned, "Boundaries!"

"Oh, relax, Char," Fanny countered with a dismissive gesture that resembled a swift, forward wave. Wrapping an affectionate arm around Ursula's shoulder and unabashedly looking into her eyes, she said with conviction, "It gives you character, young lady. Show's you're strong. *Resilient.* Be *proud* of it."

Ursula offered Fanny a muted grin. Encouraged as she was by her positive response to her deformity, she wished that someone, someday, would not even see it. Fanny gave her little time for wishing, however, as she ushered her to the couch, sat down and thumped the vacant cushion next to her.

"Now, come sit down and tell me what happened, Miss Ursula," Fanny insisted kindly. Dreading the recounting of the attack, she seated herself next to Fanny and folded her hands in her lap. The older woman looked to Charlotte and instructed her, "Char, I baked some fresh brownies for you girls. Why don't you get you and Ursula some brownies, maybe a glass of milk? Oh, wait, you're not one a' those lactose intolerant kids, are you?"

"No," said Ursula weakly with a shake of her head. Charlotte rolled her eyes, the teenager irked by her mother's intrusion on her new friendship.

"I told you, Momma, I'm not eatin' that sugary stuff," griped Charlotte. She disappeared into the kitchen, mumbling, "And no dairy, either, like I said a *hundred* times."

"That Char of mine, she's a good girl," Fanny commented without regard for Charlotte's cheek, "and I'm glad she met a nice girl like you."

Ursula blushed and averted her gaze. Charlotte soon returned with a brownie on a ceramic plate and a glass of milk. Turning a disapproving eye to her daughter, Fanny scrunched her face and wrinkled her nose.

"Skinny as a rail and won't eat a thing but chicken and vegetables," Fanny said as she took the plate from the tray and thrust it at Ursula. She gingerly accepted a huge brownie rippled with peanut butter and drizzled with melted fudge. Charlotte set the glass of milk on the end table to Ursula's left while Fanny scooted onto the edge of her seat and said, "So, tell us your story."

Ursula hesitated, the teenager feeling like a witness during a trial despite Fannie's good-natured overbearingness. She swallowed as the wonderful smell of the brownie tickled her nostrils.

"One night, after Bible study, my Aunt Vickie and I were walking back to our car, to go home, and . . . and we . . . we were attacked in the church parking lot," droned Ursula as she stared into the carpet. Suddenly enraptured by her new friend's tragic story, Charlotte leaned forward with her elbows on her knees and set her chin on her fists. She observed a trembling Ursula with watery eyes and listened intently as she added, "The man, he had a knife and he . . . he . . . ."

Ursula trailed off and gathered herself. She, as directed by Father Ray, intentionally downplayed the seriousness of Aunt Vickie's injury and omitted the revelation of her healing charism. Something about Fanny, however, made her want to confess her secrets.

"He cut my face," continued Ursula as she drifted into the memory and saw the knife gliding towards her face in slow motion. She languidly and eerily traced the scar with her finger and said with an odd composure, "He cut it here . . . and then from here . . . to here."

"You poor thing!" Fanny exclaimed as she patted Ursula on the leg. Charlotte's heart bled for her new friend but she found no words to offer. Pointing to the humungous brownie, Fanny urged Ursula, "That brownie'll make ya' feel better, darlin'. Eat up!"

A skeptical Ursula obeyed and, lifting the confection to her mouth, took a bite. Its warm, gooey sweetness did, as Fanny promised, assuage her emotions, its richness prompting her to take several gulps of the cold milk.

"It's a miracle you both survived," Fanny declared. Ursula brushed away the cobwebs of her mind and saw the hazy image of Father Ray standing above her wielding the pipe as Fanny said, "The Lord's hand defended you that night."

Ursula felt the warm rush of her love for Father Ray wash over her. She stared into the carpet and her eyes glazed over.

"Through someone else's hand," said Ursula. A buzz in her pocket wrested her from her nightmarish daydream. Reaching into it, she retrieved her phone. She offered Fanny an apologetic expression and said, "Excuse me."

Looking at the screen, she saw a notification that Tammy texted her. Ursula swiped upward on her screen, tapped on the notification and her text app popped up. Quickly maneuvering to Tammy's most recent text, she read it and scrunched her nose.

"What?" said Ursula aloud. The text contained four words, two of which were nonsensical: "*Still there? hhhuv hjh.*"

"What's 'a matter, sweetheart?" Fanny asked. Charlotte sat up and waited for Ursula's answer.

"I just got a weird text from Tammy," replied Ursula. She continued to study the text and muttered, "It doesn't, like, make any sense."

A growing sense of alarm arose in Ursula's spirit as she contemplated the purpose of the text. She tapped her screen to call Tammy. Fanny recognized her distress and again placed a hand on her leg.

"Child, what's wrong?" inquired Fanny, her own concern flourishing as she felt the strong emotion flowing from the fourteen-year-old. A chill rippled down Ursula's spine when Tammy's phone went directly to voicemail, a chill she had not experienced since the night of the attack.

"Her phone's off," said Ursula with growing worry. She set the plate aside, stood up and advised in a wavering tone, "Something's not right. Tammy's in trouble."

"Chill. You don't know that," reasoned Charlotte as she rose to her feet and grasped Ursula by her shoulders. Fanny watched her daughter comfort her new friend and pondered her disquiet. Charlotte added with a smile, "She probably just butt-texted you."

"I just know," countered Ursula as tears welled in her eyes. They fell on the landline phone on the end table behind Fanny.

"Well, then, let's call her parents, dear," Fanny suggested. The stalwart mother twisted her body and picked up the phone receiver, saying, "I'm sure she's fine but it won't hurt to make sure. What's the number?"

******

Tammy, an only child, ambled down a country road towards the rural home where she lived with her parents. The fourteen-year-old enjoyed the feel of the hot sun and the warm southern breeze yet still wore a thin, navy sweater over her school blouse. The sound of her cane hitting the dirt-and-gravel road intermingled with the wind in the soybean fields, the songs of birds flitting among the intermittent trees and the occasional bark of a dog.

Tammy walked often in defiance of her disability but the length of her trek began to fatigue her feet, legs and ankles as she neared her house. The added weight of her book bag proved as challenging as the extra miles.

"I can't believe she wanted me to wait at school 'til five thirty," Tammy said as she soldiered forward and shook off the soreness of her legs and the burden of her bookbag. Determined and independent, often to a fault, she squared her shoulders and declared, "I can walk a few miles just fine. She's so ridiculous sometimes."

Tammy stopped to admire a swarm of Cloudless Sulphur butterflies, the green-winged insects fluttering around as she approached the mud puddle at which they congregated. She smiled with delight as she watched them.

"Oh well, she'll get over it," Tammy said with a shrug. She giggled and announced to the butterflies, "Or should I say *ella conseguirá sobre él.*"

She heard a fast-approaching vehicle and looked up. It sped towards her, its velocity prompting her to step onto the narrow strip of grass between the road and the ditch. Roaring past Tammy, a dark-gray cargo van sent up a plume of dust and dispersed the butterflies.

"Hey!" Tammy shouted. She watched the butterflies disappear into the soybean field and then continued her homeward journey, shaking her head and muttering, "*Rude.*"

She smelled the fragrance of roadside wildflowers on the far side of a ditch and it instantly improved her mood. Turning a corner marked by an old, gnarled tree, she stepped onto the dirt road leading to her home.

Tammy's neighborhood was sparsely populated with only five houses spread over two miles of narrow road. Most of the surrounding land contained cornfields, their stalks reaching peak height and creating a long, concealed lane. The vehicles of non-residents rarely ventured down the long, dusty stretch.

"Almost there," Tammy encouraged herself after a half mile of progress. Seeking a distraction from the soreness in her ankles, she halted and retrieved her phone from her book bag. Tammy checked a new Facebook notification, read it and then negotiated screens to bring up her texting app. Remembering that Ursula went to Charlotte's house after school, she said, "Wonder how that's going. I wish I coulda' went. *Club español estúpido.*"

Tammy's irritation over her mother's insistence on Spanish Club rapidly dissipated when she heard a vehicle turn onto the road behind her. Glancing over her right shoulder, she saw a dark-gray van slowly rolling towards her. Tammy immediately recognized it and returned her attention to her phone.

"Mr. Polovski's back early from the VFW today," Tammy said while forging ahead. The van trundled along behind her and, as it did, the sound of pebbles and gravel crackling under its tires grew steadily louder. Tammy typed, "Still there?"

Tammy paused in the middle of her message to Ursula. Looking up to wave to Mr. Polovski, she realized it was not his opulent passenger van but instead the cargo van that ruined her butterfly viewing. It stopped next to her and the van's side door slid open. Tammy stepped away from it and into the grass beside the road.

"Hey there, sweetheart," said a tall, well-built man with stringy, jet-black hair and a matching, manicured beard. His tanned skin was leathered with age and he wore a tight, black t-shirt that revealed his rippling arm muscles, black jeans and a gold chain that hung from his neck. He glanced from side to side and inquired, "We're tryin' to buy some hay for our horses but we can't find the damn farm. Think ya' could help us out for a second?"

Tammy nervously tapped the screen of her phone. Eying the man with suspicion, she improved her grip on her cane and prepared to fight. His slick smile failed to conceal the sliminess of his spirit. Tammy's countenance soured.

"Sorry, I gotta get home," Tammy answered in a harsh tone. The man suddenly lunged forward and grabbed Tammy by the arm, the force of his attack causing her to drop her cane. She screamed while wildly tapping her phone screen in hopes of sending a message, yelling, "No!"

Tammy struggled valiantly against the man but his strength overwhelmed her. She managed to kick off a shoe as her mother taught her, however, and it fell to the road as the man hurled her into the van. Hitting her head on the far wall, Tammy's vision blurred.

"Get the cane!" barked the man. Woozy from her injury, Tammy heard the side door slam shut and, seconds later, felt a soft cloth press into her face and smelled a strange odor. All went black and Tammy saw no more, her phone still clutched in her hand.

*****

Ursula, swaddled by Aunt Vickie in a patchwork quilt hours earlier, lay on the couch and stared at the television. The surge of emotion she experienced upon learning of Tammy's disappearance now bled away and she settled into an uncomfortable and exhausted numbness. Part of the quilt remained soaked with her tears but she no longer felt the wetness press against her cheek.

"Tamara Parker was walking home from St. Judith Catholic High School in a rural area when she was abducted earlier today," said the newscaster, the mention of Tammy shocking Ursula out of her funk. His words faded away.

"She's still alive," Ursula said to herself as she realized Aunt Vickie no longer sat in her recliner. The broadcast showed the location of the abduction cordoned off with yellow police tape while police officers and two suited detectives examined the scene. She repeated, "She's *still* alive."

Unentangling herself from the quilt, Ursula rolled onto her back and cast her gaze at the ceiling. She, with her emotional energy spent, felt no urge to cry or to pray but her mind whirred to life.

"Would it've saved her?" Ursula asked herself as her guilt thrust out tentacles and wrapped them around her conscience. She glanced at the television and saw the Sheriff holding up a shoe in an evidence bag, the shoe that Tammy wore on her healthy foot. The sight of it sparked a memory and, as Ursula drifted into a light sleep, a scene from the past replayed itself in her dreams and she whispered, "A healthy foot."

She became cognizant of the pressure of bandages on her face and twinges of pain from her wounds. The pain medication waned.

"It never lasts," Ursula thought, the dream world mimicking the effect of the medication in real life.

"Well, look who's returned to the land of the living," joked Father Ray with a smile, the priest sitting in a church pew several yards from Ursula. Realizing the inappropriateness of his jest, he quickly said, "That was stupid. Sorry, kid."

Ursula gently shook her head in the negative as a sign of forgiveness. Soft, dim light illuminated the church of St. Arnulf and the sounds of medical equipment echoed throughout it. Ursula attempted to speak but failed, the bandages wrapped around her head and the pain preventing speech.

"If you're gonna ask about your Aunt Vickie, I sent her home," said Father Ray while standing up and walking towards Ursula's bed. It was positioned on the dais in front of the wooden altar. Stopping at the first step, he folded his arms and added, "She needed sleep and she sure as hell wasn't getting any here."

Ursula nodded her head in approval of Father Ray's decision while her subconscious accepted the church as the hospital. He lingered by her bed and, even in her hazy state, she perceived his uneasiness. Several times he attempted to speak but, with no words coming from his lips, he eventually meandered to the old baptismal font to the right of the altar.

"1508," said Father Ray in an odd tone as he removed his clerical suit jacket and tossed it aside. He rolled up his sleeves; first the right and then the left. Listening to him without seeing his face, Ursula felt the growing pain in her wounds as Father Ray explained, "Catechism of the Catholic Church, 1508. The charism of healing."

Ursula winced, the puzzled look she gave Father Ray tweaking her lacerations. He removed his white clerical collar and dropped it to the floor.

"A charism," explained Father Ray as he languidly yet meticulously washed his hands in the font, "is a special grace bestowed on one of the faithful for the good and the growth of the Church. And now it's been bestowed on you."

Ursula contemplated Father Ray's labeling of the power that infused her spirit. Sparingly had she used it since it manifested years earlier, the fourteen-year-old concealing her gift as she struggled to understand it. Father Ray grabbed a white towel hanging from the font, rotated around and dried his hands.

"Does anyone else know?" inquired Father Ray, his gaze penetrating and stern. Disturbed by his serious demeanor and bizarre behavior, Ursula squirmed in her hospital bed and shook her head to convey that the secret was hers alone. She turned onto her side, laid the uninjured portion of her face on the coolness of the pillow and thought of her late mother. Returning to Ursula's bedside, Father Ray placed a hand on her right shoulder and suggested, "Perhaps, for now, it would be best to keep it that way. Ya' know, keep the sword in its sheath until you're better. Just temporarily, until we figure a few things out."

Despite the pain it caused her, Ursula turned her head and looked at Father Ray. His spurious suggestion that she withhold her gift surprised and angered her, especially given his clerical station. Her expression, in turn, irked him.

"'Beware of practicing your righteousness before men to be noticed by them,'" recited Father Ray in a tone that made Ursula shiver. He took several deliberate steps, arrived at the foot of her bed and continued while staring at her, "'Otherwise you have no reward in heaven with your Father who is in heaven.'" (Matthew 6:34).

Ursula swallowed. Her lacerations screamed.

"Time for more pain medication," interjected a nurse as she swept into the room. Relieved by the respite from the tension between she and the priest, Ursula sighed and relaxed until she realized the nurse was Sister Palladia in full uniform.

Father Ray moved between Ursula and Sister Palladia and blocked the latter's view. He leaned over the teenager as if to kiss her forehead but never planted his lips, instead positioning them next to her ear. Sister Palladia turned away and readied the medication on the altar.

"Remember, Tammy," Father Ray warned in a barely audible whisper, "*. . . even the most intense prayers do not always obtain the healing of all illnesses.*" (*Catechism*, 1508).

A jarring noise from the television woke Ursula and she quickly sat up. Though her dream was filled with erroneous fragments, Father Ray's words were verbatim save for one.

"He didn't say Tammy," Ursula said while kneeling on the floor. Clasping her hands together to pray, she closed her eyes and concentrated on God.

"Was he right?" Ursula asked God. Bowing her head, she whimpered, "*Is he right*"

Remorse throttled Ursula. Her emotions rekindling and then exploding, she curled up on the couch and bawled.

"Never again," Ursula declared in defiance of Father Ray, the fate of her best friend foremost on her mind. Her failure tattooed on her spirit, she vowed through tears, "*Never. Again.*"

5 – These Two

Father Ray closed his office door, locked it and rested his head on its surface. The prayer service held at the site of Tammy's abduction was heart-wrenching and he now thought only of a stiff drink and his evening cigar.

"She's a great kid with a good heart," prayed Father Ray. Pleading for divine intervention, he shuddered in his sorrow and said hoarsely, "This can't be her end."

"Hi, Father," Judas greeted Father Ray in a voice deepening with age. The priest started but relaxed when he saw the fifteen-year-old sitting casually in one of the guest chairs with his long legs stretched out before him.

"What're you doing in here?" inquired Father Ray as his gaze fell on Judas. Meandering to his desk and feeling old in the glare of the adolescent's youthful energy, Father Ray admonished him, "You're already on Sister Genevieve's shit list and if she catches you here, *I'll* be on it, too."

Father Ray appraised Judas and the speed with which he grew into an imposing young man. He now stood six-feet-tall with developing musculature, broadening shoulders and the enthusiastic energy of youth.

"She needs to back off," Judas grumbled. Rising to his feet, he said, "It's not gonna matter soon anyway."

"We've talked about this, Judas. My support of your emancipation depends entirely on your *good* behavior," warned Father Ray with a sharp glance, a pointed finger and a raised eyebrow. Piles of books were stacked and organized on his desk without regard to size or shape and were accompanied by an open laptop. Father Ray plopped into his chair, leaned back and scolded Judas, "Going AWOL is not good behavior. Now I've had a really long day so why don't you engage in some good behavior and *go home*."

Judas's mind turned to Courtney and he struggled with his sadness and his rage. Father Ray read his emotions and relented.

"Look, Judas, I know Courtney's abduction has been hard for you to deal with," advised Father Ray sympathetically, "but that's not an excuse to do whatever the hell you want whenever you want. You've got to reign it in. *Have a little faith*."

"I'm going to find her, Father," Judas vowed. Hearing an odd undertone in his voice, Father Ray watched him walk to the window.

"There ya' go. *Faith*," Father Ray said despite his private doubts. Mustering all the false earnestness he could, he reasoned, "They think human traffickers nabbed them both so the federales are involved now. That's a lot of manpower and resources, kid. They'll find her."

"*I'm* going to find her," Judas vowed again, the gravity behind his words giving Father Ray pause. Judas, for as long as the cleric had known him, was a "crusader" with a fervent desire to protect the weak and innocent. Father Ray now sensed a different energy from his young charge, however, and it worried him. He remembered the development of Christ and compared him to Judas.

"'And Jesus kept increasing in wisdom and stature, and in favor with God and men,'" thought Father Ray to himself. (Luke 2:52). He countered as if debating with God, "But even Jesus didn't go public until thirty-three. This kid's only fifteen."

"'The exercise of justice is joy for the righteous," Judas said as he gazed wistfully out the window. Burying his grief deep, he called on the Spirit, turned to Father Ray and announced powerfully, "'But is terror to the workers of iniquity.'" (Proverbs 21:15).

Concerned realization washed across Father Ray's face. The pieces fell together, from Ethan Barnes's strange fainting episode to the reports that Dillion Buck and his friend lost consciousness during their fight with Judas.

"That thing with Ethan Barnes wasn't a one-time thing, was it?" inquired Father Ray, the priest finally daring to confirm his suspicion.

"No," Judas answered proudly and without hesitation.

"It ain't a coincidence, is it?" he silently queried his Master. Experiencing the spiritual world vicariously through the Godly gifts of Ursula and Judas was more than enough for the priest. The confluence of Spiritual power in his parish meant turmoil he did not want and he reluctantly asked, "Have you been . . . visited?"

"No," Judas said. Father Ray exhaled in relief.

"So, God has provided no direct divine sanction," said Father Ray with a smirk, "and has made your leap one of pure faith. How do you know that *you* are the one He's appointed to rescue Courtney?"

Father Ray sifted Judas like wheat but the boy did not falter under his gaze. His relief evaporated.

"Because He entrusted an angel to me, and I don't take a gift like that lightly," stated Judas with great emotion for Courtney. Taken aback by his ardent response, Father Ray remained quiet and let him expound with the command and confidence of a grizzled general, "It's time to hunt the wicked wherever they may be found."

"Look, Judas," interjected Father Ray, "I know you care about this girl, and I know you hate injustice, but you're getting way ahead of yourself. Being able to drop teenagers and winning a few high school fights doesn't make you some Catholic Jedi. Let the professionals handle it. They know how to investigate these things and track down kidnapped girls. It's what they do. They'll find her."

Judas's blood boiled so hot that Father Ray felt it against his skin. He craved his cigar.

"'Beware of practicing your righteousness before men to be noticed by them. Otherwise you have no reward in heaven with your Father who is in heaven,'" recited Father Ray as he had to Ursula months earlier. (Matthew 6:34). He opened a desk drawer and pulled out a box of cigars and a matchbook. Lighting the cigar in a plume of smoke, Father Ray advised, "I'd keep your little power under wraps for now because that's attention you don't want and, quite frankly, I don't want it either. Go home, pray for Courtney, and think about where you're taking her on your first date. They're gonna find her soon and this'll all be over."

Sensing the falsity in Father Ray's assertions, Judas decided to play the game. He composed himself.

"I'd like to pray for her in the church," Judas requested. Father Ray puffed his cigar while rummaging in his pockets for his keys. He soon produced them and tossed them to Judas.

"Knock yourself out, kid," said Father Ray. Standing up and walking to his liquor cabinet, he added flippantly, "Just don't do it to anyone else."

******

Ursula took deliberate steps as she traversed the familiar hallway that led to Father Ray's office, its walls decorated with Biblically themed paintings. A new picture hanging just outside his door caught her eye and she stopped to examine it.

"When did he get this one?" said Ursula aloud. The crudely-painted scene portrayed a joust of sorts; against a red backdrop, a man on horseback with a large, misshapen crown pierced another with a thin, white spear. She noticed her reflection in the glass, the image displaying her facial deformity. Sighing, Ursula recited the verse Father Ray taught her to buttress her strength, "'If anyone wishes to come after Me, he must deny himself, and take up his cross daily and follow Me.'" (Luke 9:23).

She donned a modest outfit for her age comprised of a red, cotton shirt with long sleeves and dark blue jeans. Ursula abruptly crinkled her nose. Father Ray, as usual, was smoking his evening cigar. The repugnant scent caused her to momentarily forget her anxiousness. Her body slackened.

"They smell so terrible," Ursula thought. Lifting her fist to the door, she paused and sighed, "I'm begging you. Please make him understand."

Ursula knocked three times in rapid succession. Ten seconds of silence ensued.

"Enter," called out Father Ray in a tired voice. Gingerly turning the handle and pushing open the door, Ursula cringed as the cigar smell intensified and thin wisps of smoke wafted towards her. An open laptop cast Father Ray's face in a haunting, white glow. Ursula's heart sank when she noticed the half-empty, condensation-glazed glass to his left.

"Maybe it'll make this easier," she thought selfishly. Father Ray smiled in adoration of his teenage parishioner and he marveled at the young woman she had become in six short months. It was her purity in an impure world, however, that he most admired and that provided him a measure of hope. Father Ray's attention caused Ursula to blush and avert her gaze.

"Hey, Urse," Father Ray replied as his eyes lit up, the cleric happy that Judas had not returned to further test him. He extinguished his cigar in the block-glass ashtray on his desk, imbibed and asked eagerly, "Any news on Tammy?"

"No," replied Ursula with her usual discomfiture over Father Ray's drinking. His mood darkened.

"Sorry, Urse," he apologized.

"Every day is the same," advised a distressed Ursula. Biting her bottom lip, she struggled with her emotions and trembled, adding forlornly, "There's never any news."

"Real faith endures in times like this," urged Father Ray as he motioned for Ursula to have a seat. She placed her hands on the back of a chair in front of Father Ray's desk but hesitated to accept his hospitality. Irked by her refusal to listen to him, he scowled and leaned forward, insisting, "Urse, sit down."

Father Ray's rare display of irritation towards her caused Ursula to ease herself into the chair to his left. She moved stiffly and sat with her hands in her lap and her gaze on the floor. The light in Father Ray's eyes vanished. He dreaded another encounter with an emotional teenager.

"I'm sorry, Urse, really," Father Ray relented. His grasped the lower half of his face in his hand and exhaled. He took another drink, frowned and uttered, "It's not the time for it."

"It's okay," replied Ursula. She ventured a glance at Father Ray but looked away when she met his gaze. Her inner turmoil made his heart bleed.

"What is it?" Father Ray asked, his own emotions palpable. Ursula hesitated as if rehearsing the words in her mind. She closed her eyes and attempted to focus her thoughts.

"It's time for me to share my gift," stated Ursula with devout conviction and without the slightest waver in her voice. She swallowed hard. Father Ray furrowed his brow as Ursula elaborated, "I don't want to wait any longer."

"We've been through this before, Urse," replied Father Ray slowly with a frustrated look, "and it's just too dangerous. We need to hold off a bit longer."

"It doesn't matter if it's dangerous. There are so many who are suffering," argued Ursula with sudden passion. She leaned forward and gesticulated demonstratively, continuing, "Maybe you could write a letter to Archbishop Wunderlich, or even to Pope Francis. They've dealt with this stuff before. The Church can help us."

"Where's all this coming from?" inquired Father Ray. He stood up and walked around his desk. Ursula flinched as he approached her but he sat harmlessly on its edge and folded his arms.

"What if I had healed Tammy's foot?" Ursula reasoned. Father Ray gave her a dubious look as she continued, "Maybe she could've run, gotten away. But she couldn't and now she's gone. I have to do something to make up for that, and sharing my gift is the way to do it."

Ursula's face illuminated but Father Ray exhaled and scowled in frustration. He mentally kicked himself for failing to manage her emotions after Tammy's abduction. Sitting up straight and grasping his forearm, she looked to him with expectant hope.

"It's time, Father," Ursula said in a determined voice.

"You know what Jesus said," replied Father Ray. His attempt to dismiss the matter was met with a glower by Ursula. Pulling free of her hold on his arm, he retreated to his desk chair and said, "'Beware of practicing your righteousness before men to be noticed by them; otherwise you have no reward in heaven with your Father who is in heaven.'" (Matthew 6:34).

The verse seemed a weak argument even to Father Ray. He knew Ursula did not seek notice or attention.

"'. . . nor does anyone light a lamp and put it under a basket, but on the lampstand, and it gives light to all who are in the house,'" countered Ursula in an ardent, compassionate tone. Rising to her feet in dramatic fashion, she continued, "'Let your light shine before men in such a way that they may see your good works, and glorify the Father who is in heaven.'" (Matthew 5:15).

Father Ray pounded his desk. Angry tears arose in Ursula's eyes but she maintained her composure as she headed for the door. She paused in the doorway and glowered at him.

"'Do not give what is holy to dogs, and do not throw your pearls before swine,'" warned Father Ray, "'or they will trample them under their feet, and turn and tear you to pieces.'" (Matthew 7:6).

Disgusted with Father Ray, Ursula exited his office. She paused in the hallway.

"Why did he send *me* the intelligent and the gifted?" Father Ray queried rhetorically, the priest unaware that Ursula loitered just beyond the doorway. Grasping his face as if his hand were a giant spider, he lamented, "These two are just over my head. I'm more suited to the dumb and the unremarkable."

"*These two?*" said Ursula with a befuddled look. She re-entered Father Ray's office and inquired, "What do you mean *these two?*"

Father Ray's eyes darted up to Ursula and he guiltily looked at her. A thousand memories from his own past inundated his present and, continuing to spare others from the mistake he made, he held up his hands and shook them in a dismissive gesture.

"Urse, it's late and it's been a long day," Father Ray implored her, "so let's sleep on this and talk about it tomorrow. You know, the whole clearer in the rays of the morning sun thing, or whatever the hell the saying is."

Ursula steamed. Whirling around, she exited Father Ray's office.

"Good night, Father," she bleated before fleeing down the hallway.

"This was a small, quiet parish with an aging and declining membership. We had just enough money, were WAY under the community radar and ignored by the Archdiocese. There was no reason for anyone to interfere and I should've been able to hide here in wonderful obscurity until the parish closed and I retired," said Father Ray while indulging in his cigar. Picking up his drink, he looked to the ceiling and sighed in exasperation, "*Thanks*."

******

Judas kneeled silently in the last pew of the darkened church, the young man intermittently fuming and praying. He acutely felt the burning frustration of his youth, the inferno fueled by the ever-strengthening, violent tides of the adult world.

The interior of the Church of Saint Saturnin was a true spectacle to behold. Three sections comprised the elaborately decorated, cavernous building: the main chamber with its vaulted, two-and-half-story ceilings and one-story side chambers atop which were built galleries. Pillars supporting the galleries lined the main chamber as if herding the wooden pews towards the altar.

The flash of someone in Judas's peripheral vision startled him and he leapt to his feet. Racing down the center aisle of the church, Ursula wept and wiped tears from her eyes as she ran. Judas watched her as she reached the steps of the altar and, after falling prostrate upon them, she broke down. Struggling to crawl closer to the altar, her body seemed weak with despair as a multitude of silent, stained-glass saints observed her.

"Please, bring her back!" wailed Ursula as she lifted her head like a whipped slave who expected the next lash at any second. Gazing upon the golden tabernacle, her copious tears fell like slivers of silver in the moonlight. She begged in a whisper, "Just bring her back."

Judas stood rooted to the floor. He pitied Ursula and wished to comfort her but also hesitated to intrude on her private moment with God. Her body crumpled and she squalled uncontrollably. The woeful sight compelled Judas to approach her.

"You gotta do something," Judas implored himself. Ursula's gaze fell upon the statue of the crucified Christ suspended by chains from the ceiling, the reminder of her Savior's suffering blunting her emotions and slowing her tears. Judas noticed her stirring and he halted halfway down the aisle, thinking, "Or not."

His heart would usually war with his mind during moments like this but, in an unexpected twist, his heart warred with itself and his mind remained quiet. Ursula's crying intensified.

"'Blessed are those who mourn, for they shall be comforted,'" called out Judas as he walked up to Ursula. (Matthew 5:6). His commanding voice paralyzed her and, to her surprise, soothed not merely her emotions but her very spirit.

"I'm sorry," apologized an embarrassed Ursula as she cowered and hid her face. She also attempted to conceal her sorrow but the pitch of her voice and her occasional sobs betrayed her. Forcing herself to display feigned composure, Ursula uttered feebly, "I thought I was alone."

"So did I," Judas replied with a nod to the cross, "but I guess He's always with us, whether we remember it or not . . . and He put *us* together."

Judas cringed at the import of his careless words as his kindness kindled Ursula's guilt and resuscitated her bawling. She buried her head in her arms on the top step and her tears soaked into the sleeve of her shirt.

"Nice move, Judas," Judas muttered, the teenager bemoaning his constant failure in communicating with the opposite sex. He whirled around to leave. Ursula's head popped up as Judas took several soft steps in retreat.

"Your name's Judas?" queried Ursula as she swiped her eyes with her sleeve and removed several tears. Her crying lessened, the mention of the traitorous apostle distracting her from her angst. Judas stopped in his tracks and glanced back.

"Yeah," answered a perplexed Judas. He rotated around.

"You mean like *betrayed Jesus* Judas?" asked Ursula with distaste and a sour mien. She sniffled several times and again wiped her eyes, this time using her hand.

"Uh, well, yeah, that's *one* of 'em in the Bible," countered an irked and embarrassed Judas, "but I prefer the brother of Jesus. Ya' know, Matthew 13:55. Mark 6:3. That guy."

"Oh, yeah," replied Ursula, the fourteen-year-old feeling very uncomfortable in her own skin. She shrugged and said, "Sorry."

An awkward silence followed. Gradually turning her head to the left, Ursula tried to acquire Judas in her peripheral vision. She greatly desired to see his face but feared any revelation of her scarring.

"Well, you know my name but I haven't even seen your face," Judas said with a smirk. It faded when Ursula remained silent and motionless; she, in fact, felt embarrassed by her weakness and the brief lapse of her trust in God. Unwilling to surrender, Judas walked closer to her and offered, "Or we could just start with your name."

Judas intrigued Ursula and her sadness slowly evaporated. Pressing her lips together firmly, she pondered her response for several seconds.

"It's Ursula, after Saint Ursula," said Ursula as she fidgeted. She wished to get away from Judas and stay with him at the same time. The emotion paralyzed her and even had she decided to flee she would not have been able. Ursula shifted her weight and added, "But it's nothing to be proud of. They're not even sure she really existed."

Judas smiled. A strange elation percolated within him.

"So, Ursula who doesn't exist, can we exchange faces now?" Judas asked. He stepped onto the first stair but Ursula scooted away from him and hid her face.

"I-I . . . *I can't*," pleaded Ursula. Her tears returned and her shame over her appearance overwhelmed her. Mustering her inner strength but continuing to cry, she placed her faith in God and prayed silently, "It's okay, God, I understand. I will deny myself, and take up my cross daily, and follow your Son."

"Whoa, what happened?" Judas asked nervously with outstretched hands. Quickly stepping off the first stair, he looked on Ursula with puzzlement and said, "What'd I do?"

"Nothing. It's not your fault," whimpered Ursula as she curled her body and buried her face in her chest. Expecting him to leave, she mewled, "I'm sorry. I just can't."

"Uh, well, let's see," Judas said as he wracked his brain. He yearned to see her face and, after a few moments of thought, the light bulb clicked on and he suggested, "Hey, wait. Here's an idea. Why don't I close my eyes and *you* can look at *me*? That way you'll at least know what I look like."

Ursula ceased crying, lifted her head and relaxed her body. Judas's unique approach piqued her interest.

"How do I know you'll keep them closed?" inquired Ursula skeptically. She felt herself tremble as she thought of Judas seeing her facial deformity.

"You'll just have to trust me to do what's best for you," Judas answered. The sincerity in his tone encouraged her.

"Okay," said Ursula hoarsely. Exhaling to center herself, she rose to her feet in a gradual, deliberate manner.

"They're closed," Judas advised Ursula. She reluctantly turned towards Judas and peeked at him to ensure he upheld his end of the deal. Confirming his compliance, she studied his young, handsome face with a fluttering heart and a partially averted gaze. He raised his arms in a gesture of display and quipped, "Nothing special, right?"

"*No*," disagreed Ursula as she raised her chin and smiled. Risking two careful steps forward, she felt her excitement outstrip her fear. She felt the urge to reach out and touch his chest as she thought, "He's really cute."

Ursula's arm raised an inch before Judas's eyes popped open. She yelped, dropped her arm and prepared for flight; however, she stopped in her tracks when she noticed Judas's expression.

"You didn't flinch," said Ursula with astonishment. She felt as if she stood naked before him but strangely experienced no fear or shame. She thought, "He's looking at me like people used to look at me. Like no one else ever does anymore."

"Why would I flinch?" Judas replied with continued sincerity in his voice. Stars formed in Ursula's eyes, stars identical to the ones in the eyes that looked back at her. Holding out his hand, Judas smiled sheepishly and asked, "You drink coffee?"

Ursula returned Judas's grin and nodded but said nothing. She, in truth, hated coffee but accepted the invitation. Gingerly taking his hand, she let him lead her down the center aisle of the church.

"Judas and Ursula," scoffed Ursula to herself. Indulging in the firm grip of Judas's hand and with a girlish smirk, she thought, "Sounds like a bad indie movie."

******

"It's not supposed to be this cold in October," griped Ursula as she shivered. She and Judas sat on opposite ends of a wrought-iron bench with the illumined statue of the Virgin Mary before them. Each teenager held a large Styrofoam cup in one hand though Ursula handled her coffee as if it were a scorpion. Judas noticed and smiled.

"You don't drink coffee, do you?" asked Judas. Ursula averted her gaze for several seconds before returning her attention to Judas and shrugging.

"Not really," admitted Ursula with a guilty grin, "and I can't believe you do, either."

The pair chuckled but their mirth was soon washed away by the running fountains. Judas, *sans* coat, ignored the cold night but Ursula dressed warmly in black, her ensemble including a fluffy down coat, a ski hat topped with a grey puffball on top and gloves. He scooted closer to her when she shivered again.

"Who were you asking God to bring back?" queried Judas. He knew he risked upsetting her but proceeded anyway, his desire to comfort her brushing aside his discretion. Growing cold and quiet like an ice sculpture, Ursula bowed her head.

"Tammy Parker's my best friend," Ursula stated. She managed to suppress even the involuntary twitches of her face by biting into her lower lip and focusing on the pain.

"*Oh,*" replied Judas. He recalled the recent news reports of a missing fourteen-year-old girl and her smiling face arose in his mind. The thoughts of Tammy led to thoughts of Courtney and, wracked with pity for Ursula and remorse for being alone with her, he said, "I'm sorry. I lost a friend recently, too."

Ursula's composure fizzled and she burst into tears. Jumping up and dropping her coffee, she fled to the cobblestone path leading away to the gate. Judas stood up as she departed and, as he did, his sense of duty buttressed his strength.

"Ursula, wait!" called Judas in a powerful voice, its tone loud and clear. Ursula turned around on the path and viewed him with mouth agape. Judas looked like a holy knight of the Middle Ages, the fifteen-year-old backlit by the dim glow of the shrine. The immense statue of the Virgin Mary loomed over him and seemingly implored him to action, the scene appearing like a compelling Catholic painting. Judas promised, "I'll find her."

"What?" Ursula mewled with tears streaming down her pale face. She wiped them away with her sleeve and sniffled.

"I'll find Tammy," Judas vowed with stern conviction. Approaching Ursula with firm, deliberate footfalls, he kneeled in front of her and took her trembling hand in his own. He looked on her with piercing eyes and pledged, "I promise. I'll find her and bring her back to you."

Ursula felt her trepidation subside and her hope surge. Sensing no falsity or uncertainty in Judas, she grasped him by the cheeks, leaned down and kissed him. The gentle caress of their lips meeting forever bound them to one another, a link that immediately caused them heavenly joy and hellish sorrow. One incredible second later, Judas saw Courtney in his mind and pulled away.

"She wasn't just a friend," Ursula said as she read Judas's face. Mortified that she let her guard down only to be rejected, she released Judas and stepped away.

"Well, kind of. I don't know. Maybe," said Judas. Flames of mortification engulfed Ursula while the competing forces of Ursula and Courtney tore at Judas. Fearing that Ursula might flee, he grasped her by the shoulders and advised her, "It was Courtney Melendez."

Ursula's emotions melted away. The night grew quiet as the fountains ceased.

"This isn't a coincidence," Ursula said while contemplating their intertwining destinies. She inquired calmly, "But what can we do other than have faith in God and pray for them?"

"Now we will arise, and we will set them in the safety for which they long," replied Judas. (Psalm 12:5). Ursula nodded in agreement. Disregarding the complexities of their relationship and the dangers of the real world, they sealed their pact with an embrace.

******

"I hope their pain is worth it," Father Ray prayed as he watched Judas and Ursula hug one another via the Marian shrine's security cameras. Ruing his failure to keep them apart, he sighed, "It was only a matter of time, I guess."

The priest resisted Aubrey Stillerson's suggestions that he install the cameras and construct a control room in the Church but, as usual, she ignored his objections. He now appreciated their usefulness.

"Thank you, Aubrey," Father Ray muttered.

"It's not like you to leave doors unlocked, especially at night," said Sister Palladia as she stepped into the open doorway of the Church's control room. The nun was dressed in her full regalia.

"I wonder which one's the chaser, the one who's going to bleed when they crash and burn," Father Ray said acerbically but without looking away from the screen.

"Excuse me?" said Sister Palladia. Entering the room, she proceeded to Father Ray and caught a glimpse of the teenagers' embrace. She attempted to hide her surprise but he heard her catch her breath. Father Ray slowly turned his head to gloat at her.

"Now why would a simple hug between two teenagers bother you?" Father Ray queried haughtily. Sister Palladia maintained her ruse and smirked.

"It doesn't concern me in the least, Father," replied Sister Palladia, "other than the fact that it's a hug between two unsupervised teenagers of the opposite sex."

The quality of her performance caused Father Ray to consider that Sister Palladia might know of Judas's abilities and, if she did not, the efficacy of revealing them to her. He, for the first time in years, saw a peaceful path to retirement and his self-interest warred with his concern for his young charges.

"Three birds with one stone and they'd all be better for it," Father Ray urged himself. The words of Aubrey and a selfish idea arose in his mind. Sister Palladia noticed his mental calculations as he said to himself, "And it opens up the *other* option."

"To be able to read your mind," said Sister Palladia as she attempted to do so through the windows of Father Ray's eyes.

"Ditto, sweetheart," Father Ray snapped. He whirled around and snarled with a glower, "Why don't you cut the bullshit and tell me why you're really here?"

"To tell you the truth would be to violate the vows I've taken to God and the Church," answered Sister Palladia calmly and respectfully despite her trust in Father Ray. Taking a seat in one of the control room chairs, she motioned for him to do the same and stated, "But I can tell you what you already know."

"How does that help?" Father Ray asked suspiciously while declining Sister Palladia's invitation to be seated. Her civility and her strange response puzzled him and his vitriol disappeared.

"God has blessed Ursula with the charism of healing," replied Sister Palladia earnestly, "and shortly thereafter, Reynald, I arrived."

Father Ray's countenance grew grim and he returned his attention to the monitor. Sister Palladia patiently watched him as he watched Ursula and Judas, the pair again sitting on the bench and engaging in a serious discussion. Father Ray gradually perceived the spiritual connection developing between them. He grinned.

"Well, you might wanna break that up then," Father Ray said with a nod to the screen, the priest enjoying the wrench God threw into Sister Palladia's plans. Conflicted as to whether he should reveal Judas's gift to her, he continued to avoid her gaze by watching his mentees.

"Why is that?" asked Sister Palladia with a tilt of her head. The complications of Judas's and Ursula's fledgling relationship escaped her and, deciding to maintain at least one advantage, Father Ray played his cards to the vest. He glanced at Sister Palladia.

"She just can't see it. *Good*," Father Ray thought with devious delight. It proved to be short-lived, however, as looking back to the screen, he noticed Judas and Ursula were gone.

6 – Turning The Wicked To Ruin

"Get in," Ursula instructed as she raised the tailgate of Aunt Vicki's Traverse. She scanned the parking lot and the church for any signs of her aunt as Judas clambered into the vehicle. Covering him up with a blanket and piling other debris on top of him, she whispered, "Now stay there. I'll come get you after she thinks I'm asleep."

"Ursula!" shouted Aunt Vicki as she exited the church and quickly walked to her with Father Ray in tow. Seeing the oncoming adults, Ursula slammed the tailgate shut and scurried over to them to keep them away from the car. Aunt Vicki was visibly upset but the priest seemed unusually reserved.

"What's wrong?" Ursula replied, the teenager silently praying that Judas would remain undiscovered.

"Where've you been, young lady?" inquired Aunt Vicki brusquely as she arrived in front of her niece and embraced her. She then released Ursula and gesticulated wildly while scolding her, "You can't just disappear like that! You scared me! Especially with all the kidnappings going on around here. What were you thinking?"

"I just went to the shrine with Judas," Ursula advised. Father Ray said nothing and gave no indication that he witnessed Ursula's conversation with the boy. She assured Aunt Vicki, "I was perfectly safe."

"Who's Judas?" demanded Aunt Vicki.

"He's the boy at St. John Berchmans that I mentor," interjected Father Ray.

"The one who gets in trouble all the time?" asked an incredulous Aunt Vicki. She threw an angry, sidelong glance at Father Ray.

"He was just being nice to me, Aunt Vickie," Ursula said in defense of Judas. She added in a high-pitched voice, "His girl . . . ."

Ursula stopped speaking to hide her feelings but not before Father Ray heard the infatuation in her voice and subtly cringed. The thought of Courtney being Judas's girlfriend wounded her but she composed herself.

"His girlfriend was kidnapped just like Tammy," Ursula stated. Aunt Vicki's anger cooled as she remembered the news reports of the second victim. Collecting herself, Ursula explained, "We both lost friends and we were just talking about it. That's all."

"Speaking of Judas, where is he?" asked Father Ray with narrowed eyes. Something was off about the situation but he could not put his finger on it.

"I spilled my coffee at the shrine and he went to get something to clean it up," Ursula lied. Father Ray remembered her dropping of her cup and, for the moment, it made him believe her story. She silently prayed again, this time for forgiveness, and with feigned confusion queried, "Didn't you see him inside?"

"I'd better go track him down," said Father Ray, his departure serving the dual purpose of locating Judas and escaping Aunt Vicki's wrath. He added with a tilt of his head, "So, if you'll excuse me, I'll see you two ladies at Mass tomorrow."

Hurrying off, Father Ray soon disappeared into the church. Aunt Vicki spun Ursula around and ushered her towards the car.

"We're not done, Ursula," said Aunt Vicki, her pushing swiftly becoming dragging. Arriving at the car, she opened the front passenger door and motioned for Ursula to get inside, continuing, "No more wandering off without telling me and no more wandering off alone, *period*. And I *don't* want you hanging out with this Judas. Do you understand me?"

"*Okay*," Ursula whined. Squelching her urge to defend Judas, Ursula entered the car, sat down and absorbed the jarring noise of her door slamming shut. Aunt Vicki's lecture continued the entire way home but Ursula remained quiet. Satisfied that the noise helped conceal Judas's presence, she stifled a grin and thought, "This may actually work."

******

Confident that Aunt Vicki slumbered soundly, Ursula climbed out of her bedroom window. She eased it closed and cautiously descended from the second story to the first.

"Sneaking out of your window at night?" Sister Palladia greeted Ursula as she neared the ground. Startled by her teacher's appearance, she jumped down the last three feet and spun around to face her. Sister Palladia, with her hands folded, said, "That doesn't seem like you, Ursula."

The nun did not look like a servant of God to the fourteen-year-old. Sister Palladia wore her hair in a tight ponytail and dressed in black from head-to-toe save for a maroon turtleneck sweater. Succumbing to the change in weather, Sister Palladia also wore black gloves and a jacket.

"What're you doing here?" hissed Ursula. She instinctively pressed her body against the siding of the house although she felt no threat from Sister Palladia. A dog barked several houses over and it caused Ursula to twitch.

"I need to speak with you before you make this decision," Sister Palladia replied without acknowledging the dog.

"It couldn't wait 'til Monday?" answered Ursula impatiently. She desperately desired to free Judas from Aunt Vickie's car and Sister Palladia's impromptu visit delayed their plans. She looked in the direction of the Traverse even though she could not see it.

"Unfortunately, no," Sister Palladia said. She stepped towards Ursula, who shivered with adrenaline, and added, "You and Judas have forced my hand on this."

Ursula's heart sank and she went pale. She experienced a sudden, intense fear for Judas but buried it deep along with her anxiousness.

"If you wanna talk to me, then you let him go," replied Ursula defiantly. Scowling at Sister Palladia, she braced for the trouble to come and said, "Or I'm not listening to you."

"I'm not here to stop Judas," Sister Palladia advised. She sympathized with Ursula's plight and gave her a look of sincere pity. Her response proved better than Ursula expected; however, she still intended to defend Judas at all moral costs.

"But you're here to stop me, and I'm going with him," answered Ursula bitterly. She felt her tenuous grasp on Judas slipping away but, resolved to protect him, she set her feet and declared, "You have to let him go. That's the deal, okay?"

"I'm here to offer you a choice, Ursula, not force you into one," Sister Palladia said while placing a reassuring hand on her arm. Ursula squirmed beneath the affection as Sister Palladia added, "You only have to listen and then make that choice. Judas's destiny is his own and I won't interfere with it. But his destiny doesn't have to be yours."

"*What do you want?*" said Ursula with tears welling in her eyes and angst welling in her heart.

"I know of your gift," Sister Palladia said, her expression expectant yet cautious. The revelation paralyzed Ursula. Squeezing her arm, Sister Palladia stated, "And I'm here to help you share it with the world."

Ursula's anxiousness faded. She sensed the waves of kismet washing over her but remembered Father Ray's zealous admonitions.

"What if I told you there's a way for you to use your gift in secret?" asked Sister Palladia as if reading her mind. She joined Ursula in leaning against the house and said, "To heal the ill and the infirm and serve God in the shadows."

"You're not a Sister of the Holy Family of Nazareth, are you?" inquired Ursula as she stared at the ground in front of her. Her curiosity burgeoned.

"So precocious," Sister Palladia commented, the nun outwardly measured but inwardly rejoicing in the Holy Spirit's presence in Ursula. Reaching into her turtleneck, she produced her necklace and held its wooden charm in her fingers. Sister Palladia methodically massaged it and asked, "Are you familiar with the Crusades, Ursula?"

"Yeah, a little," answered Ursula though her uncertainty belied her answer. Sister Palladia's tangent agitated her and she grumbled, "From when I took World History."

"So you know about the First Crusade, when Catholic armies from Europe recaptured the City of Jerusalem from its Muslim rulers in 1099?" Sister Palladia queried. A bewildered Ursula gaped at her as, again with hands folded, she inquired, "And that crusaders from all walks of life would 'take the cross', meaning that they committed themselves to the crusade in exchange for remission – *forgiveness* – of their sins?"

"I don't know *that* much about it," replied Ursula, the teenager feeling as if she were back in her World History class and bored to tears by Sister Marie. She contemplated escape from Sister Palladia's bizarre lecture and said with poorly veiled annoyance, "But I guess I'll take your word for it."

"Good," Sister Palladia replied with a wry smile. Ursula shifted her weight and looked at the ground as the nun expounded, "The physical representation of 'taking the cross' was a small cross of textile or other material sewn onto the shoulder. Now the only *woman* known to have taken the cross is Emerias of Alteias, said to be a rich French noblewoman by some sources, and by others, a Catholic sister."

Ursula fidgeted. Her patience and her attention frayed with every passing word.

"It's believed that in the year 1098, Emerias sought out Izarn, Bishop of Toulouse in France, to receive his blessing for her journey to the Holy Land. He reportedly dissuaded her from that perilous journey," Sister Palladia continued. Peeved by Ursula's drifting focus and body language, she stepped in front of her, smacked her face and demanded, "Pay attention."

Taken aback by Sister Palladia's physicality, Ursula obeyed. She offered the nun a look of contrition.

"Thank you," Sister Palladia said tersely. She began pacing back and forth in front of Ursula as she explained, "Now, as I said, he reportedly dissuaded her from that perilous journey and, instead, ordered that she re-establish the ruined Church of St. Orient. The Church was donated by local noblemen, and Emerias was tasked with serving our Lord there by serving the poor. She supposedly accepted the Bishop's command, but there is nothing else recorded about her."

Sister Palladia ceased speaking and let the nighttime calm creep around them. The conflicted expression on Ursula's face caused her to break the silence with a chortle.

"I know what you're thinking, Ursula," Sister Palladia said, her sternness fading. Walking up to her, she continued, "You're wondering, 'What in heaven's name does this have to do with me?'"

Ursula bowed her head and said nothing but Sister Palladia took her chin in both hands and raised it. Gazing on her with great faith, she addressed her gravely.

"That story is accurate with one very important exception," Sister Palladia stated with great satisfaction and pride. Releasing Ursula's face but not her attention, she said, "You see, Ursula, Pope Urban II visited Toulouse during his preaching tour to recruit for the First Crusade. He arrived there on May 24, 1096, and met a woman – young, strong, and standing as tall as a man – who offered her sword in service to the Church. Yet, more importantly, she possessed great faith and love for her Lord, and *something else*: a gift of the Holy Spirit. It was that gift that convinced the Pope that she was destined for the Holy Land."

A single tear ran down Ursula's face. Sister's Palladia's glacial explanation now overwhelmed her as it picked up speed and turned in her direction.

"Emerias, possessor of the gift of healing, took the cross from Pope Urban himself that very day, and, by secret papal bull written that night, the Emerian Order was formed," Sister Palladia said with a seriousness that struck Ursula's very spirit.

"What happened to her?" asked Ursula. Wrapped up in the hidden tale of Emerias, she gripped Sister Palladia's hands tightly.

"She left with the contingent of Raymond IV, Count of Toulouse, in October 1096," Sister Palladia answered, "and was in Jerusalem when it fell in 1099 . . . ."

Sister Palladia's voice faded as a spasm of pained sorrow rippled across her face. Appearing as if she might cry, she wobbled but Ursula steadied her and felt the lean muscularity of her arms and shoulders.

"A story for another time," Sister Palladia muttered as her face turned to stone. She remained silent for ten seconds, her visage slowly regaining its humanness. She looked up and continued, "Emerias's sister, Celsa, remained in France and, in 1098, took the cross in her sister's name and faithfully served the poor until her death. And that is from where the story arises, as ordered by the Pope so that the Emerian Order would remain a secret. And so it has remained, known to only a precious few for nearly a thousand years."

Both women remained silent for over a minute as Sister Palladia treasured her vocation in her heart and Ursula pondered her options. The older woman set her troubles at the feet of her Lord and smiled.

"There is one more detail that might interest you," Sister Palladia said. Leaning towards Ursula, she explicated, "The 1096 meeting between Pope Urban and Emerias occurred after he consecrated the altar of a church in Toulouse. It was the altar in the Basillica of St. Sernin, first Bishop of Toulouse, or, as others called him, *St. Saturnin*."

Astonishment washed over Ursula's face and her head reeled as she absorbed knowledge of God's will for her life. Her tears flourished and rolled down her face. Her wish to serve Him through the use of her gift had been granted.

"But I'm not tall, or strong, and I can't fight," argued Ursula. She greatly feared Sister Palladia's offer as evidenced by her quivering bottom lip. Suddenly remembering her pact with Judas, she inquired in distress, "And what about Judas?"

"You have faith in God and the charism. That's all you need, Ursula. The body can be made strong and one can learn to fight," Sister Palladia replied. She turned her back on Ursula and walked towards a line of trees on the edge of the property, saying, "As for Judas . . . to join the Emerians you must take a vow of chastity."

Sister Palladia's last statement shocked Ursula out of her distress. Ursula wiped away her tears and composed herself.

"The Lord is requesting your service, Ursula," Sister Palladia advised. Ursula's reluctance concerned her and she asked solemnly, "How will you answer Him?"

******

Stealthily maneuvering through the cornfield, Judas repeatedly squeezed the handle of his .357 caliber pistol in anticipation of the violence to come. He set the gun on the ground, kneeled in a low patch of corn and raised his binoculars. A remote, abandoned motel consisting of dilapidated individual units arose directly ahead of Judas, each one black-roofed and hastily wrapped with white, discolored siding.

"One, two, three occupied units," Judas thought to himself as he counted faint glows behind the shades of the units' rear windows. He attempted to stretch out his spiritual perception but the distance between he and the units proved insurmountable. A shadowy figure patrolled the cement walkway running along the front side of the units, the red, circular glow of his cigarette periodically detectable as he moved between buildings.

"Only one guarding the front and no one covering the back," Judas said as he allowed himself a few more steps. He seethed over the traffickers' arrogance and added, "They're not even worried about getting caught."

Heavy footfalls arose behind Judas and, in response, he held up his hand. Steve ceased his lumbering approach, the sandy-haired behemoth carrying a scoped hunting rifle that looked like a toy in his massive hands. He kneeled on one knee behind Judas and supported himself with the butt of the rifle.

"Mike says there's one in an SUV in the barn across the street," whispered Steve, "and the guys' cars are in there, too. So we gotta wait 'til they're gone and then we can do it."

"No," Judas corrected Steve as he detected the anxiousness in his friend's voice. He lowered his binoculars and said, "I'm going in now."

A sudden, stiff breeze ushered in the chill of early morning. Despite it being the middle of fall, the wind revealed that the day would be colder than normal. Steve shivered. Judas did not.

"We can't go in there when there's *five* of 'em," protested Steve. He scooted closer to Judas with a look of incredulity on his broad face and added, "Besides, they're not the ones running it."

"But their perversions feed the beast," Judas replied with a sneer. His righteous wrath welled within him and he stated, "They're just as guilty, just as deserving of punishment."

"Three teenagers against five grown men? Those odds suck," complained Steve. His whisper became a hiss as he argued, "We're just kids, man! And Ursula's not gonna be able to help. We should call the Sheriff and get outta here, Jude."

"My name is Judas," announced Judas as he abruptly whirled his head around and chastised Steve with an unforgiving glare. It cowed the gigantic teenager, his fear palpable despite his size.

"I'm not going in there until they're gone," objected Steve, the mountain of a young man speaking with a wavering in his voice. Judas offered him a sympathetic expression and, shuffling towards his friend, placed a reassuring hand on his wide shoulder.

"You're not going in there at all," Judas instructed him. He determinedly met Steve's troubled gaze before rotating back around and saying, "Radio Mike and tell him to stay put no matter what happens, and you do the same. You hear me? *No matter what happens.*"

"You can't go in there alone!" replied Steve in an elevated tone. He stood up and gestured emphatically as he added, "How do you even know that's what they're doing?! Wouldn't the cops know about it by now?"

"Shut up!" Judas hissed as he motioned for Steve to lower his profile. Steve obeyed and returned to his crouched position. Many silent seconds ensued as Judas stared forward without fear or reluctance. He finally raised his chin and said, "You hear rumors about this place everywhere, Steve. All you gotta do is listen . . . and put the right pieces together."

Ursula crept up behind them and immediately caught Judas's eye. She wore her black winter hat, her jacket and her gloves, the adolescent looking as if she were on a ski vacation. Judas's gaze lingered on her and then darted back to Steve. He seemed uneasy whenever he looked at Ursula as evidenced by the veiled sourness on his face.

"I'm not letting it happen anymore, *not here*, not when God's given me the power to stop it," Judas stated eerily. He allowed his words to sink into Steve's mind and then asked, "You're good with that rifle, right?"

"Been shooting it since I was eight," answered Steve proudly as he patted the rifle. He straightened himself and pressed its butt into his shoulder with the barrel pointed at the ground.

"Good," Judas said as he glanced back at Steve. He stowed his binoculars in his backpack, nodded to Ursula and said, "All you need to do is protect her and keep your eyes open. And, if you can, cover me if I come back in a hurry. But remember, I may not be the only one coming back."

Steve nodded in the affirmative. Ursula wanted to send Judas off with an embrace but fought the urge.

"Be careful," mouthed Ursula. Judas selfishly hoped for another kiss but she maintained her distance. Ursula's inaction gave him pause.

"I will," Judas mouthed back feebly, the two words all he could muster as he turned away from her. The breeze picked up and blew steadily for over a minute. Judas stirred when it died, the youth removing two gloves of a thin, tough material from his backpack and sliding them onto his hands. He then produced a ski mask, pulled it over his head and picked up his handgun.

"'The righteous one considers the home of the wicked, Turning the wicked to ruin,'" Judas recited as he ventured into the darkness alone. (Proverbs 21:12).

******

The Great Star Motel was, at one time, a quaint and well-maintained stop for those traveling U.S. 223 towards Adrian, Michigan. Abandoned for decades, however, it degraded into a ramshackle eyesore and overgrown nuisance that no entity had interest in tearing down.

Approaching the last building in a line of seven, Judas placed his fingertips on the muntin bar of the rear window and gently eased the sash upward. It, to his surprise, was not locked and lifted with little effort. He carefully cracked the window one inch and listened carefully.

"Overdid it, huh?" asked a man inside, his words accompanied by the slow creaking of mattress springs. Judas focused intently on the sounds and attempted to determine their distance from the window.

"Ovuh di wha?" replied a young, female voice in a spacey, slurred tone. The irregular creaking continued as if she squirmed on the bed. Judas engaged his spiritual perception and, concentrating on its use, he detected the presence and locations of two people inside the unit. He was acutely aware of their life forces as if the back wall was absent and he looked directly upon them.

"Just go to sleep, baby," urged the man as the creaking ceased, "I'll do all the work."

A rage detonated within Judas as his suspicions were confirmed. Projecting his consciousness forward, he throttled the spirit of the man and smothered it. The sounds of a muffled thud and an abrupt creak reached his ears, the noise causing him to withdraw his power. Judas paused and felt the man's weakened life force.

"He's out, and so is she," Judas thought. Opening the low window the rest of the way, he sat on the sill and swung his legs over it. He quickly maneuvered around the closed shade, the teenager insinuating himself between the wall and a small, round table in front of the window. Scanning his surroundings, he saw the poor condition of the building and inhaled the foul smell of cigarettes and alcohol. Traces of other unpleasant odors also floated around the room, the stank causing Judas to scowl and think, "Gross."

A lamp without a shade emitted dull light in the corner to Judas's left while a door to his right opened onto a dank, dingy closet of a bathroom. Stepping forward into the main living area, he confirmed that only two people occupied the unit. A full bed surrounded by dirty, worn carpet extended from the right wall into the center of the room and upon it, beneath a grizzled, wiry man clad only in unfastened jeans, lay a teenage girl. They were both unconscious.

Moving fluidly and quietly, Judas grabbed the man, pulled him off his red-headed paramour and lowered him to the floor. He retrieved a roll of duct tape from his backpack and dexterously bound the man's ankles, wrists and hands. Judas also made several passes around his head to gag him. He stood up.

"She's alive," Judas whispered as, loathing any contact with the dirty blankets and sheets, he examined the girl carefully while hovering above her. Her breathing, while shallow, was regular, her skin was flushed and a trickle of mucous leaked from her right nostril. Heroine and related paraphernalia lay scattered about a bedside table along with an ash tray, several packs of cigarettes and a bottle of vodka. Determining the girl, who appeared no more than fifteen, to be stable, he said, "Keep breathing, *please.*"

The man stirred but did not awaken. Satisfied that he was incapacitated, Judas locked the front door and then hurried to the window. He climbed out of it and closed it.

"One down, two to go," Judas thought as he crept to the corner of the building and quickly looked around it. Peering into the space between the units, he saw nothing. He pulled back his head and attempted to sense the presence of the guard and, after several seconds of concentration, he felt him moving at the front of the building. Peeking around the corner again, he watched him pass while taking a drag on his cigarette. Judas said to himself, "Lead the way."

Shadowing the guard on the opposite side of the buildings, he eventually arrived at the fifth motel unit. Mimicking his earlier attempt, he tried to open the window. It failed to budge.

"Locked," Judas thought as he scowled in frustration. He sensed two presences inside and it prickled him that he could not intercede. Focusing on the guard's spiritual energy, he waited until he passed the fifth unit on his return route and then scurried to the next building. Its window, though locked, possessed a faulty locking mechanism and Judas opened it by applying extra force to a cautious upward thrust. His success prompted him to pray, "By the grace of God. *Thank you.*"

"That's it, take it off," urged a male voice. Using the same method as with the first john, Judas located the man, interrupted his spiritual energy and incapacitated him. He paused after hearing a muffled squeal but, when the silence returned, he slithered through the window with all possible speed. The unit was cleaner than the first one though still shabby and unkempt and it also lacked a table. Noticing a thin, blonde teenager cowering on the bed, Judas held his index finger to his lips.

"Who are you?" whispered the frightened girl in a high-pitched tone. She pulled up the covers to hide herself and scrunched up against the tattered headboard. Saying nothing, Judas tapped his finger on his lips four times. The girl shivered and obeyed but closely watched him as he approached. The bedside table was, like the first one, littered with drugs, cigarettes and alcohol.

Brandishing his duct tape, he restrained the man in the same manner as he did the first. The man awoke just as Judas wrapped the gray tape around his head. Grasping the man's nose between his thumb and forefinger, Judas invaded his personal space and glowered at him.

"Behave yourself," Judas whispered. The man struggled briefly and, with a reddening face, screamed, his yelling causing the girl to start and cry out. His resistance ceased when Judas again interrupted his life force.

The front door was thrown open and the guard – the tall, well-built man with stringy, black hair and a matching beard – entered with a .38 caliber revolver drawn. Brandishing his own weapon with incredible celerity, Judas aimed it at the guard and fired twice. Both bullets struck the guard in the chest and he stumbled backward out of the door as the terrified teenager shrieked.

Judas, with proverbial ice water in his veins, remained stationary and immediately extended his spiritual perception as far as it would go. He sensed six life forces in the line of motel units and another fast approaching from the direction of the barn across the street.

"Rick . . . Rick!" beckoned a harsh voice amid the pounding of feet on the crumbling pavement of the parking lot. The door of the fifth unit creaked open but was met by the voice which demanded, "Get the hell back in there!"

Three shots rang out, their booms followed by the shout of a man and the slamming of a door. Holding his ground, Judas waited patiently for the second guard.

"Both of you, come out! Now!" ordered the guard. The girl looked to Judas who shook his head in the negative and motioned for her to move to the floor. She complied and eased herself downward while pulling the bedding with her. The guard hit the side of the house and growled, "Come out, Gina!"

Bursting into the room, the guard wildly fired two shots from a nine-millimeter pistol. He, too, fell victim to Judas's aim and his .357, the burly man falling backwards in the doorway after being struck twice in the chest.

"*Courtney*," Judas said as he remembered the bullets fired into the fifth unit. Leaping to his feet, Judas sprinted towards it.

******

Huddling into herself, Ursula battled both the icy breeze and her concern for Judas. She yearned to chase after him and protect the courageous teenager despite having no idea how she would accomplish such a feat.

"Okay, he's inside the first one," reported Steve as he watched Judas through his binoculars. He continued to kneel on one knee with his rifle leaning against his shoulder.

"He shouldn't be doing this alone," Ursula protested as she moved next to Steve. The quiet night made his heavy breaths sound like peals of thunder in her ears.

"He told us to stay here, *no matter what happens*," countered Steve with an anxious glance at Ursula. She stoically returned it.

"He told *you* to stay here," Ursula said.

"Yeah, but he also told me to keep an eye on you," grumbled Steve with waning patience. Taking his point, Ursula exhaled in frustration and returned her attention to the first unit.

"I should've went with him," Ursula thought. Waiting for minutes that seemed like hours, she bemoaned every second until Judas reappeared. She clasped her hands together to cease their trembling but the attempt failed.

"See," said Steve while handing the binoculars to Ursula, "he's fine."

"Really?" Ursula asked as she whisked the binoculars out of Steve's hands. She observed Judas sneak to the corner of the first unit and peer around it. He then pulled back his head, paused for what Ursula thought to be a lifetime and peeked around the corner again. She inhaled sharply as Judas and the guard walked nearly parallel on opposite sides of the buildings.

"What's going on?" demanded Steve. He attempted to retrieve his binoculars but Ursula nimbly evaded his large hands.

"He's trying the window on the fifth one," advised Ursula as she nudged Steve away, "but it looks like it's locked. Now he's moving on to the next unit. The guard's going the other way now, so he should be okay, for a little while anyway."

Judas forced the window open on his second attempt. His success prompted Ursula to pray.

"By the grace of God. *Thank you*," she whispered.

"C'mon, let me see," griped Steve as he grabbed the binoculars. Proving no match for his strength, Ursula struggled and dodged him for but a few seconds before surrendering. Steve looked through the binoculars and hissed, "He's gone!"

Leaping to her feet, Ursula yanked the binoculars from Steve's hands and raised them to her eyes. She shook with fearful anticipation as she searched for Judas. Three minutes later, they heard a faint cry from the direction of the sixth unit, followed shortly thereafter by two gunshots and a screech.

"*Judas*," Ursula mewled. Dropping the binoculars, she forgot everything but the fifteen-year-old crusader and sprinted towards the motel.

"Ursula," begged Steve, "wait!"

Ursula heard the shouts of a deep voice and more gunfire. She tripped on a rock in the field and tumbled to the ground. Ignoring the pain of a sore knee, she jumped up and continued towards the motel.

"Both of you, come out! Now!" ordered a man's voice as Ursula arrived at the rear of the sixth unit and flattened herself against it. Someone hit the side of the house and the voice growled, "Come out, Gina!"

Rounding the back corner of the building, Ursula heard the front door thrown open and two more gunshots followed closely by two more. A sickening thump of something hitting the ground paralyzed her for several seconds.

"God, please, no," Ursula whimpered quietly. The thought of Judas being wounded spurred her to action. She overcame her terror and ran to the front of the building.

******

Arriving at the fifth unit's front door, Judas met a portly, half-dressed man fleeing the scene. He cold cocked the middle-aged john with a powerful, left-handed punch and dropped him where he stood. The man remained motionless after hitting the ground but a mobile phone slid out of his hand and clattered on the cement porch.

Judas paused and looked at the phone. Stooping and picking it up, he stepped over the john's body and entered the building. Another teenager with yellowish hair, exhausted eyes and wearing only her bra and panties lay on the bed. She lazily turned her gaze to Judas and his heart immediately sank: Courtney was not at the Great Star Motel.

"I'm bleeding," said the dazed girl. She held her right shoulder which oozed blood.

"Damn it," Judas said in exasperation. Sensing a presence behind him, he whirled around and lifted his gun. It was Ursula.

"It's just me," blurted Ursula as she held up her arms in surrender.

"You were supposed to stay with Steve," Judas replied, the teenager irked by her disobedience and risk-taking. Noticing the girl's wound, Ursula shoved Judas out of her way and sat next to her on the bed. The authority with which she acted shocked Judas and he exclaimed, "What're you doing?!"

"I can help her," answered Ursula firmly as the girl lost consciousness. Focusing only on her ward, she removed her right glove, held her hand to the bullet wound, bowed her head and prayed for God's healing grace. Judas marveled at Ursula's courage and the way the flow of blood stopped. She removed her hand from the girl's shoulder and, to Judas's great surprise, only intact, blood-and-dirt-smeared skin remained.

"How did you do that?" Judas inquired in astonishment. Ursula caressed the girl's forehead and then turned to him.

"You're not the only one who's been blessed by God," said Ursula. Marching forward, Judas grabbed her by the arm and ushered her out of the unit. She struggled against his efforts and objected, "Hey! *Judas*, stop it!"

"Go back to Steve, now," Judas demanded. Hurt by his gruffness and rough treatment, Ursula wriggled out of his grasp and pushed him away.

"Why?!" asked Urusla. Judas realized the harshness of his tone and relented.

"*Please*. Just trust me and go," he pleaded. Giving her a quick kiss on the forehead, he drained her of her angry resistance. Judas maneuvered her to the space between units four and five and placed his lips near her right ear.

"I'll be back soon," he promised with a gentle nudge, "now *go*."

******

Judas duct-taped the middle-aged john on the porch of the building with his mind racing a circuit of his current situation, Ursula and Courtney. The girl in unit six watched him from the doorway with nervous brown eyes. She was enveloped in a blanket and wore nothing on her feet.

"Who are you?" asked the girl again as she shifted the blanket on her body. Judas looked up to her.

"It doesn't matter," he answered. He felt nauseous as he contemplated the girl's age and the circumstances into which she had been forced. Scooping up the man's cell phone, he tossed it to the girl, who caught it, and said, "Call 9-1-1 and then stay in here with her and lock the door. I'll tape this guy up and then you'll be safe."

The girl hesitated. She watched Judas with mistrust while he finished restraining the john.

"It's over now," Judas assured her. Giving the john a swift kick, he looked up to her and said, "See, he's not going anywhere. Make the call."

The girl dialed 9-1-1 and conversed with the operator as Judas dragged the man into unit six. She, to the chagrin of the operator, ended their conversation by setting the phone on the bed. Judas finished his task and prepared to flee before the police arrived. The operator called out for the girl.

"Wait," begged the girl. Judas halted and turned around. She, with watery eyes, removed her necklace. Grasping both ends of the chain, she held its charm aloft so that it shimmered in the weak light.

"'Vindicate the weak and fatherless; Do justice to the afflicted and destitute,'" she read from the charm, "'Rescue the weak and needy; Deliver them out of the hand of the wicked.'"

Her compelling words instantaneously and permanently branded Judas's heart and spirit with the mission set forth in Psalm 82. Placing the necklace in his hand, the girl closed his fist with both hands and nodded gently.

"It was my Dad's. My Gramma gave it to me, before I ran away," explained the girl. Tightly wrapping the blanket around her body, she bowed her head in disgrace and whimpered, "I'm sure she hates me now."

Judas hugged the girl and she greedily accepted the comfort. Courtney's face arose in his mind, however, and he simultaneously mourned for her.

"'Return to your house,'" Judas whispered in the girl's ear, "'and describe what great things God has done for you.'" (Luke 8:39).

A siren suddenly rang out in the distance, its shrillness piercing the chilly night air. Judas, without another word, disentangled himself from the girl's embrace and rounded the corner.

"Wait!" begged the girl. Judas turned his body halfway and watched her over his shoulder. The girl, with sorrow etched on her face, trembled and said, "There're other girls. I heard them talking. They're at a farm somewhere in Ohio. It's not that far away from here."

Judas's adrenaline soared as he considered the possibility that Courtney was being held at the site. His next target chosen, he disappeared into the night.

7 – The Hall Of Guilt

Fourteen-year-old Mike drove off in his grandmother's old minivan, Judas's underage accomplice tasked with sneaking the vehicle back into her garage. Ursula watched the van's taillights dwindle and then disappear as it rounded a corner.

She and Judas sat on a ring of landscaping blocks circumscribing a large, leafless tree in her neighborhood's park. The breeze died and everything from the trees to the playground equipment appeared frozen in time. Ursula turned to Judas and observed him staring at the ground.

"We did it," said Ursula hopefully though the declaration of their success felt odd as it passed her lips. Their first triumph, at least in her young mind, seemed inadequate and stained by the taking of human life. Judas did not respond to her comment and, sensing that he walked far afield in his thoughts, Ursula called out, "Judas?"

He remained inert. Seized of his first victory against the iniquity of human trafficking, Judas felt no comfort. His efforts did not save Courtney and the failure gnawed at his gut.

"*Judas,*" called Ursula again as she grasped the sleeve of his jacket and shook it. Awoken by her touch, he slowly exited the realm of deep reflection but kept his eyes downward. Ursula placed her left hand under Judas's chin and lifted it, asking, "What's wrong?"

A dejected Judas indulged in the comfort of her warm attention. He trembled, the adolescent seeing Courtney's exotic blue eyes in his mind and Ursula's unremarkable brown eyes in his reality.

"Oh. Courtney. Sorry," said Ursula awkwardly. She released her grip on his chin and stood up. The loss of her touch pained Judas but the image of Courtney guilted him into inaction. Reading the conflict on his face, Ursula set aside her own feelings, thrust her hands into her coat pockets and assured him, "We're going to find her, Judas."

"I know," Judas replied after a hard swallow. Maneuvering away from his conflicting emotions, he pondered loftier issues and uttered, "But will it be too late?"

Judas noticed Ursula shiver. He stood up and offered her his hand.

"We should get you home," Judas said. Ursula withdrew her right hand from her pocket to accept Judas's offer but stopped in the middle of her reach.

"Why didn't you go with Mike?" inquired Ursula.

"Because I need to get you home," Judas answered while continuing to hold out his hand, "and we couldn't risk dropping you off at your house."

Judas extended his hand further towards her. Ursula gripped it and the pair exited the park.

"Shouldn't *we* be a little more careful then?" asked Ursula as they stepped on the sidewalk and turned right.

"I'm tired of sneaking around tonight, and I think we're good now, anyways," Judas answered. He squeezed her hand and added, "If someone catches us, we'll just tell them we're going out and snuck out to see each other."

Ursula's heart fluttered. Everything about them fit together perfectly: their hands, their appearance as a couple, their gaits. Her desire to kiss him again kindled her guilt and she tried to wiggle her hand free of his grip. Judas refused to let it go.

"We probably shouldn't be doing this," said Ursula, the teen prickled by the fact she walked hand-in-hand with another girl's boyfriend.

"Courtney and I were never together," admitted Judas without looking at Ursula. She glanced at him cautiously while he expounded, "I just wanted us to be together, and there was a chance we were gonna be. That's all."

Ursula felt encouraged yet saddened by Judas's revelation. They walked in silence for two blocks before turning the corner onto her street. A thought struck her when she saw her house and it dulled the pain in her heart.

"You're not going back at all, are you?" queried Ursula shrewdly, the teenager suddenly and terribly worried about Judas.

"No," Judas stated matter-of-factly. He continued their steady march down the street.

"Why?" asked Ursula, her distress evident in her voice.

"From now on, I gotta move forward, not back. *Ever*," answered Judas. Halting in front of a line of high hedges, he said, "They'll only try to stop me and it'll slow me down. Way down. And every hour I waste is another hour that Courtney, Tammy and all the other girls suffer. It's another hour we risk losing them."

"But where are you gonna go?" queried Ursula with growing angst. She searched for the right words to dissuade Judas from his plan but none were forthcoming.

"It doesn't matter," Judas answered. He attempted to continue their walk but, dissatisfied with his answer, Ursula jumped in front of him. Judas sidestepped her but she mimicked his movement and again blocked his advance.

"Maybe we're going too far," suggested Ursula without believing it. Gesturing as she spoke, she reasoned, "We promised we'd find Tammy and Courtney. That's it. That's all we have to do right now. We can do that without you running away. Let's just find them and wait for God's guidance."

"'Vindicate the weak and fatherless; Do justice to the afflicted and destitute,'" he said as he produced the necklace given to him by the girl and held it aloft. He seemed to grow taller and project greater command as he stated, "'Rescue the weak and needy; Deliver them out of the hand of the wicked.' That's the command He's given me, Ursula. That's His guidance."

Given the intensity of the Holy Spirit radiating from Judas, Ursula expected the necklace to shine brightly. Instead, it merely glimmered in the light from the streetlamp. Something about the necklace frightened her and, overwhelmed by Judas's seriousness, she bowed her head and fought off tears.

"One of the girls we saved tonight gave me this," advised Judas, the holy fire burgeoning within him, "a girl who had to live in those shitty conditions day after day, and was hooked on heroin, and forced to have unsafe sex. *She* gave it to me. It's a sign of His will, and I'm gonna carry it out."

Ursula embraced Judas forcefully and buried her face in his chest. He reluctantly wrapped his strong arms around her.

"I know I can't," said Ursula as she clung to him, "but I wanna come with you."

"I wish you could," Judas replied forlornly while moving her away from him, "but it's too dangerous and, if too many of us disappear, they'll find out what we're up to. They'll find us. So, for now, the three of you need to pretend like nothing happened and wait. Once I find that farm, I'll let you know."

"D-d-don't you d-dare go alone," warned Ursula while poking an index finger into his chest. Her shivers became constant and her teeth chattered. She threatened, "I m-m-mean it, Judas."

"I won't, I promise," Judas said with a smile. Nudging her forward, he escorted her to her house and said, "Now let's get you inside before you get sick. I'll give you a boost and-."

"I climbed out of the house without you," interjected Ursula with a smirk. She shoved him playfully and said, "And I can climb back in without you, too."

Enjoying her good-natured and slightly impish rejection of Judas, she scurried away to the house and scaled its side. He watched her ascent until she crawled through and closed her bedroom window. Moving to the line of pine trees, he observed her light come to life.

"What if, when all this is over, Courtney decides she doesn't want me," thought Judas as he continued his vigil outside Ursula's window. She soon extinguished the light but he remained hidden in the trees and ruminated over a decision he was not ready to make.

****

Father Ray groaned and rolled over as his mobile phone screamed at him from the bedside table. He made several errant attempts to grasp it and knocked the lamp to the floor.

"Damn it," Father Ray complained while failing to corral his ringing phone. It tumbled to the floor and bounced under the bed, its evasiveness prompting him to ask, "Why the hell do I leave that ringer on?"

Leaning over the side of the bed, Father Ray swept his hand underneath it and grasped the phone. His momentum caused him to slide to the floor, however, and he landed on his stomach.

"Awesome," he groaned. His vision was too blurry to read but he eventually swiped the glowing screen, held the phone to his ear and said, "Hello."

"Hello, Father, it's Sister Genevieve," said the nun in a distressed tone. The priest laid his forehead on the floor.

"What did he do?" Father Ray inquired defeatedly. Content to lay on the carpet, he rolled onto his back and braced for the bad news to come.

"Please forgive me for calling at this hour but, but . . . Judas is gone!" exclaimed an agitated Sister Genevieve.

"Hold on," Father Ray said as he sat up. He set down the phone, rubbed his eyes and then retrieved it. The time on the screen was 5:23 am. Returning the phone to his ear, he uttered, "Whaddaya mean he's *gone*?"

"He is nowhere to be found in this house or on the grounds, Father," said Sister Genevieve as if Father Ray should have known the answer. He raised himself from the floor and sat on the edge of the bed while the nun expounded, "He retired early last night, said he wasn't feeling well. Given the disappearance of Ms. Melendez, I didn't think much of it. He's gone to bed early every night since it happened and . . . ."

"Uh, oh," Father Ray thought as his blood ran cold. He tapped the speaker icon on the screen, set it on the bedside table and returned the overturned lamp to his nightstand while Sister Genevieve launched into a monologue about Judas. He sat on the mattress again and said to himself, "He didn't forget to lock up last night and return the keys. He never came back. *Damn it.*"

"Father Ray? *Father Ray*!" bellowed Sister Genevieve angrily. Father Ray silently cursed himself for his inattention and clicked on the lamp.

"I'm here," Father Ray snapped. He stood up and asked accusatorily, "Did you call the police?"

"Of course I called the police!" growled Sister Genevieve with offense evident in her voice. Father Ray rolled his eyes as she stated, "They were my first call and a car should be here any moment."

"Good," Father Ray replied. He stretched and said, "Put some coffee on. I'll be there shortly."

Tapping the icon to end the call, Father Ray tossed his phone over his shoulder and it landed on the bed. He exhaled, clapped his hands and then rubbed them together.

"Okay. Donuts to dollars he's huntin' down Courtney," said Father Ray aloud. Walking to his closet and throwing open the doors, he added, "I've gotta move that kid's thought processes north of his heart."

****

Strolling into the parking lot despite the cold Sunday morning air, Father Ray popped his cigar in his mouth. He struck a match but, being wired from too much coffee, he failed to keep his hand still and the flame disappeared. He retrieved another match and swiped it along the box.

"It's gonna be that type of day," Father Ray griped as he lit his cigar and then extinguished the match. Glancing over his shoulder, he made sure he was clear and then tossed the match to the pavement. He puffed on the cigar and emitted smoke like the proverbial chimney, saying, "Got me outta saying Mass today, though. Thank you, Judas."

Three Monroe County Sheriff cruisers were parked at St. John Berchmans Home for Boys as the deputies questioned the staff and residents of the facility. Father Ray intentionally provided little information to the officers, the priest hoping to track down Judas himself and set the boy straight without the intervention of law enforcement. He pondered his whereabouts and enjoyed his cigar while pacing in the parking lot.

"Now, the last time I saw him was at the Marian shrine talking to Ursula," Father Ray said. He froze when realization slapped him in the face. Several seconds later he uttered, "Duh. *Ursula.*"

Reaching into his jacket, he pulled out his phone. Unlocking it with his PIN and maneuvering through several screens, he found Aunt Vickie's number and tapped the "Call" button.

"Please don't be in church," Father Ray said as he lifted the phone to his ear. Listening to it ring, he pleaded, "Please don't be in church."

"Hello, Father," answered Aunt Vickie in a puzzled voice. Father Ray subtly pumped his fist as she said, "It's eight thirty. Why aren't you in Mass right now? Is everything okay? Are you sick? Ursula's sick, too, in fact."

Impatiently absorbing Aunt Vickie's verbal barrage, he grimaced. He switched the phone to his other ear as she yammered.

"Really," Father Ray said when Aunt Vicki halted to take a breath. He queried with a hint of suspicion in his voice, "What's she got?"

"Hard to say. She's zonked out on the couch right now, poor thing," replied Aunt Vickie. Father Ray shook his head as she continued, "She's lethargic, a little nauseous, and she looks absolutely exhausted. My guess is she's been bitten by the flu bug. It's getting to be that time of year."

"Yeah, probably," Father Ray agreed despite believing otherwise. He blew out a cloud of cigar smoke and thought, "Or maybe she was out all night with a certain hooligan that I've taken under my wing."

"Did you need something, Father?" inquired Aunt Vicki, his parishioner's curiosity piqued by his unexpected call. Turning towards the house, Father Ray watched a deputy descend the porch stairs and enter his vehicle.

"Nah, never mind," Father Ray said. He watched the taillights of the deputy's car light up as he said, "You just take care of Urse and tell her my prayers are with her, as always."

"Are you sure, Father?" asked Aunt Vickie. Disquieted that she could not assist her pastor, she advised, "She's okay to stay here by herself for a little while if you need me."

"Thanks, Vickie, but don't worry about it," Father Ray assured her. He grinned haughtily and said, "Now that I think about it, I actually think it's better if I figure it out myself."

******

The Church of St. Saturnin contained two small wings running at forty-five-degree angles from the front of the building. The one to the left of the main entrance housed the sacristy and related rooms while the other housed the confessionals and a small chapel. The chapel provided penitents with an area to reflect and pray before undergoing the Sacrament of Reconciliation.

"Juuuu-das," beckoned Father Ray as he entered what he jokingly called The Hall of Guilt. The vacant Hall led past the confessionals and to the dimly lit chapel at its far end. Father Ray called, "Where ya' at, my little miscreant?"

His gaze fell on the large cross of burnished metal that hung above chapel's small, wooden altar. Sauntering through the Hall, Father Ray passed the confessionals and then the pews running parallel to the aisle. He stopped to admire the elaborate stained-glass window that comprised most of the rear wall.

"If only the Archdiocese knew what Aubrey paid for it," Father Ray said with a chuckle. He turned around in the chapel. A brief darkness passed over him as he remarked, "They'd probably just hock it to pay settlements."

Scanning the confessionals, Father Ray noticed that their indicator lights were in operation. All of them glowed green to convey that they were unoccupied save one, its red hue signaling that it was in use.

"Well whaddaya know," Father Ray said as he approached the priest's booth to the right of the occupied confessional, "I actually got one right."

Father Ray produced a gold key, unlocked the priest's booth and entered it. Closing the door behind him, he returned the key to his pocket and sat down. He slid open the small door so that only the confessional screen separated he and the penitent.

"Good afternoon, Judas," said Father Ray, his mood surprisingly jovial. He suspected this administration of the Sacrament of Reconciliation would differ greatly from Judas's usual confession of minor violence in defense of schoolmates. He smirked and advised him, "I've been expecting you."

"Bless me, Father, for I have sinned," Judas said grimly with a bowed head. His tone gave Father Ray pause. He added with poorly veiled angst, "My last confession was seven days ago."

"What's wrong, Judas?" Father Ray asked while leaning towards the screen. Judas's morose demeanor concerned him deeply, especially given the teen's encounter with Ursula the previous night and his subsequent disappearance.

"Please, Father, read to me from Scripture," requested Judas earnestly. There was desperation in his tone.

"All right, now I know something's wrong," Father Ray replied. He moved his mouth to within an inch of the screen and demanded, "Where the hell were you last night? Are you okay?"

"Did you read The Monroe Evening News this morning?" inquired Judas cryptically. He knew Father Ray read the online Sunday edition without fail each and every weekend. The cleric sat up in his chair and massaged his temples with his thumb and middle finger.

"No, because Sister Genevieve summoned me to deal with the latest antics of her most troublesome resident," Father Ray countered, his ire with his young protégé burbling to the surface. Pulling his phone from his jacket pocket, he accessed the internet and asked, "And what's that got to do with anything, anyway?"

"You should read it now," suggested Judas. The maturity in his voice befuddled Father Ray but his puzzlement soon ended. Bringing up The Monroe Evening News website, he felt his spiritual energy flicker and fade as he read the news report of the vigilante hit on a human trafficking ring.

"You could've been killed," the priest excoriated Judas, "or, worse, you could've gotten others killed, too."

"But I didn't," Judas snapped. Confounded by Judas's courageous-yet-misguided foray into vigilantism, Father Ray exhaled in frustration and scowled. Judas stated powerfully, "And now those three girls are *safe*. For them, it's *over*."

"I can't argue that point," said Father Ray with adrenaline pumping through his body. He felt the disquietude radiating from Judas and perceived the conviction in his spirit, his perception of it causing him concern for the troubled teenager. Father Ray contained his wrath, put his face next to the screen and asked, "Was she with you?"

Judas hesitated.

"Yeah, she was," Judas answered thickly. The question irritated him but he understood Father Ray's disapproval.

"*Idiot*," growled Father Ray as he struggled to calm himself. He balled his hands into fists and clenched his jaw.

"One of the girls got shot," explained Judas, "and she would've died if Ursula wasn't with me."

Father Ray stewed. Judas felt the heat of his displeasure but remained undaunted.

"So you know, too. *Great*," Father Ray complained, the priest lamenting the unraveling of his carefully laid plans. He leaned forward, placed his elbows on his knees and clasped his hands in front of him. Contemplating the possible outcomes of Judas's folly, he instructed his young charge, "All right. Let's do this the right way. Tell me the sins you've committed."

"I snuck out of the Home without permission . . . ," began Judas. His voice became mockingly official as he continued to expound upon his sins, saying, " . . . I was the passenger in a vehicle driven by an underage driver, I conducted a raid on a human trafficking location that was unauthorized as I am not a law enforcement officer, I broke into and entered two units of an abandoned motel and I'm a minor in possession of an unlicensed handgun."

"Anything else?" Father Ray asked while throwing his arms up in exasperation.

"I killed two men this morning and restrained three others," Judas stated flatly, "although I believe those actions constitute legitimate self-defense under the Catechism of the Catholic Church, Article 5, Sections 2263 and 2264. I don't think they're sins."

"Oh, ya' don't, do ya'?" Father Ray replied. Astonished and amused, he sneered and inquired, "And why is that?"

"The men I restrained were attempting to have sex with underage girls and threatened their safety," answered Judas without remorse, "and the guys I killed came at me with guns. I've got a right to defend my own life, right?"

Pausing to turn over Judas's compelling defense in his mind, Father Ray folded his arms and leaned back in his chair. Several seconds later he grasped his chin with his right hand.

"Sounds right to me," Father Ray responded with a shrug though, despite his equivocal answer, he knew the Catechism well and deemed Judas's actions legitimate self-defense. He abruptly winced when he remembered Courtney and asked, "She wasn't there, was she?"

Judas bit his lip and stifled his sorrow, albeit with great difficulty. He shook with a kaleidoscope of emotions.

"No," answered Judas with a heavy heart. Wracked with guilt, he took a minute to compose himself and added sadly, "Tammy wasn't there, either."

Perceiving the crossroads on which he stood and the need for an immediate decision, Father Ray reached out to God and prayed for guidance. Consequences long considered by the priest now seemed inevitable: Father Ray cast his die and placed his faith in his Master.

"All right, kid," Father Ray uttered gravely and with an expectation of disaster, "whaddaya need from me?"

******

His attention drifting, Father Ray scanned the abnormally large Sunday crowd. The twelve o'clock service, the last mass of the day, drew to a close as the lector droned through a lengthy list of parish announcements. Images of fresh donuts and strong coffee danced in Father's Ray mind and his stomach growled.

"*Shit*," Father Ray muttered under his breath as he noticed Archbishop Konrad Wunderlich leaning against one of the pillars at the rear of the church. He massaged the radix of his nose and thought, "So much for donuts."

The aging Archbishop failed to wear his violet skull cap and its absence prompted Father Ray to remember his superior's usual admonishment on the subject: "It's called a zuchetto, Father Reynald, not a skull cap. You *must* learn to use the proper terminology."

"Here's what you can do with your zuchetto," Father Ray said to himself. Archbishop Wunderlich, a spry and wiry seventy-eight-year-old, had harried Father Ray since his installment as leader of the Archdiocese of Detroit. Bringing his by-the-book practice of Catholicism and military-style leadership methods to bear on his subordinate seemed to thrill him. His eyes were a piercing greyish green, his thinning hair a greyish-white and his skin simply greyish.

"When it rains, it floods," Father Ray said to himself. He nodded to Archbishop Wunderlich who responded with a tilt of the head and an expression of rebuke. Exhaling in frustration through his nostrils, Father Ray looked away and thought, "The till's always full, old man. What could you possibly want now?"

The Archbishop's failure to wear his ceremonial bishop's outfit in favor of black clerical clothing worried Father Ray, the reason being that the old man usually indulged in the attention that accompanied his station. He leaned towards Tommy, the altar boy sitting on his right, who appeared to be sleeping with his eyes open.

"The Commandant's here," Father Ray whispered in the boy's ear. Tommy snapped out of his reverie with a barely perceptible start. Gently nudging him with his arm, Father Ray added, "You know the drill."

Tommy struggled to suppress a skeptical look. Father Ray leaned closer to the mop-headed twelve-year-old to hear his reply.

"We used the fire alarm *last* time," griped Tommy in a hissing whisper. The terseness of his response drew several glances but, after both Father Ray and Tommy displayed stone faces, the gazes returned to the lector.

"Use the bells," Father Ray instructed Tommy in a careful whisper, "program setting one."

"I want Emily Carnes in my Catechism class again," bartered Tommy. Noticing the renewed attention of the parishioners, Father Ray shot Tommy a sidelong glance of veiled ire. The lector read the last announcement so, with the clock approaching zero, the priest accepted the deal with a few nods of his head.

"Here we go," thought Father Ray as the lector finished and he stood up, his brain churning with all the possible reasons for Archbishop Wunderlich's visit. Fortunately, he learned and perfected the mass by rote and could say to his audience with little mental energy, "The Lord be with you."

"And also with you," replied the congregation after rising to their feet. The air in the room, at least to Father Ray, became stuffy and warm.

"May almighty God bless you," Father Ray stated as he performed the sign of the cross in the air, "the Father, and the Son, and the Holy Spirit."

"Amen," said his parishioners in unison. A tall, willowy figure loitered in the vestibule just outside the inner doors. Father Ray acquired it in his vision as he spoke.

"The mass has ended," he said with his eyes flitting between the congregation and the familiar face, "Go in peace to love and serve the Lord by loving and serving one another."

"Thanks be to God," said the congregation. The organist commenced the recessional music.

"Thanks be to God, indeed," Father Ray thought as he nudged Tommy again. He whispered in the altar boy's ear with a haughty smirk, "Don't worry about the bells. The cavalry just arrived."

******

"Well hello there, Padre," Aubrey greeted Father Ray as he entered the vestibule. She wore a pants suit of the latest fashion and an immodest blouse that matched her eyes. Tommy and his fellow altar boy banked to the right followed closely by the lector. Aubrey embraced Father Ray for longer than appropriate and kissed his cheek, cooing in his ear, "Long time, no touch."

"Uh, Aubrey, uh, hello," stammered Father Ray as he nervously scanned the vestibule for Archbishop Wunderlich. Her public display of affection caught the disapproving eyes of several parishioners as the congregation exited the church. Dislodging himself from Aubrey's arms, he stepped back, greeted an elderly woman with a welcoming hand on the shoulder and said, "Hi, Mrs. Rice. How are you today?"

"Fine, Father, fine," replied Mrs. Rice as she eyed Aubrey with disdainful suspicion. Aubrey returned her contempt with a scornful smirk.

"Glad to hear it," said Father Ray as he patted the old woman on the shoulder and waved to another parishioner. Turning his attention back to Aubrey, he addressed her in puzzlement, "I didn't expect you back so soon. Weren't you in some backwater part of China?"

"I was," Aubrey responded while batting her dark lashes at Father Ray and closing the distance between them, "but I missed my spiritual advisor."

A spidery hand clamped down on Father Ray's arm and caused him to jump. Aubrey lifted an eyebrow in irritation.

"Good afternoon, Father Reynald," said Archbishop Wunderlich though his words sounded more like an announcement of his presence than a greeting. He paused to revel in the glances of the church's patrons as they exited the church. Looking down his nose at Aubrey, he inquired, "And who might you be?"

"More than you can handle, Padre," Aubrey retorted while folding her arms and shifting her weight to her left foot. Father Ray winced.

"I am not a mere priest, young lady," snapped Archbishop Wunderlich as his face hardened into a scowl. Stepping into Aubrey's orbit, he declared pridefully, "I am Konrad Wunderlich, the Archbishop of the Archdiocese of Detroit."

"I don't care if you're the Archbishop of my-," Aubrey interjected. Father Ray stepped between them and interrupted her insult.

"Who wants coffee and donuts?" asked Father Ray as he placed one hand on the shoulder of both Aubrey and Archbishop Wunderlich.

"I need to speak with you, *immediately*," stated Archbishop Wunderlich as he removed Father Ray's hand from his shoulder. His hawkish eyes bored into Aubrey.

"I was here first, Archie," Aubrey snarled. Insinuating herself into Father Ray's orbit, she pulled his arm over her shoulder and wrapped her arm around his waist. She suggested snidely, "Why don't you grab coffee with one of these blue-hairs and give me and the Padre thirty minutes?"

"Tommy!" exclaimed Father Ray as he noticed the altar boy approaching him. Still clad in his white surplice and black cassock, he cringed and turned pale when he saw Father's Ray's predicament. The cleric slithered out of Aubrey's grasp but the heat of Archbishop Wunderlich's wrath remained palpable.

"*Suck*," murmured Tommy as he hesitantly heeded the priest's summons. Forcing an angelic expression, he thought bitterly, "He's gonna owe me *bigtime* for his."

"Archbishop, this is Tommy, one of our fine altar boys here at St. Saturnin," said Father Ray. He ruffled Tommy's hair and received daggers in response.

"Hello, my boy," said the Archbishop with a disinterested nod. His wizened countenance fell upon Father Ray like a bird of prey and he stated, "As I said, I need to speak with you post haste."

"Tommy, why don't you take the Archbishop to my office and get him some coffee?" instructed Father Ray. Addressing his superior and gesticulating, he continued. "I'm going to say goodbye to Ms. Stillerson and then I'll be right in, Your Excellency. That way I can give my undivided attention to whatever matters we need to discuss."

Archbishop Wunderlich pondered Father Ray's suggestion. He relented, his expression softened and he gestured towards the rectory.

"Very well. Lead on, young man," said Archbishop Wunderlich. Tommy threw a dubious look at Father Ray.

"Oh, and Tommy," said Father Ray. Tommy offered him a sour expression but it faded when Father Ray said, "I can get you in the Catechism class you wanted. *All set*."

Tommy nodded in agreement and led Archbishop Wunderlich towards the rectory. Father Ray sighed in relief.

"Aubs, that man is my superior," scolded Father Ray with a finger pointing towards the departing Archbishop, "and you *cannot* pull that shit when he's around. I need ya' to back off on this one, okay?"

"Sorry, handsome," Aubrey objected with a feigned smile of innocence. Patting Father Ray on the cheek, she said, "But I think it's time to put that old geezer in his place. I built this place and I'm in charge around here."

******

Aubrey sauntered into Father's Ray's office as if she owned it with the priest trailing her by several steps. Intent on preventing a clash between his benefactor and his boss, he forgot to close the door.

"What is *she* doing here?" demanded a disgusted Archbishop Wunderlich as he rose to his feet and pointed a bony finger at Aubrey. She dodged Father Ray's attempt to grab her arm and marched up to Archbishop Wunderlich. Going nose-to-nose with him, she let the greenish fires of her eyes blaze with anger.

"Let me explain something to you, *Archbishop*," Aubrey sneered with vitriol dripping from her tongue. The old cleric leaned away from Aubrey as if she were a campfire that suddenly grew too hot. Father Ray cringed. Glowering at the Archbishop and holding her ground, she continued, "I'm a billionaire. A billionaire who pours cash into this parish. *Barrels of cash*. And that, *Archbishop*, is why this parish is your top moneymaker and will be year after year after year. I've seen the numbers. No other parish comes close. So I think I've earned a seat at the table when it comes to St. Saturnin . . . and to *any* decision regarding Father Ray."

"I demand you leave at once or I'll have you arrested for trespassing," threatened Archbishop Wunderlich. He sat down in his chair in an attempted gesture of dismissal but Aubrey clearly intimidated him.

"You're just upset because I could get a meeting with your boss before you could," Aubrey said with unrestrained hauteur. She reveled in her victory with a smirk and her hands on her hips.

"*Anyone* can get a meeting with my boss," said Archbishop Wunderlich with a nod to the ceiling. He retrieved his saucer and coffee cup and drank from it.

"Enough!" barked Father Ray in an abrupt, emotional explosion. His audience glared back at him though, given the passionate energy radiating from the priest, they failed to interrupt him and even Aubrey sat down. Pacing back and forth and gesturing emphatically, Father Ray lectured them, "Despite having the lowest attendance in the diocese, mainly because we're out in the middle of nowhere, this church brings in *far* more money than it needs to operate, just like Aubrey said. Masses are conducted, Sacraments are administered, I don't molest kids and the coffee and donuts are out every damn Sunday. Not that I ever get to enjoy any of 'em, of course. But the point is that no one's complaining. *About anything.*"

Archbishop Wunderlich gazed on Father Ray in utter shock while Aubrey, though taken aback, grinned a muted-yet-adoring grin. Father Ray's chest heaved, his respiration heightened, his heart thumped and the adrenaline coursed through his veins. He ran his right hand through his hair.

"So, what's the problem?" inquired Father Ray sharply. Placing his hands on his hips, he swiveled his head from side-to-side as if discombobulated. The irritated priest narrowed his eyes and withdrew into himself before recovering. He looked back to Aubrey and Archbishop Wunderlich, exhaled and grumbled, "I know you're both here because you *want* something. And given the way my life's been going lately, my guess is, your somethings are related, though you probably don't even know it."

Father Ray walked to his desk chair and plummeted into it. Several tense seconds of silence passed. Archbishop Wunderlich stirred first.

"There are two photographs on your desk," advised Archbishop Wunderlich as his conceit returned. He rested his elbows on the arms of the chair and interlocked his fingers in front of his smug face.

"All right," replied Father Ray blithely. Looking down, he saw the two photographs neatly placed next to each other. He inhaled sharply when he saw the one on the left.

"You were recently visited by a nun who is not from this Archdiocese," stated the Archbishop in a deliberate tone. Aubrey glanced at him as he elaborated, "The picture on your left is her leaving the rectory late one evening."

The photograph, though shadowy, captured Sister Palladia's departure on the night she and Father Ray reunited. The failure of his efforts to tamp down the tides of destiny struck him hard and his face became grim. Deeply satisfied with the extent of his knowledge and its effect on Father Ray, Archbishop Wunderlich smirked.

"So who is she, Ray?" queried Aubrey with a jealous glare. She moved from her chair to the edge of Father Ray's desk, took a seat and said, "You see, I've got my own picture of Sister Mystery."

Reaching inside her jacket, Aubrey produced a photograph and handed it to Father Ray. He initially refused to take it but, after she angrily thrust it at him, he accepted it. Father Ray looked at it and, as he suspected, it was a photo of Sister Palladia leaving the rectory from another angle. Comparing the two photographs side-by-side, he shrugged with an unimpressed expression.

"It's just Sister Palladia Esseltine, or, as I originally knew her, Marybeth Esseltine," scoffed Father Ray with a chuckle as he launched into his performance. Tossing down the picture, he obtained a cigar from his desk drawer and expounded, "She's with the Sisters of the Holy Family of Nazareth and's been serving in the Ukraine for over a decade now. We were friends – *just friends* – in college. She's a lover of French language and history and was interested in having one of my teenager parishioners take a class she's teaching this semester. That's it."

Aubrey and Archbishop Wunderlich exchanged puzzled glances as Father Ray lit his cigar with a match. Confident in his performance, he blew out a billowing cloud of smoke and smiled incredulously.

"Now, who wants to be the first to tell me why *the hell* they've had PIs on my butt and why a nun visiting a priest is such a big deal?" asked Father Ray in a tone of mock cordiality. Enjoying his cigar and his deft deflection of his guests' accusations, he picked up the second of the Archbishop's pictures. He managed to stifle his shock as he viewed it and tossed it away like the final nub of a cigar, thinking, "Well, that's not good."

"Father Ray, can I see you?" Ursula asked as she breezed through the open door of his office.

"Speak of the devil," thought Father Ray. Turning her head quickly to the left, Ursula noticed Aubrey and Archbishop Wunderlich gazing at her and started.

"I'm so sorry. I didn't know you had visitors," apologized Ursula with a dubious glance at Aubrey.

"Not at all, Ursula. Come in, come in," replied Father Ray while waving her further into his office with thin smoke trailing from the end of his cigar. The timing of Ursula's arrival seemed yet another throw by the hand of fate and he deemed the interruption advantageous. Watching the faces of his guests meticulously, he said, "Archbishop, meet Ursula Baumé, one of our pious young parishioners and the reason Sister Palladia paid me that visit."

Ursula felt the usual embarrassment as his guests noticed her and her scar, Archbishop Wunderlich with a mien of condescending pity but Aubrey with instant recognition and thinly veiled disgust.

"You've already met Ursula, Aubrey, though it's been a while," Father Ray said. Aubrey nodded and forced a grin. Relieved that his guests' reactions were to Ursula's scar and not Ursula, Father Ray took a celebratory puff of his cigar.

"Hello, my dear," greeted Archbishop Wunderlich.

"Hello, your Excellency," replied Ursula. The Archbishop smiled in approval at the use of his official title.

"They don't know a damn thing," Father Ray said to himself. Zoning out as his three guests muddled through an exchange of mostly insincere pleasantries, he turned his thoughts back to donuts.

8 – Make No Oath At All

"I appreciate you making this a priority," Father Ray said uneasily as the room service attendant popped the cork on a bottle of red wine. He and Aubrey dined in the Presidential Suite of the Renaissance Center Marriott which overlooked the Detroit River and the City of Windsor, Ontario.

"Anything for you, Padre," replied Aubrey with her usual suggestiveness. The attendant filled her glass with wine.

"Wine, Father?" asked the attendant.

"Sure," Father Ray answered with a polite smile, "thank you."

"Will that be all, Ms. Stillerson?" inquired the attendant dutifully after filling Father Ray's glass.

"Yes," answered Aubrey without looking at him. He set down the wine bottle and melted away like a trained personal servant.

"Aren't you supposed to tip him?" Father Ray asked, the priest slightly embarrassed by Aubrey's cold treatment of the attendant.

"Trying to spend more of my money?" replied Aubrey, her tongue a rapier striking at Father Ray's ego. He parried.

"This dinner is a little pedestrian for the Billionaire Queen," Father Ray commented. The meal, while of the finest quality, was a simple one: T-bone steaks, Au-gratin potatoes and long green beans in a butter sauce.

"I know my guy, and he's the steak-and-potatoes type," said Aubrey, her green eyes glimmering with adoration. Father Ray winced, his face flushing and his cheeks warming with embarrassment. Pressing her advantage, Aubrey inquired, "Have you considered my offer?"

"No," lied Father Ray in irritation. Her question made him uncomfortable and she knew it.

"Well, there will always be a place for you in my organization, so when you're ready – and you *will* be ready at some point – just let me know," Aubrey said with her usual hauteur. Father Ray looked at her but said nothing, his silence prompting her to table the issue and ask, "So, what made you so eager to get into my hotel room?"

"You said if I ever needed anything, anything at all, that I should call you," Father Ray reminded Aubrey while she sipped her wine. He sighed and forced himself to say, "Well . . . I need something."

"You mean something other than that monstrous church and new rectory I built you, right?" asked Aubrey with a smirk. She loved toying with Father Ray but, on this occasion, she wished to weigh his state of mind. He glowered at her.

"Hey, look, if you're just gonna mess with my head, dinner's over," growled Father Ray and he stirred as if to stand.

"Easy, Ray," replied Aubrey with her left hand raised and her palm facing outward in a gesture of parley. She sipped from her glass and asked, "What does my favorite priest need?"

Father Ray exhaled and prepared himself to make the request. The words came but only with great arduousness.

"I need an . . . well, an . . . *off-the-record* favor," Father Ray began. Aubrey's eyes flashed as she gave him the same look a lion gives an antelope when it takes one unwitting step too close. Knowing he walked into a potential trap, Father Ray continued gravely, "No one can know I'm involved. Lives depend on it."

"*Do tell*," said Aubrey with rapt attention as she straightened up in her seat. She set down her glass and subtly leaned towards Father Ray. Aubrey's predatoriness caused him to reconsider his audience with her but, cognizant of Courtney's and Tammy's peril, he took the risk. The billionaire and the priest commenced their meal and settled into the groove of an old, married couple.

"Do you remember one of my parishioners, Tammy Parker?" asked Father Ray. Producing a picture of Tammy from his jacket pocket, he handed it to Aubrey. She accepted it and studied Tammy's face.

"How could I forget *this* one?" answered Aubrey bitterly as Father Ray put his napkin in his lap and sliced into his steak. She sneered, "The little orange-haired cripple with the sharp tongue."

"C'mon, Aubrey," Father Ray admonished her. He took a bite of his steak.

"Tell me what part of that isn't true," said Aubrey with an incredulous look. She indulged in a forkful of potatoes.

"She was abducted nine days ago," Father Ray replied. Merely stating the fact caused him considerable distress yet also stoked his anger.

"I know," said Aubrey without concern. She cut into her steak.

"You know?" inquired Father Ray in mistrustful disbelief.

"I make it my business to know what's going on in your world," advised Aubrey before taking another bite. The revelation disturbed Father Ray but he gave no outward indication of it.

"I think she's being held at a farm in Northwest Ohio," Father Ray explained while intentionally omitting the source of his information. He stopped eating, set his utensils on his plate and said, "I need the location of that farm."

"And what would you be planning to do with that information?" inquired Aubrey with a peculiar, amused expression.

"Don't ask," Father Ray pleaded. Aubrey laughed.

"Why don't you just leave it to me, Padre?" suggested Aubrey. She washed down her steak with more wine and reasoned, "Go back to your big church and shepherd your little flock. I'll have some of my people find your little handicapper."

Father Ray considered Aubrey's offer. The thought was tempting; Aubrey's people were professionals, at least in some sense of the word, while Judas was a fifteen-year-old with little experience and much to learn. The Holy Spirit, however, warned him against it.

"I just need the location," Father Ray said as he braced for a fiery response. Aubrey's mirth dissolved and her face grew stern.

"This wouldn't happen to have anything to do with Sister Palladia, would it?" queried Aubrey while barely containing a scowl. Seizing his opportunity, Father Ray fanned the flames of her jealousy.

"No, no. Of course not," Father Ray answered with a poorly feigned lie designed to prickle Aubrey. He casually drank his wine and then returned to his meal before asking, "So, can you help me out here?"

"Like I said," replied Aubrey with a chilling smile, "*anything* for you, Padre."

******

"What in the names of heaven and earth are you doing in here?" inquired Archbishop Wunderlich as Aubrey unabashedly entered the sacristy of The Cathedral of the Most Blessed Sacrament in Detroit. The blonde firebrand caught the Archbishop as he put on his clerical vestments but he paused to chastise her with his eyes. Undaunted by his enragement, Aubrey shut the door behind her to the sound of the old cleric's rebuke, "I'm about to celebrate Mass."

"Do you think God has a sense of humor, Archie?" Aubrey asked. Clad in skin-tight, designer jeans, a white blouse and a casual blue blazer, she clacked across the floor in red high heels.

"Get out or I'll have you removed," demanded Archbishop Wunderlich. Standing in front of a long counter beneath which were numerous drawers, he looked from wooden door to wooden door in search of the best escape route.

"See, I think he does," Aubrey continued as she walked to the table between them. Sitting down in one of its four chairs, she placed her elbows on its armrests and stretched out her legs in front of her. Aubrey folded her hands on her stomach and said, "Because you and I hate each other with a passion and yet He's given us the unique opportunity to call a truce and join forces for our mutual benefit."

Archbishop Wunderlich's anger slowly evaporated though he maintained his skepticism. Stepping forward, he placed two gaunt hands on the back of the chair across from Aubrey and gripped it with white knuckles.

"You have two minutes to interest me before I have you arrested for trespassing," warned Archbishop Wunderlich. He resumed his preparation for Mass by donning his stole.

"Always with the threats," Aubrey said with a wrinkled nose and a wry smile. Ignoring an offended glower by the Archbishop, she stated bluntly, "Your investigator sucks. My guy has pictures of your guy pissing in the bushes outside the church."

"My investigator is quite competent, I assure you," countered Archbishop Wunderlich, his ire stoked by Aubrey's use of profanity.

"Really? Does he have any of these?" Aubrey said as she brandished a stack of photographs, fanned them out with a flick of her thumb and forefinger and then tossed them down on the table. Taking a moment to glare at her before moving, Archbishop Wunderlich quickly shuffled the pictures into a neat stack and studied them with growing astonishment. His eyes darted up to Aubrey.

"The girl," said Archbishop Wunderlich with an expression of withering intensity. The pictures, some of which appeared to be taken by a drone, documented several of Sister Palladia's visits to Ursula's house. They also verified Aubrey's claim of the Archbishop's private investigator relieving himself on church property.

"Exactly," Aubrey replied. Throwing her arm over the back of the chair, she said, "I don't know why yet . . . *but I will.*"

"Want do you want?" asked Archbishop Wunderlich with suspicion as he closely studied his potential ally.

"Ray," Aubrey answered with the lust of a predator, "and I don't need any old girlfriend picking my pocket. But I have a feeling you're gonna run Sister Palladia outta town and I'm going to help you do it."

"She took a vow of celibacy, as did he," advised the Archbishop dismissively, "though his is less an obstacle than hers, of that I'm certain."

Archbishop Wunderlich deemed Aubrey's yearning for Father Ray trivial and debasing. His mind churned, however, as he nonetheless planned to use her desire to his advantage.

"But I say to you, make no oath at all. Instead, say yes or no, because anything else is evil," Aubrey responded, her words a paraphrasing of Matthew 5:34-37. She tilted her head to the side, smirked and said, "You see, even JC realized how easily vows are broken, and I, like you, prefer certainty."

"You read Scripture?" inquired Archbishop Wunderlich, the seventy-eight-year-old stunned by Aubrey's resort to the Gospel.

"No," Aubrey answered, "but I pick up a little by half-listening to Ray when he's babbling about it."

"May I keep these?" inquired Archbishop Wunderlich. It pleased Aubrey to watch him salivate over the pictures so she let several seconds pass.

"They're all yours, Archie," Aubrey replied before visibly running her tongue along the bottom of her teeth. She stood up and continued, "So, Wunderlich gets his wunderkind and the nun gets run out on a rail. Acceptable?"

Archbishop Wunderlich's eyes flipped up to Aubrey. She smiled evilly.

"Acceptable," replied the Archbishop.

******

The metal statue of Mary silently stood guard over Ursula though the fountain at her feet sang its usual song. The fourteen-year-old, as always, took comfort in the presence and protection of the Blessed Mother. She sat on a bench in front of the statue, a raincoat shielding her from the light drizzle and mists in the air. The temperatures soared into the sixties that afternoon and, together with a half-day of school, permitted her to wait several hours in hopes of a visit from Judas.

"Don't let him do it alone," Ursula prayed to The Virgin Mary. She had neither seen nor spoken to Judas since the morning raid on the Great Star Motel and she worried about him every second of every day. Disheartened by their seemingly diverging paths, she begged, "I know I can't have him, but I can't lose him, either."

"Our Lord blessed Judas's efforts, at least this time," said Sister Palladia as if reading Ursula's mind. She dressed as a civilian with her hair pulled into a tight bun. Unaffected by the drizzle, she added, "But the taking of human life without official position or sanction is disturbing. He was reckless."

Ursula's countenance hardened. She watched Sister Palladia in her peripheral vision but did not turn her head.

"He wasn't reckless," Ursula countered with a bitterness that gave Sister Palladia pause. A sudden dislike for the nun flared within her and she said, "They were evil men and they attacked him first."

"Judas's actions are not for you to judge," rejoined Sister Palladia as she brushed aside Ursula's defense. The youth stood up quickly and glared at her.

"But they're for you to judge?" Ursula snapped, the teenager's ire stoked by Sister Palladia's criticism of Judas.

"It remains to be seen if Judas is acting for God or for himself," replied Sister Palladia dismissively. She walked towards Ursula and said, "Father Ray has certainly instilled impulsive decision-making in him."

Ursula moved to the Marian Shrine, stopped at the edge of the fountain and stared into the turbulent waters. The scene was surreal; the fourteen-year-old stood before the towering Blessed Mother as the mists drifted around her.

"I've given you the time you requested. Have you made your decision?" inquired Sister Palladia. She took several measured steps towards Ursula who remained silent and still, urging, "God is calling you. Will you not answer Him?"

"How important am I to the Emerian Order?" Ursula inquired, the adolescent emitting a peculiar vibe that disconcerted Sister Palladia. Taking a few seconds to compose herself, she then moved shoulder-to-shoulder with her protégé.

"Why do you ask?" responded Sister Palladia. Her attempt to intimidate Ursula fizzled; the girl had grown in courage and height since she first met her in the summer. Teacher and student raised their eyes to Mary's comely face, each woman hesitant to begin the impending conflict between them.

"I don't think I can leave Judas," Ursula said. Turning to Sister Palladia, she declared, "I won't leave Judas. He needs me."

"Or is it that you need him?" asked Sister Palladia, her characteristic patience fraying. She turned her head to sternly gaze at Ursula and warned, "It's God's will that you join the Order. Your gift proves it. Will you turn your back on Him for a mortal man and the trivialness of teenage infatuation?"

Sister Palladia turned towards Ursula. The anger between them boiled over and caused Ursula to clench her fists.

"It would be unfortunate if Judas's identity was revealed," threatened Sister Palladia, her Australian accent thickening.

"What if *your* identity was revealed?" queried Ursula with snide ferocity.

"How dare you!" exclaimed Sister Palladia. She lunged at Ursula to slap her cheek but the teenager dodged the attempt. The threat to Judas bolstered her courage.

"If I say no, and you turn in Judas, they'll arrest him, and interfere with God's plan for his life," explained Ursula defiantly, "and I can't let you do that."

Shocked by Ursula's cold, grave demeanor, Sister Palladia stared at her in disbelief. She saw shades of herself in the child.

"I *won't* let you do it," Ursula continued. Launching into a spirited monologue, she expounded, "There are so many girls out there, girls like my friend Tammy, whose bodies are being defiled and whose minds and hearts are being ruined by evil men. They live every day in fear. Without love. Without hope. It's slavery. *Slavery of children.* But Judas is their champion, their crusader, and I'm not giving up on them or him. Ever."

Pulling off her hood and shedding her rain jacket, Ursula let it drop from her fingers and hit the ground. The nun said nothing and remained motionless.

"If you want me to join the Order then Judas's fight is our fight," Ursula advised with a remarkable wisdom, "but, if you're not gonna do that, then you don't get me, and you're not leaving here until you swear to me you'll leave Judas alone. *His call is greater than mine.*"

Ursula ceased speaking for ten seconds. The words on Judas's necklace trickled into her mind.

"'Vindicate the weak and fatherless; Do justice to the afflicted and destitute,'" Ursula recited once confident of the exact verses, "'Rescue the weak and needy; Deliver them out of the hand of the wicked.'" (Psalm 82:3-4).

Sister Palladia sensed the strengthening of Ursula's will and the influx of the Holy Spirit into her young body. The powerful transformation of the fourteen-year-old left no doubt in the nun's mind as to her destiny or to the future of the Emerian Order.

"You, Ursula, truly don't know what you're asking of me," said Sister Palladia, her words and her tone causing Ursula to tense and step back into a defensive posture. Remaining stationary, she sighed and relented, advising her student, "I don't have the authority to agree to your terms, even if I wished to agree with them. There is only one man on earth who does. I will take your demands to him, but it will require great sacrifice on your part."

Ursula, her clothes and hair damp from the light rain, picked up her raincoat. Walking past Sister Palladia, she arrived at the cobblestone path leading away from the shrine and paused. Her heart bled.

"You will take a temporary vow of chastity, for three years," said Sister Palladia. She moved closer to Ursula and stated, "You will take it here, you will take it now, and, if you do, I will keep my knowledge of Judas's activities to myself until you make a final decision."

The rain intensified and soaked Ursula though she did not acknowledge it. Sister Palladia waited patiently as her clothing became waterlogged and her hair wet and stringy.

"Fine," Ursula replied after a minute of excruciating consideration. Cognizant that one word did not constitute an official vow, she said loudly and clearly, "Today, before God, I take a temporary vow of chastity for three years. *Satisfied*?"

Ursula shivered. Drained of all energy, she slowly proceeded down the path and disappeared into the mists.

******

Hugging her soaked pillow for dear life, Ursula bawled into it to muffle the sound. She curled up beneath her covers and shut out the world; the prospect of standing by Judas's side without the ability to be any closer wounded her deeply. A knock at the door caused her to stifle her sobs and listen intently.

"Ursula, dear," called Aunt Vickie in a careful tone. She knocked again and asked politely, "Ursula, honey? Can I come in?"

Given away by her sniffles, Ursula nonetheless pretended as if she slept. Aunt Vickie waited for thirty seconds before knocking again.

"Ursula?" said Aunt Vickie in a heightened tone.

"This is taking too long," Charlotte griped. The sounds of a short commotion emerged from behind the door and it was soon thrown open. Charlotte burst into the room while Aunt Vickie lingered in the doorway, the fourteen-year-old asking, "*Girl*, what's goin' on with you?"

Ursula remained still but continued to sniffle. Charlotte looked at her incredulously with her hands on her narrow hips.

"Perhaps she needs a little more time," suggested Aunt Vickie.

"I got this," Charlotte assured Aunt Vickie while nudging her out of the bedroom with the door. The older woman offered light resistance but soon surrendered and the lock clicked shut. Turning towards Ursula, Charlotte folded her arms and ordered, "I know you're awake, Urse. Get up."

"Just leave me alone," mewled Ursula despite wanting to be comforted. She did not want, however, to draw anyone else into her misery and feared that doing so would twist the knife of finality in her relationship with Judas.

"Nope," Charlotte countered. Marching to Ursula's bed, she tore off the covers and revealed that Ursula still wore her wet clothes. Charlotte crinkled her nose and inquired, "Where've you been?"

"Go away!" protested Ursula as she assumed the fetal position with her hands clutching her pillow. She pressed her face into it.

"I'm not leaving. Momma and your Aunt Vicki already said I could spend the night, so you might as well just tell me what's goin' on," Charlotte advised her grief-stricken friend. Walking to the door, she opened it and reached outside. Charlotte retrieved an overnight bag, tossed it to the floor and closed the door again. Lowering her voice, she asked, "Did you see Judas?"

The mention of Judas sent Ursula into another downward spiral of weeping. She adjusted her grip on the pillow, scooted away from Charlotte and huddled against the wall.

"Just go!" whined Ursula while wiping away tears with her sodden sleeve.

"I'm not leaving," Charlotte stated determinedly. Sitting down on the edge of the bed, she queried, "Did you see him or not?"

"No," whimpered Ursula. The desire to see him burned within her. Frustration burned within Charlotte.

"Tell me what's going on," Charlotte demanded as she rolled Ursula over. Bleary-eyed and pallid, she hugged her damp pillow to her chest and averted her gaze. Charlotte invaded Ursula's personal space and said, "I'm waiting."

"Judas and I went looking for Tammy," confessed Ursula after a five-second delay. It took another five seconds for Charlotte to understand the import of her words.

"Oh my god," Charlotte uttered, the teenager remembering the local hubbub over the vigilante attack on The Great Star Motel. She sat up and queried in amazement, "That was you guys?"

Ursula frowned and nodded in the affirmative. Pondering her newfound knowledge, Charlotte stood up and paced the floor. Ursula watched her in silence until she stopped in front of her.

"I want in," Charlotte insisted.

"No!" objected a distressed Ursula. She cringed at the loudness of her voice. Lowering its volume, she explained, "It's dangerous, Char. They shot at

Judas and tried to kill him. One of the girls almost died . . . I can't lose you, too."

"You won't, and you're not losing Tammy, either," Charlotte scolded her. Ursula's eyes flashed to her but she said nothing. Grasping her friend's shoulders and lifting her into a sitting position, Charlotte read the expression on her face and asked slowly, "But you weren't talking about Tammy, were you?"

Ursula's waterworks resumed. She leapt to her feet and forcefully embraced Charlotte who wrapped her in her long arms and let her cry for several minutes.

"What happened?" Charlotte finally inquired. She ushered Ursula to the bed and they both took a seat on it. Taking her hands in her own, Charlotte squeezed them and continued, "Did you ask him out? I told you to wait until he's over Courtney. It's too early."

The mention of Courtney sent Ursula into another round of bawling. Charlotte once again let her cry out her sorrowful energy on her shoulder and, once she had expended it, resumed her questioning.

"Did he say he doesn't like you or something?" Charlotte asked. She said with growing annoyance, "Ursula, just tell me,"

"I gave him up," said Ursula with a pronounced exhale. Responding to Charlotte's furrowed brow, she repositioned her pillow and laid down on her queen bed, expounding sadly, "And now it's over. He's Courtney's now."

Confused by Ursula's cryptic explanation and convinced sleep would be in short supply that night, Charlotte grabbed a pillow and tossed it against the wall. She propped herself up with it and sat perpendicular to Ursula with her lengthy legs hanging off the bed.

"I'm gonna need more than that," Charlotte said. She hugged her knees into her chest.

"Things are gonna start changing," said Ursula and, with that, they talked long into the night of religious orders, crusades, vows and charisms. Most important for Ursula, however, they discussed her love for Judas and her refusal to leave his side.

******

"*Judas*," sighed Ursula when her eyes fell upon him. Charging the object of her affection, she threw her arms around him and squeezed him tightly. Judas seemed, in her mind, taller, more handsome and more muscular than the last time she saw him. Her body tingled.

"Geez, did you miss me?" asked Judas with an adoring grin. Their reunion occurred in Father Ray's "war room", an elaborate reception room specially designed for him by Aubrey's team of interior designers and built into the new rectory's basement. Charlotte appeared in the doorway a second later and immediately drew the attention of Steve and Mike. She leaned against the door frame and folded her arms.

"I was worried," admitted Ursula nervously while dodging Judas's question. Remembrance of her vow of chastity prompted her to reluctantly release him and step back. Judas noted her retreat but did not react to it.

"He's with me, Urse," Judas assured her with unwavering confidence, "He's with *all* of us now."

Ursula nodded and offered Judas a reserved smile. Her vow seared her heart like a white-hot branding iron and the wound ached unbearably.

"So, you gonna introduce me or what?" interjected Charlotte with a sharp tilt of her head. Ursula spun around.

"Sorry," apologized Ursula, the fourteen-year-old embarrassed by her fawning over Judas. Walking over to Charlotte, she took her by the arm and led her into the room, saying, "This is Charlotte, guys. She wants to help. She and Tammy and I were best friends."

The mention of Tammy in the past tense deflated everyone in the room save Judas. He studied Charlotte while the others recovered.

"*Are* best friends. I'm Judas," Judas corrected Ursula as he gestured towards himself. He then pointed at Steve and Mike and said bluntly, "Steve. Mike"

"Sup," Mike greeted Charlotte with a cocky nod. Steve, unable to muster words, simply waved at her.

"Hey," replied an unimpressed Charlotte.

"All right, listen up," Father Ray barked as he swept into the room and interrupted further pleasantries. He held a glass in one hand, a lit cigar in the other and a large, rolled map under his left arm.

"Isn't it a little risky to meet here?" inquired Charlotte with attitude. Father Ray looked to her with an annoyed smirk before setting down his glass and tossing the map on a large, dark-wood dining table.

"I'm being watched twenty-four hours a day, for reasons that have nothing to do with any of this," Father Ray began, "so, from now on, you're all members of the youth group I've started for high school students. We meet right here on Wednesday evenings to discuss the gospels and how they affect your everyday lives. I don't smoke or drink during these meetings, and we have no idea where Judas is. Got it?"

"He's right here," said Steve quizzically. Charlotte rolled her eyes.

"You must be Steve," Father Ray replied while pausing to look at the mountain of a young man. The adolescent fidgeted and furrowed his brow.

"Yeah," answered Steve, "and you're Father Ray, right?"

"Wow, two-for-two, big guy," said Father Ray. He spread out a detailed map of northwest Ohio on the table. Ursula dutifully grabbed some heavy, marble coasters and secured the edges of the map.

"Thank you, Urse. Now, gather 'round, you hooligans," Father Ray instructed them. He waited for the teenagers to follow his direction and then pointed at a small town. Judas and Ursula exchanged glances of warmth and amusement. Father Ray seemed like a World War II general, the cleric smoking his cigar and imbibing from a condensation-coated glass.

"This is Pettisville, which is part of Henry County, Ohio," Father Ray explained. Sliding his finger southeast across the map, he traced a line to the location of the barn and twice tapped an area circled in permanent marker. He allowed himself a gulp of whiskey and then continued, "The barn's right here, south of County Road C."

"How did you find it so fast?" asked Ursula, the teen puzzled by his swift unearthing of the location. Judas glanced at Father Ray but the priest kept his eyes on the map.

"A friend," Father Ray answered cryptically. Leaving no time for further questioning, he puffed on his cigar and continued, "The barn's used to store hay, which, in turn, is used to hide a secondary, two-story structure built into the north end. That's where they're keeping the girls."

Indecision temporarily paralyzed Judas. He greatly desired to question Father Ray about Courtney but, with Ursula at his side, he loathed even the thought of the hurt it would cause her. He punted instead.

"How many guards?" inquired Judas while staring intently at the map. Father Ray slid a smaller satellite image of the area out from underneath it. The group closed around the table.

"Varies," Father Ray answered, "but it's usually five, and they're always moving. Seems like your first assault got 'em riled up because they're definitely on alert."

"And the girls?" asked Judas while ignoring Father Ray's pointed look. He hoped the priest would address Courtney's whereabouts of his own accord.

"Not sure," Father Ray said, "but the invest- . . . my source saw two taken inside and one taken out. A different one. So it might be a clearing house."

"A clearing house?" queried Ursula. She waved away a curl of cigar smoke that drifted near her.

"It's where they bring the girls together after they're abducted," Father Ray explained grimly. Placing one hand on his left hip and gesticulating with the other, he continued, "They're then ferried out to different locations in the area for, well, you know . . . ."

Waves of nausea washed over Father Ray and he scowled. Ursula cried intermittent tears, Charlotte's eyes moistened and Steve and Mike bowed their heads and remained silent.

"We're going in tomorrow night," Judas declared as plans and contingencies developed in his mind.

"I hate to be the bearer of bad news, Batman," said Father Ray as every face turned to him, "but this crazy weather's shifting again tomorrow. We've got eight inches of snow on the way starting tomorrow night."

"Good," Judas said with a satisfied smile. All the faces turned to him as he reasoned, "The weather'll cover my approach."

"*Our* approach," growled Ursula with an unforgiving nudge. Judas avoided her angry gaze and ran his finger along a line of trees to the east of the barn.

"Our approach," Judas conceded, the thought of Ursula by his side encouraging him.

"You're looking at a two- to three-hour drive in the storm," said Father Ray. He placed his open palms on the table and warned, "This isn't like the last time where all of you can sneak out and then sneak back in before your parents wake up."

"Whiteford and Summerfield High Schools are doing a joint lock-in this Saturday at Whiteford," suggested Charlotte matter-of-factly, "and our school's been invited, too. We could all go and then sneak out."

"That'll work," Judas replied without concern. He and Charlotte shared glances but Father Ray rolled his eyes. Indicating with his finger on the map, Judas said, "We can come in from the trees, and, if the snow's heavy, they'll never see us. Steve, you'll cover us from the treeline, as best you can in the snow, and Mike, you'll stay with the van and be ready to bail like last time."

"Forgetting someone?" asked Charlotte indignantly. Placing both hands on the table and leaning towards Judas, she sneered, "And the right answer to that question is that I'm hitting the barn with you."

"Athletic ability and attitude won't be enough," Judas warned.

"What about a black belt in Tang Soo Do and a .38?" countered Charlotte. A stunned Ursula gaped at her friend while Steve and Mike watched her with burgeoning infatuation. Judas remained unmoved.

"Maybe. Do you know how to use it?" Judas asked. He recognized the warrior within Charlotte and realized it was a gift from God.

"Yep," replied Charlotte in a snarky tone. She produced the pistol from her waistband, set it on the table and slid it towards Judas, saying, "That's what gangbanger daddies teach their kids during parenting time."

"I like her," Father Ray said with a wry smile as he shook his finger at Charlotte. He drained his glass. Judas picked up the gun and examined it.

"If she's going in, then I'm going in," insisted Steve despite being terrified by the prospect. Mike squirmed, the young man wanting to volunteer for the assault but unable to force himself to speak.

"Then that's it," said Judas while observing the determined faces of his companions. The bonds of the Holy Spirit began forming between all of them. He stated with conviction, "We hit the barn tomorrow night."

Hope infused Judas. The mustard seed was growing.

******

Father Ray ended the call and set down his phone on a chairside table. Retrieving his second cigar of the evening from a marble ash tray, he crossed his legs and leaned back in a leather chair. A fire blazed in the gas fireplace and warmed the war room considerably.

"Well, unfortunately, I have an Anointing of the Sick tonight," said a suddenly melancholy Father Ray. Judas sat on the other side of the table in an identical chair, the youth listening to the priest's words but failing to comprehend them. Father Ray inhaled, held in the cigar smoke and then exhaled it, saying, "Mr. Priebe's got brain cancer to go with his kidney cancer, so a helluva lot of prayers went unanswered. *'Your will be done.'* In any event, the PIs will follow me when I go and then you can leave." (Matthew 6:10).

Turning to Judas, Father Ray remained silent and watched him stare into the flames. The teenager was deep in thought and, with the exception of his adolescent attire, appeared like a young statesman. Father Ray allowed Judas his thoughts for ten minutes while he quietly enjoyed his cigar and reflected on Judas's rapid ascent into manhood, incomplete as it was.

"I know it comes from God, but what *is* my power?" asked Judas. Recalling a similar conversation he had with Ursula, Father Ray exhaled a plume of smoke high into the air. He extinguished the nub of his cigar in the ashtray.

"It's called a charism – at least I believe that's what it is, especially given that Ursula possesses the charism of healing and, as they say, your destinies seem *intertwined*," explained Father Ray in an odd tone. Contemplating the unique nature of Judas's charism, he said, "Of course, healing is more common, if you can call any charism common. Yours? I can't find a record of anything like it."

"What's a charism?" interrupted Judas impatiently. He gripped the ends of the arms of his chair slowly and tried to drive Ursula from his thoughts. Father Ray noticed the conflict within him.

"It's a special grace bestowed on one of the faithful for the good and the growth of the Church," Father Ray answered. His response piqued Judas's interest and allowed him to chase Ursula to a distant corner of his mind. Father Ray added, "In short, you've been given a gift from God, one that you must use to help the Catholic faithful and, for better or worse, their shepherds."

"But I'm not helping the Catholic faithful, or the Church," argued Judas as his focus shifted from Ursula to his unique ability to influence the spiritual energy of others.

"Not yet, at least," Father Ray replied while running his hand over his face. Standing up and walking to the edge of the fire, he let its warmth make him uncomfortable and said, "If anything, this little crusade of yours is cutting more than a few Catholic corners."

Father Ray lifted his head abruptly. The word "crusade" prickled him like a hedge of thorns and he wished to distract Judas from his use of it.

"That Charlotte seems like quite the ballbuster," Father Ray said with grin. He folded his arms and declared, "I'd take her into a fight over that lug Steve any day."

"She's going to be a big part of this," advised Judas presciently. Envisioning Charlotte primarily as Ursula's loyal guardian, he said, "She'll do great things in God's name."

"What makes you say that?" Father Ray asked while throwing Judas a curious, sidelong glance. The teenager rose to his feet and positioned himself next to his mentor.

"The Holy Spirit is with her," replied Judas without the slightest trace of doubt in his voice. The cleric stirred.

"Like the Force?" Father Ray quipped with a chuckle. The disapproving look on Judas's countenance prompted him to move indirectly to a topic of greater interest to him.

"She's a good-looking kid," Father Ray commented. Judas said nothing but fidgeted. Though agreeing with Father Ray's assessment of Charlotte, only two women possessed any claim to him. Father Ray nudged Judas with his shoulder and suggested mischievously, "The two of you'd make one badass couple."

"When are you leaving?" inquired Judas as he turned around and walked away from Father Ray.

"So I guess that means you're not interested," Father Ray pressed him while losing himself in the dancing flames. Judas whirled around angrily.

"How can you even talk about that while Courtney's out there, alone, terrified and being raped every day?! What the hell's wrong with you?!"

barked Judas. He felt his hands trembling with rage and balled them into fists. Father Ray languidly rotated around to face him.

"Take it easy, Judas," Father Ray demanded in a deep, raised voice. Evaluating Judas's anger, he closely studied him and decided on a more direct approach. He said soberly, "I know you have strong feelings for Courtney, but I also know, like you do, that she's not the only one on your radar."

Judas's eyes widened and his face grew pale. Father Ray's insinuation brought Ursula back to the forefront of his mind.

"Let me advance your knowledge on the subject," Father Ray said, "and listen carefully because it's important. Sister Palladia's not here to teach French, she's here for Ursula, or more specifically, Ursula's charism. And if she gets her way, which she's really damn good at, Ursula will be on her way outta town and you'll be left with your . . . well, let's just say you'll be left holding the bag."

"You know about us?" asked Judas. His use of the word "us" was invigorating and terrifying at the same time.

"I know the two of you are a bad idea," Father Ray growled, his own romantic past percolating to the surface. Quelling with difficulty the pain and anger of Palladia's betrayal, he continued, "You're young, ya' don't know how it all works, and you're getting drawn into the Church, which destroys relationships."

"Maybe that's how I end up serving the Church," suggested Judas.

"Yeah, maybe," Father Ray conceded. He began to gesticulate and ranted sardonically, "But before you go running after her into the Church, remember this. Sister Palladia's a nun. Nuns take vows of chastity. Vows of chastity, for nuns, involve celibacy, and that means no sex, but they also mean no romantic relationships."

"So what?" snapped Judas as a spasm of anger passed over his face.

"Use your head, kid," Father Ray scolded him while stepping forward. He placed a hand on Judas's shoulder and expounded, "*Palladia's recruiting her.* They want her to join their Order. She'll be giving herself to God, which means his Church gets Ursula and you get *nothing*. See how it works? I tried to protect you, Judas, but I failed."

"Whaddaya mean, tried to protect me?" inquired Judas sharply. The gears of Judas's mind churned and he remembered all the excuses, the hurried escorts home and the abrupt refusals of visiting privileges. Realization struck him like a thrown rock and, with a sneer, he bucked Father Ray's hand off his shoulder and snarled, "You kept us apart."

"For your own damn good, kid," Father Ray said, his gaze stern and unrelenting. Judas overturned the leather chair in which he earlier sat and roared in a fit of rage. Father Ray held his ground despite the tsunami of Judas's wrath and threat of his charism.

The adolescent then punched a support column, the strike obliterating the paneling and the drywall, and then stormed out of the room. Father Ray ignored the wake of Judas's tirade and slumped into his chair.

"For your own damn good," Father Ray muttered.

9 - He Must Deny Himself

Sitting on the floor of the Whiteford High School gym beneath a huge bobcat head, Ursula and Charlotte waited for the right moment to sneak out. High school students mingled and buzzed around them and any sudden commotion would provide the perfect smokescreen for escape. Steve and Mike, in fact, managed to enter the lock-in, check into the event and, in a flood of students, walk right back out the front doors. A nervous Ursula checked her phone.

"Will you relax?" scolded Charlotte as she pushed Ursula's phone away from her. Scanning the crowd, she said, "He's not gonna contact you on your real phone. Besides, one fight and we're outta here."

"It's not that," Ursula countered, her self-consciousness plaguing her more than usual. She endured several quick glances as students from the other high schools noticed her disfigurement. Charlotte stood up and glared at a passing herd of boys as they gawked at Ursula's scar. The group altered its course and hurriedly walked off.

"C'mon," beckoned Charlotte with an outstretched hand. Ursula hesitated but then stowed her phone and accepted her friend's offer. Charlotte pulled her to her feet and felt the sweatiness of her palms. Releasing Ursula's hand, she wiped her hand on her jeans and asked, "Why're you so nervous? Judas said you don't have to go in with us if you don't want to."

"He's gonna leave without us," Ursula growled, her anxiety bubbling over in a flash of anger. It subsided as swiftly as it arose and she said, "I'm sorry."

"Why would he leave without us?" inquired Charlotte. She snagged Ursula by the sleeve and led her into an adjacent hallway.

"To protect us," Ursula answered as she yanked her arm free of Charlotte's grasp. Trembling, she expounded, "He wasn't gonna take anyone in with him last time. It'll be more dangerous this time, and he knows that. I'm telling you. He's gonna leave without us."

Charlotte said nothing. She closed her eyes and exhaled in frustration.

"*What?!*" Ursula demanded. The higher pitch of her voice caught the attention of a several passing students so she ducked into a recessed doorway.

"How are you gonna do this?" replied Charlotte as she followed Ursula.

"*Do what?*" Ursula queried while spinning around in the doorway and throwing her hands in the air.

"Be with him but not be with him," answered Charlotte bluntly. The question paralyzed Ursula. Grasping both sides of her head, Charlotte held her fast and ranted, "What're you gonna do if we find Courtney tonight? You said he's been crushin' on her since like last year and if he saves her life . . . girls kinda dig that stuff, Urse. *They're gonna go out.*"

"That's fine," Ursula stated as she feigned composure. She backed into the wall, rested the rear of her skull against it and lifted her foot so that it pressed flat against its masonry blocks. Staring upward, she said with a barely quivering lip, "He doesn't have to be alone just because I took the vow."

"Uh, you only took it for like three years," argued Charlotte. The group of boys that Charlotte dispatched began a spirited, good-natured shouting match with a group from another high school and the sounds of their voices echoed throughout the hallway. She offered Ursula a mischievous expression and added, "They ain't gonna last that long."

Ursula smiled sheepishly for Charlotte's benefit but knew Sister Palladia would push for entry into the Emerian Order and a permanent vow of chastity. Charlotte nodded over her shoulder.

"Looks like those idiots are starting somethin'," declared Charlotte. She exited the doorway as she added, "Time to go."

Ursula followed Charlotte closely. The pair slipped quietly down the hallway as a teacher marched past them to intervene in the intensifying ruckus.

******

Another round of snow fell in southeast Michigan and northwest Ohio but, fortunately for Judas's group of adolescent vigilantes, only two-to-four inches were expected through the night. The roads, however, were still slippery and a stiff wind blew from the west.

Mike, who recently celebrated his fifteenth birthday, handled the deteriorating road conditions splendidly despite his age. Steve sat next to him in the passenger seat after being banished from the middle seat by Charlotte.

"You're huge, and you're like, invading my personal space," she admonished him. Charlotte now sat with her back to the side of the vehicle and her legs stretched out. Steve repeatedly glanced into the mirror to catch glimpses of her, the last glance prompting her to glower at him and bitingly say, "*Stalker.*"

Judas and Ursula sat together on the rear seat of the van, their bodies as close as possible without touching one another. Battling a kaleidoscope of emotions, Ursula dreaded every mile of their journey into Ohio. Each one brought her friends closer to danger and Judas closer to Courtney. Ursula wished her no ill will but the thought of helping Judas cement his relationship with her mercilessly tore at her heart.

"What did the priest call these again?" asked Charlotte as she fiddled with a cheap mobile phone. Father Ray purchased pre-paid phones for the group so that they could dispose of them after their covert endeavor.

"Burners," Judas answered.

"Burners," repeated a bored Charlotte with an emphasis on the "B".

"He's taking a really big risk for us," said Ursula worriedly. Father Ray supplied them with winter clothing suitable for their mission, including ski masks, and cash in addition to the phones. She took hold of the seat back and shifted her body to face Judas, asking, "What if he gets caught?"

"He's taking a risk for *them*, just like we all are," Judas replied without emotion. Charlotte pretended to be oblivious to their conversation but listened to it carefully. Judas returned to ruminating over his plans.

"*Judas*," said Ursula while shaking his arm to demand his attention. His irritation with her spiked but, as always, it was short-lived. Taking several seconds to calm himself, he looked at her with pity.

"He'll be fine, Urse," Judas insisted. Seeking to assuage her concerns, he continued, "God's with us, and He'll be with Father Ray, too."

"This is just so dangerous," said Ursula. She, to her great surprise, did not fear for her own safety; instead, she feared for the safety of Judas and her friends.

"People are gonna die, Urse, and not just the bad guys," Judas gravely warned her while squeezing her hand. His touch lessened her anxiousness but his words provided no reassurance as he continued, "It *will* happen. That's something neither of us can stop."

Ursula quickly looked out the window, the teen haunted by Judas's assertions for the rest of their journey. The mere thought of losing any more of her friends alarmed her. Returning to her original position, Ursula recalled Father Ray's incessant Scriptural citation.

"'If anyone wishes to come after Me,'" Father Ray recited *ad nauseum*, "'he must deny himself, and take up his cross daily and follow Me.'" (Luke 9:23).

"Do I hafta be a Catholic for this?" inquired Charlotte to break the tension. Judas's angry eyes flashed to her but, amused and undaunted, she added, "Because I'm a Lutheran."

"It'd help," Judas grumbled, the teenager irked by Charlotte's cheek. Her hostility towards him, though veiled and minor, was constant. Judas attributed it to his complicated relationship with Ursula and her desire to protect her friend. He added, "We'll convert you later."

The moratorium on speaking resumed. Reaching over the seat, Judas retrieved his backpack from the rear of the van and began checking his equipment for the third time.

"Watch over them," Ursula prayed in earnest.

******

The snow intensified and whirled around the trees, the precipitation tossed by the icy wind blowing from the west. Intermittent squalls obscured the barn and shielded it from prying eyes, its exterior lights the only consistently visible feature. Judas raised his hands to stop the group just inside the tree line and everyone obediently lowered themselves into crouching positions.

"Okay, Mike, you're up," Judas thought. Thirty seconds passed before he noticed the lights of the van traveling the road on the west side of the barn. Mike, as directed by Judas, reconnoitered the area and would then return to their rendezvous point. The lights soon disappeared and the group, hidden in the woods, waited silently for his report. Judas's burner phone lit up several minutes later.

"Car @ house across street," read Mike's text. Judas wiped snowflakes off the phone before a second text appeared on the screen, "Barn dark inside."

"Stay put. Going in," Judas texted back. He stowed his phone in his backpack and pulled out his binoculars. Lifting them to his eyes, he surveyed the vicinity of the barn but failed to detect any guards or movement. Judas lowered the binoculars and, stretching out his spiritual perception, he tried to discern their location. Unlike his attempt during the assault on The Great Star Motel, he was able to overcome the distance and perceived seven presences in the barn. Judas, though uncertain, believed he sensed a differentiation in the spiritual energies and thought, "Three girls. Four guards."

Judas attempted to scan the house across the street but his spiritual perception would not extend that far. He returned his binoculars to his backpack and slipped his arms into its straps.

"One or two in the car," Judas said to himself. He raised his hands and displayed six fingers to the rest of the group. He then motioned forward with his right hand and proceeded across the field. Ursula and Charlotte followed closely behind him.

Steve took up a position at the edge of the tree line, the massive teenager concealing himself behind a huge tree stump. He rested his scoped rifle on it, produced his own set of binoculars, and watched his friends approach the barn. He dropped the binoculars due to the slipperiness of the melted snow and they fell to the ground. Gunfire made his blood run cold.

"I shoulda went with them," thought Steve as he, with difficulty, reacquired the binoculars and watched Charlotte's long, lanky form disappear into the barn. He bristled at Judas's order to remain behind and cover their retreat, especially when he heard a muffled crash. The passing seconds weighed heavily on him and, resolved to intervene, Steve declared defiantly, "I'm going."

Casting aside Judas's command, Steve stood up and grabbed his rifle. He hesitated for several seconds but, swallowing his trepidation, he forced his feet to move and lumbered across the snowy field.

*****

A warning alarm sounded in Judas's spirit. Halting Ursula and Charlotte on the east side of the barn, he rounded its southeast corner and approached a small entry door in its southern face. He breathed deeply and watched the wind carry away his breath.

"They know we're coming," Judas thought. He threw open the door. Shots rang out from several locations in the darkness, the shooters' positions betrayed by the muzzle flashes of their weapons. Pinpointing and squelching their spiritual energies, he incapacitated four guards in a heartbeat. He heard a sickening thud as one fell from the rafters.

Cognizant of the guards in the vehicle across the street, Judas turned his attention to them. He felt them rapidly closing on the barn and throttled their life forces. Though he did not see it, Judas heard their car crash into a deep ditch on the west side of the road.

Confident that the guards were disabled, Judas cautiously entered the barn. The dim illumination from the southern exterior light revealed meticulously stacked hay bales on either side of a makeshift hallway, the floor of which was strewn with loose hay. The aisleway led to the middle of the barn where it turned on a ninety-degree angle. He returned to the door and gave an "all clear" wave to Charlotte who peeked around the corner of the barn. She and Ursula swiftly entered and Charlotte closed the door behind them.

"They're unconscious," Judas informed them as he produced two rolls of duct tape and a handful of police-grade zip ties from his backpack. Handing one roll and some zip ties to Charlotte, he pointed and instructed, "There's one around the corner, one up in the hay there and another on that side. Let's get 'em bound before they wake up. Then we'll get the two outside and-."

"On it," interjected Charlotte. She grabbed the tape and zip-ties and marched to the door with Judas's angry glare following her. Charlotte opened the door, hung a sharp right and slammed it closed.

"I'll take those," insisted Ursula as she stole the roll of duct tape and the remaining zip ties from Judas. She knelt next to the guard who fell from the rafters and zip-tied his wrists.

"Hold on. I don't want you to-," began Judas. Ursula's stinging look prompted him stop in the middle of his sentence. Judas searched his backpack for more zip-ties and muttered, "No wonder you two are friends."

"Charlotte!" called out Steve as he crashed through the small barn door, his raw strength tearing the door from its hinges. Judas drew his gun on him and Ursula squealed with fright.

"Damn it, Steve!" Judas castigated him as he lowered his weapon. Ursula quickly recovered and zip-tied the man's ankles. Keeping his mind on the task at hand, Judas grumbled, "Charlotte's getting the two in the car. Get out there and help her."

Noticing the damage he caused, an embarrassed Steve averted his gaze. He picked up the ruined door, set it against the hay bales and tromped outside.

"Get the other one, too," Judas said with nod towards the other guard. He pointed at the two guards on the hay bales and said, "I'll get these guys."

Judas effortlessly climbed the mass of hay bales and began the work of binding the guard. Ursula, her hands shaking due to the cold and her nervousness, zip-tied the next guard's wrists and ankles.

"No!" yelled Charlotte. A gun fired outside the barn and a second firearm responded with two shots of its own. Charlotte screamed, "Ursula!"

Terror on her young face, Ursula looked to the only untied guard and then to Judas. Her expression begged for guidance.

"Go!" Judas barked as he hurled his zip-tied guard to the floor. Sprinting out the door, Ursula disappeared. Judas let his spiritual perception scan the area to the west of the barn. He registered only two conscious persons outside. Pausing for the briefest of moments, he made his decision.

"They can handle it," he said aloud. The untied guard stirred and he stifled his spiritual energy. Judas leapt down to the floor and then ascended the other mass of bales, muttering, "They've gotta handle it."

******

Hopping into the shin-deep snow of the ditch, Charlotte opened the driver side door of the sedan and confirmed that the guard was unconscious. She then shifted the car into park, turned the key to kill the engine and deftly zip-tied his wrists and ankles. Steve appeared trudging through the snow and towards the car.

"Get the other one!" Charlotte ordered him as she duct-taped her guard's mouth and then used the tape to reinforce the zip-ties on his wrists. Steve clumsily descended into the ditch, approached the passenger door and set his rifle against the car. Fumbling with the handle, he eventually managed to open the door.

"No!" Charlotte bellowed as the other guard lifted a Glock. He fired it into Steve's thigh, the teen shouting in pain and tumbling backwards. Acting with lightening reflexes, Charlotte drew her pistol and fired two shots into the guard's chest before he could aim and squeeze the trigger a second time. He lifelessly slumped forward, his corpse held up by his seatbelt. Charlotte screamed, "Ursula!"

Charging around the car, Charlotte struggled through the deep snow of the ditch. The wind and snow battered her but she persisted and, upon reaching Steve, she sat him up. He groaned and held his large hands over the bleeding wound.

"He shot me!" exclaimed Steve.

"I know, genius!" Charlotte replied. Steve groaned again as Ursula crested the edge of the ditch and scampered down into it. She tugged on his huge hands but was unable to dislodge them.

"What're you doing?!" queried Steve in a strained tone.

"Move your hands and stay still," Ursula demanded. Steve obeyed and, after a bubbling up of blood, she quickly placed her hands on Steve's wounded thigh. Her prayers caused his pain to evaporate as he and Charlotte watched in wonder.

"How did you do that?" inquired a flabbergasted Steve.

"Get him back to the van," Ursula urged while locking her determined eyes on Charlotte. Her friend silently nodded. Leaving Charlotte to assist Steve, Ursula climbed out of the ditch and ran back to the barn.

******

The four guards were laying in a row along the main aisle when Ursula entered the barn, each one zip-tied at the wrists and ankles and wrapped in copious amounts of duct tape. Judas was nowhere to be found.

"Judas!" Ursula called as she clambered over the guards and ran down the aisle. Turning left, she entered another short, hay-lined hallway with light shining into its far end. She ran down it and arrived at an even shorter hallway leading to an open door set in a cinder-block wall. Ursula called out again, "Judas!"

There was no response. Ursula walked forward and neared the door. Her entire body shuddered as a wave of stale heat and cigarette stink crashed into her.

"Judas?" she said, her voice faltering into a hoarse whisper. Stepping into the first room of the inner structure of the barn, she realized it was a makeshift lounge for the guards. There was an old, dirty couch on one wall, next to which sat a large refrigerator, and a folding table with four metal chairs around it on the other side of the room. Cards, ash trays and beer cans littered the table while light, albeit dimmer, entered the room from an open door in the far wall.

"He got them all," Ursula thought as she contemplated what lingered in the hallway and beyond. Forcing one foot in front of the other, she proceeded at a snail's pace to the door and entered the hallway. She called out softly, "*Judas?*"

The long, narrow hallway granted access to four small rooms on its right side while another cinder-block wall bounded its left side. Ursula moved to the first door and peered inside. Three scantily clad teenage girls huddled together on a mattress on the floor. Ursula hurried to them but they bleated and recoiled as she approached.

"It's okay, you're safe now," Ursula assured them. She performed a cursory check of their bodies but, worried about Judas, she asked impatiently, "Are you hurt?"

"N-n-no," whimpered one of the girls. Though leery of Ursula, the other two shook their heads in the negative.

"I'll be right back," Ursula promised. She exited, crept down the hallway and checked the other rooms, the next two the same as the first but unoccupied. She arrived at the fourth room and stepped into its doorway but stopped cold when she saw Judas hovering over Courtney. Ursula swiftly raised her left hand to her lips to stifle a gasp. She prayed desperately, "God, please, *no*."

Kneeling next to Courtney, who wore a dingy, black t-shirt and purple panties, Judas laid his head on her stomach and wept. Rigor mortis hardened her lifeless body and the coldness and pallor of death hung heavily on it. Tears formed in Ursula's eyes.

"I'm so sorry, Courtney," he mewled, the fifteen-year-old allowing himself to mourn and ponder what might have been. Judas outwardly composed himself and declared, "I wasn't fast enough. I didn't get it right, and now you're dead. Because of me."

Judas stood up. Leaning over Courtney, he caressed her cheek and kissed her forehead in a painful goodbye. He then swallowed his emotions.

"'The eye is the lamp of the body . . . ,'" Judas uttered grimly. (Matthew 6:22). Placing two fingertips on her eyelids, he forever shuttered the lamps of Courtney's body. The tides of time provided Judas no more time to contemplate his loss. He buried his grief deep and turned to face Ursula.

"We've gotta get outta here," Judas said. He picked up a mobile phone lying on the bed which he pilfered from a guard and dialed 9-1-1. Staring at its screen, Judas inquired, "Is Steve okay?"

"Yeah," replied Ursula. She struggled with the moment, the fourteen-year-old desiring to comfort Judas but unable to find the proper words or actions.

"And the guard?" Judas asked. His dourness deterred Ursula from embracing him.

"He's. . . ," said Ursula, ". . . *he's dead.*"

Judas said nothing more. Tapping the "SEND" button on the phone, he laid it on the bed. He then, with the 9-1-1 operator chattering in the background, took Ursula's hand and led her away.

******

Judas and Ursula once again found themselves in her neighborhood's park on a cold night, albeit a much snowier one than on their last visit. They sat on the same ring of landscaping blocks circumscribing the same large, leafless tree, its branches now covered in snow.

"We should get you home," said Judas, the teenager using the same words he used on their last foray into the park. The snow continued to fall around them though the winds eased.

"It's not your fault," Ursula stated while wiggling her hands into the pockets of her coat. She looked to Judas but he refused to return her gaze and stared into the ground. Scooting closer to him, Ursula intentionally bumped into his body.

"It is my fault," replied Judas in response to the contact. A violent shiver ran through him.

"How can it possibly be your fault?" Ursula queried, her tone thick with disbelief. Standing up, she moved in front of Judas and bent over to go face-to-face with him, saying, "You risked your life to save her. You at least gave her a chance."

"Never mind," Judas said dismissively. He lowered his head to avoid her gaze. She promptly placed her fingers under his chin and lifted his eyes to her own.

"You're *not* doing that to me," Ursula warned Judas. He looked away but she turned his head right back. Grasping his cheeks to hold him steady, she insisted, "If you really believe it's your fault then you have to tell me why."

Judas went cold. Gripping Ursula's hands tightly, he removed them from his cheeks.

"Instead of shooting those guys at the motel, I should've knocked them out and, when they woke up, made them tell me where Courtney was," explained Judas with weak, heavy eyes. He rose to his feet and pulled Ursula's hands into his chest. Dumbfounded by his bleak countenance, she listened as he continued, "They had to've known where she was. But I didn't think about that. I just acted. *I messed up.* If I'd 'a just got there a little earlier, maybe just by a few hours, she'd be alive, Urse. But I didn't think. And *that's* why it's my fault."

"They could've killed you," Ursula argued with incredulity. Pulling her hands away from Judas, she insisted, "It was self-defense."

"That's not an excuse," uttered Judas.

"Judas, you've saved six girls from being sex slaves," Ursula reasoned ardently, "but you can't save all of them. *You* told me that. *You* told me we can't stop all of them from dying."

"I wanted to save Courtney!" barked Judas, the explosion of his ire stunning Ursula. Wounded and angered by one too many mentions of Courtney and irked by Judas's obstinance, she yanked off her glove and slapped Judas with her bare palm.

"You saved me!" Ursula shouted. She paused, glowering at Judas, and then launched into a monologue replete with tears and sobs, the teen yelling and gesticulating, "What if you didn't shoot them, and something went wrong and they shot *me*? Would you feel better then? Would you be happy with your pretty Courtney and her perfect face? If you'd have waited a few more seconds, *I* could be dead. Would you like to trade my life for Courtney's? I'd do it, ya' know. *For you.* But I can't bring her back, and you can't either."

Ursula turned away from Judas and bawled. Remorseful for his focus on Courtney, he tried to embrace Ursula from behind. She dodged the attempt.

"Hey, come here," said Judas as he tried to hug Ursula again. She darted away and spun around.

"Go home, Judas!" Ursula shouted. Each time he attempted to approach her, she took an equal number of steps backward. Ursula sniffled and begged, "You're hurting and you're tired. You need to get some sleep. Please, just go home."

"At least let me walk you to your house," pleaded Judas. Ursula wiped away tears with the sleeve of her coat as he added, "I wanna make sure you get home okay."

"I'll be fine," Ursula mewled. She begged him again, "*Go home.*"

Judas hesitated but soon relented under Ursula's determined gaze. He shrugged.

"Okay," said Judas. He meandered across the park towards the car Father Ray provided him. Unable to watch Judas's departure, Ursula hurried home as she wept. She, however, did not see him turn around and follow her at a distance.

******

Father Ray dozed in one of his war room chairs while flames flickered and danced in the fireplace. The stubs of two long-extinguished cigars rested in an ash tray on the table next to him. He wore his black clerical garb and held an empty glass in his hand. Judas suddenly collapsed in the chair opposite Father Ray and his body deflated.

"You're alive," Father Ray uttered as he lingered on the edge of sleep. He opened his eyes and set his glass on the table, adding, "That's good."

Judas scowled to ward off sobs. His lack of response prompted Father Ray to sit up and glance at him. Reading the hybrid expression of anger and sadness on Judas's face, he began sobering up.

"What happened?" Father Ray demanded. He rose to his feet, the rapid ascent causing him to sway due to his fading inebriation and drowsiness.

"Courtney's dead," answered Judas. He clenched his jaw and continued to scowl to hold his emotions in check but the tremors of his countenance betrayed his sorrow.

"How?" Father Ray asked in shock. He grasped his chin and sighed in disappointed disgust.

"She was dead when we got there," droned Judas, the teenager staring aimlessly into the fire. Looking drawn and haggard, he said, "Probably OD'ed. They're hooking the girls on heroin."

"Ursula?" Father Ray inquired, his spine tingling with anticipation. The mention of her name expended the last feeling of which Judas was capable and he felt a pain in his chest.

"She's fine . . . they're all fine," continued Judas without emotion. He explained in a monotone, businesslike fashion, "Steve got shot but Ursula healed him. We caught five guys but Charlotte killed one. We saved three girls. It's probably on the morning news right now."

Judas did not move, the youth too exhausted to do anything but gaze into the fire and breathe. Pitying his mentee, Father Ray walked to him, grasped his shoulder and dug his fingers into his flesh. Judas felt intense pain but absorbed it without reaction.

"Listen to me, Judas," Father Ray ordered with a sneer. Maintaining his hold on Judas's shoulder, he expounded grimly, "Courtney's with God now. Her pain? Her fear? They're over, as is her part in this little war of yours. You should thank God for that. And she knows what you did for her, the risks you took to save her life. But she's gone now, gone forever. And your pain? Your fear? It's just beginning. If you're really serious about all of this, about saving all these girls, about busting up the ring, then get over your loss, get your shit together and get to it so that no other girl suffers Courtney's fate."

The priest's harsh words rocked Judas to his very foundations. His emotions regenerated and overwhelmed him in a rush of sorrow, of disgust and of anger.

"Otherwise, go home," Father Ray instructed Judas as he released his grip and patted his shoulder affectionately. The priest added eerily, "Either way, you've got a long road ahead."

*****

Returning to his office, Father Ray sat in his desk chair as a throbbing hangover headache and a night of fitful sleep wore on him. Clicking the mouse pad of his computer, he watched as the screen reappeared and revealed a letter typed in Microsoft Word. He slumped into the chair and exhaled.

"Re: Request for loss of clerical state and dispensation from the obligation of celibacy," Father Ray said as he read the subject line aloud. Feeling ashamed, he muttered, "I'll get him a little farther, and then others can take over. I gotta correct my own mistakes. I gotta get the hell outta here while I still have the opportunity."

Father Ray chuckled. His momentary mirth, however, did not help him shed his remorse and his smile faded.

"'Sorry I couldn't do better,'" he said as he quoted Lando Calrissian in *The Empire Strikes Back*, "'but I got my own problems.'"

10 - Every Tear That Falls

Father Ray positioned two pillows against his headboard and slid under the covers of his bed. Plucking the remote off the bedside table, he clicked on his television and extinguished the lamp. He glanced at his phone: it was 11:01 pm.

"Tonight, three more teenage girls are safe with their families after The Great Star vigilante strikes again, this time at a farm in Northwest Ohio," said the news anchor as she opened the eleven o'clock news. Turning to a second camera, the fortysomething blonde continued, "The vigilante's efforts have now shut down two suspected human trafficking sites in the last month."

"Oh, great, *this*," Father Ray complained. Shifting uneasily in his bed, he grumbled, "Why couldn't I have left it on ESPN?"

"The three abducted teenagers were found alive by local police last night in a barn on the property after an anonymous 9-1-1 call," said the anchor, "but a fourth girl was found dead of an apparent drug overdose when they arrived. Authorities are not releasing the girls' names due to their ages, but they are believed to be between fourteen- and sixteen-years-old."

The reference to Courtney sickened Father Ray and he shivered. The screen split to accommodate both the studio and a field reporter: a young, attractive Hispanic woman standing against the snowy backdrop of the farm.

"We go now to Stephanie Aguilerez who is at the farm tonight," said the newscaster. She greeted her coworker, "Good evening, Stephanie."

"She's cute," Father Ray commented with a thoughtful expression. He temporarily forgot his nausea.

"Hello, Aida," said the reporter who was bundled up to combat the cold. Yellow caution tape, whipped about by a stiff wind, cordoned off the area and kept the media far from the barn. Stephanie stood defiantly against the wind and explained, "Behind me is the farm near Archbold, Ohio where, last night, The Great Star vigilante captured five suspected human traffickers, killed one and rescued the three young women being held there. Those five men are now in the custody of the FBI, which has taken over the investigation."

The image of Stephanie Aguilerez gave way to a pre-recorded segment detailing Judas's assault on The Great Star Motel. Video of the abandoned structure surrounded by sheriff's deputies began the segment.

"This is The Great Star Motel, an abandoned motel in Summerfield Township, Michigan. It's here that the vigilante, now dubbed The Great Star vigilante, first struck, the mysterious savior killing two human traffickers, rescuing three underage girls held as sex slaves and capturing three men who engaged in sex with the girls."

Father Ray's attention waned as the Sandman worked over his eyelids. He knew more than the FBI and nothing reported was news to him. Stephanie Aguilerez reappeared on the screen and raised her microphone.

"And, new tonight, we've learned from the special agent in charge of the investigation that one of the victims reported a second, *female* vigilante," advised Stephanie, "while also confirming the presence of a tall, young male. That description is consistent with the perpetrator of the first incident."

"Well, that's not good," Father Ray muttered, the priest's understatement not indicative of his anxiety. He sat up and rubbed his face with his hands. Finished with the day, he turned off the television, tossed the remote onto the bed and laid down, his mind spinning as to what clues Judas's band of minor vigilantes left at the scene. Wrestling his pillow into the proper position, he thought, "I may need to get outta here sooner than I thought."

******

"Your insistence that we meet here is utterly ridiculous," complained Archbishop Wunderlich. Grabbing the cream-colored drapes that bisected the room with a greyish, gaunt hand, he yanked them aside and glared at Aubrey. The Archbishop responded to her amused grin by chastising her, "Though I have no doubt you are in dire need of confession."

The unlikely allies met in the one of the confessionals of the Cathedral of the Most Blessed Sacrament. Half of the room was wood-paneled and drab with a crucifix hanging on the wall behind the confessor's chair. The other half, in which the priest sat, possessed eggshell-white walls, a narrow cathedral ceiling and a high-set, mitre-shaped window.

"Aw, c'mon, Archie," Aubrey replied with a sinister smile. Waving her hands and arms about to convey the presence of ghosts, she said, "It's just like in the movies, all suspenseful with God floating around us as I spill my guts and you pronouncing your draconian Catholic judgments on me. I've been a very bad girl. Maybe you should spank me."

Aubrey laughed. Archbishop Wunderlich fumed.

"A confessional is a sacred and vital part of the Sacrament of Reconciliation!" barked the Archbishop. He continued with unveiled vitriol, "And if you refer to me as 'Archie' again this meeting is over."

"But I've got news for ya', Archie," Aubrey advised him in a tone of feigned contrition. The cleric released the curtains and let them separate he and Aubrey again. She reclined in her chair and crossed her legs.

"I already know that Sister Palladia left the country," said Archbishop Wunderlich dismissively. He, too, reclined in his chair, the priest placing his elbow on the armrest and pressing his index finger into his temple. He cleared his throat and explained with disapprobation, "It's innocuous. One of the nuns in her Order – a close friend of hers, in fact – is dying, and she returned to the Ukraine for her final days. Sister Palladia is not concealing her whereabouts."

"That's odd, because yesterday one of my people saw Sister Mystery in Rome," Aubrey announced pridefully. She could not see the surprised expression on Archbishop Wunderlich's face but she felt it. It provided her considerable satisfaction.

"*Ridiculous*," snapped the Archbishop in disbelief. Sounding flustered, he argued, "I have it on good authority that she was in the Ukraine yesterday morning, our local time, of course."

"Oh, she was, Archie," Aubrey replied. Letting the moment fester, she waited fifteen seconds and then added mockingly, "But she was in Rome last night . . . our local time, of course."

"Innocuous still," declared Archbishop Wunderlich with a dismissive wave of his hand. He stood up and said, "The Order's Generalate is on the outskirts of Rome. It is entirely plausible she had legitimate business there. Perhaps she's being reassigned which solves your problem, does it not?"

"I assume Generalate means headquarters," Aubrey said with a sneer. She stood up and turned to observe the crucifix on the back wall, expounding with annoyance, "Now pay attention, *Archbishop Wunderlich* . . . she's no regular nun. She's had some type of training, CIA, or MI6 or something like that. She slipped my guys in Kiev and managed to get all the way to Rome, and that's not easy to do, I assure you. But unfortunately for Sister Mystery, I had someone waiting and watching there."

"How did you know?" demanded Archbishop Wunderlich. Aubrey's gaining of the upper hand rankled him.

"Easy there, Archie," Aubrey snarled as she whirled around and glowered at Archbishop Wunderlich through the curtain. They stood on opposite sides of it, the pair shielded from one another's eyes but not one another's ire. Aubrey calmed herself, returned to her seat and said, "I played a hunch, that's all. She abandoned her little French program pretty fast for someone who loves it so much, and only after she met with the girl several times. She was going back to report to someone about the kid . . . and I think I know who it was."

Aubrey and Archbishop Wunderlich both silently pondered the identity of Sister Palladia's superior. A neuron fired in his brain and a memory percolated to the forefront of his mind. The Archbishop stirred.

"There is something that you might interest you about her," advised Archbishop Wunderlich with slow, thick words. He thrust one hand in his pocket and shook a pointed finger in the air, saying, "The girl and her aunt were attacked in the parking lot of St. Arnulf last Spring."

"So that's where she got that nasty scar," Aubrey replied with a grimace.

"Yes, yes it is," said Archbishop Wunderlich. Clasping his arms behind his back, he paced in the small room and said, "But, more importantly, Father Reynald's report indicated he called 9-1-1 after disabling the attacker."

"That's my man," Aubrey remarked proudly. She placed her elbows on the armrests of the chair, stretched out her legs in front of her and folded her hands on her stomach.

"You're incorrigible," snapped Archbishop Wunderlich.

"Always," Aubrey said with a smirk.

"And the 9-1-1 recording?" inquired the Archbishop angrily.

"Didn't your 'quite competent' investigator dig it up already?" Aubrey countered with a tilted eyebrow. She raised her folded hands and rested her chin on them.

"He couldn't find the recording," admitted Archbishop Wunderlich reluctantly. The undertone of his voice conveyed the investigator's fate as he said, "I have since terminated his services."

"And you figured my people could find it for you," Aubrey replied. She paused, considered her options and then acquiesced, "Fine, Archie. I'll get you the recording. But it'll cost you."

"What did you have in mind?" queried Archbishop Wunderlich, the old man unconcerned with the price.

******

Kneeling on the steps leading to St. Saturnin's altar, Ursula experienced an anxious and heightened awareness. No tears fell from her eyes despite the sorrow she felt and she implored God for strength.

"Where the hell've you been?!" Judas exclaimed as he burst through the narthex doors and entered the church proper. Ursula leapt to her feet and spun around to face him. Marching up to her, Judas berated her for her avoidance of him, asking, "Why won't you text me back?"

"I just need a little space," replied Ursula, the teen in clear distress. She moved behind the altar and used it as a shield, pleading in a jittery voice, "Just for a little while."

"I am *not* communicating with you through Charlotte anymore," Judas declared as he hopped onto the dais. He slowed his pace but continued around the altar, asking, "What's wrong?"

"Nothing. I'm fine," insisted Ursula. Her actions belied her words, however, as she kept the altar between she and Judas. They circled it several times until Judas head-faked in one direction, reversed course and charged around the altar. Ursula ran from the dais but tripped on her descent. Judas caught her in the middle of her fall and lifted her into his arms.

"Let go of me," demanded Ursula. She struggled in his embrace but his strength proved insurmountable.

"I won't be doing that ever again," Judas replied as he moved his face towards Ursula. His blue eyes paralyzed her.

"What about Courtney?" queried Ursula in desperation. Never in her young life had she dreaded and desired something as much as Judas's kiss. His eyes became hazy as he drifted away but they soon cleared.

"Courtney was beauty and mystery. I cared about her, I did, and I'm sad that she's gone," Judas admitted as he held Ursula fast. He withdrew into himself again, thought of Courtney and then returned to Ursula. Hypnotized by his mere presence, she listened and marked each word as he explained, "But she was just the match that started the fire, God's guide that led me to this path. I'll never forget her and I'll always be thankful for her sacrifice. But now she's gone, and you're here, and you're more than beauty and mystery. You're strength, and mercy, and *destiny*. You're the one who's supposed to walk the path with me, not as two together, but as one."

Ursula floundered in the temptation of Judas and the promise of a loving relationship with him, the urge to forsake her vow growing with every second she indulged in his commanding touch. She squirmed and steeled her will to resist.

"*Not as two together, but as one,*" scoffed Ursula with a shake of her head. Despite falling in love with the words, she continued to squirm and sardonically objected, "Did you get that from *Twilight*?"

"How do you explain our gifts, and how we first met, and the incredible things we're doing in God's name?" Judas interrupted her.

"None of that means we're supposed be with each other," argued Ursula, the fourteen-year-old loathing every word that passed her lips. Her insides churned and twisted and, wishing to ward herself from temptation, she conjured a powerful lie to break his spirit. She prayed silently, "Forgive me. It's what he has to believe."

"Tell me," Judas dared Ursula as he pulled her closer, "tell me you don't want me. Tell me and I'll stop."

"You could've chosen me over her, but you didn't," explained Ursula, her words intended to encourage Judas's remorse. The ploy succeeded and he faltered. Wriggling out of Judas's arms, she said, "That's okay, I swear it's okay. But you just lost her, and you're upset, and hurt, and you don't want really want *me*. You'll see that someday. You don't want *me*."

"Bullshit," Judas snapped, his resort to profanity evidencing his own desperation. He attempted to reestablish his grasp on her arms but she evaded him and retreated several steps.

"Please don't touch me," pleaded Ursula, the request slicing into both teenager's hearts. Her rebuke wounded and angered him. Leaping forward with seemingly supernatural speed, he forcefully embraced Ursula and engaged her in an ardent kiss. She melted into it, her vow of chastity suspended by her love for him.

"No!" protested Ursula as she broke free of the kiss and Judas's grip. She ran towards the rear of the church, her abrupt flight surprising him long enough to allow her escape.

"Where're you going?" shouted Judas. Banking to the left, she ran into the confessional area with Judas in pursuit. She entered the first confessional on the right, slammed the door and locked it. Judas arrived a second later and yanked on the door handle, demanding, "Ursula, open the door!"

"No!" refused Ursula. Her faithfulness to God was all that succored her in her reluctant deflection of Judas's advances. Sitting with her arms wrapped around her knees and her feet on the confessional chair, she added, "Not until you promise you won't touch me anymore. We do this together but *not* as one. *Promise me.*"

Horribly wounded by Courtney's death and now crushed by Ursula's rejection, Judas leaned forward and rested his forehead on the confessional door. He realized that, in less than a week, he had lost both Courtney and Ursula. Remaining quiet for over a minute, he allowed himself to wallow in his depression.

"Judas?" said Ursula, the youth watching the back of the confessional door as if she could see through it.

"'Vindicate the weak and fatherless; Do justice to the afflicted and destitute,'" Judas recited in his mind, "'Rescue the weak and needy; Deliver them out of the hand of the wicked.'" (Psalm 82:3-4).

The recitation of the command of his Lord rescued Judas from his personal failures and losses and his deep disappointment in himself. Subordinating his own desires and emotions to the will of his Master, Judas stood up with grim determination. He turned and departed.

"Judas?" Ursula called again. Unlocking the door in a panic, she threw it open. What she saw haunted Ursula for many years to come: the spot where Judas once stood was empty.

******

Aubrey lounged in the cabin of her private jet and indulged in fifty-year-old scotch whiskey, the spirit costing a mere $60,000 a bottle. She sat in an opulent, oversized chair and stared at the equally-opulent-and-oversized desk in front of it. An open laptop, an unlabeled CD in a clear plastic case and an open file folder containing several documents lay on its surface. Aubrey exhaled.

"All right, Ray," she said. She extracted the CD from its case, opened the drive door and inserted it. Setting the case aside, she closed the door. Her media player opened and, a few touchpad taps later, it played the CD. Aubrey sipped from her drink and said, "Let's see what you've been hiding from the world."

"9-1-1, what's your emergency?" asked the 9-1-1 operator.

"What're you doing?" Father Ray inquired.

"Sir, what's your emergency?" queried the 9-1-1 operator again.

Aubrey's face hardened as she concentrated on the recording. She heard the wind against the phone receiver.

"There's . . . there's been a knife attack at St. Arnulf in Summerfield Township," Father Ray answered harshly despite his heavy breathing, "and we need an ambulance and a Sheriff, yesterday!"

"Is the attacker still there?" asked the operator.

"Yeah, but he's unconscious," Father Ray said. The priest continued, "Two people have serious knife wounds. We need that ambulance."

"Two?" asked Aubrey aloud as she stopped the recording. She searched through the documents and pulled one out of the stack. Aubrey read it carefully as a sinister smile gradually spread across her lips. Dropping the document on her desk and reclining in her chair, she said, "Gotcha, Ray."

Aubrey gulped down some of her scotch and then held the glass with two hands. She pondered the new information for over a minute before restarting the recording.

"1508," Father Ray uttered.

Aubrey heard a movement in the background. She sat up in her chair and again stopped the recording. Rolling her chair closer to her desk, she clicked Internet Explorer and brought up a window.

"1508 healing," Aubrey said as she typed the number and the word into the address bar. She, after hitting "Enter", watched the search results appear on her screen. She scrolled through them, clicked on the last entry of the first page of search results and uttered with a hint of excitement, "Let's see what the Vatican has to say about it."

A webpage on the Vatican's official website appeared. Aubrey scanned the page for "1508" and quickly found it. The text began: "<u>1508</u> The Holy Spirit gives to some a special charism of healing so as to make manifest the power of the grace of the risen Lord."

"Mystery solved," Aubrey said with a cold, self-satisfied sneer. Ursula's apparent healing power and its implications for the existence of God, however, unsettled her. She drowned her uneasiness in scotch whiskey and restarted the recording.

"Now it's your turn, kid," Father Ray begged Ursula desperately, "C'mon, kid, do it. Ya' gotta do it."

"Let no one seek his own good, but that of his neighbor," said Ursula in a strong, clear voice.

"How noble," Aubrey commented contemptuously. Father Ray's compassionate rescue of Ursula stoked her jealousy.

"Ursula!" called Father Ray. Vickie screamed. More commotion followed and Father Ray yelled, "We need that ambulance!"

"Sir, what's happening?" asked the 9-1-1 operator with growing concern. Vickie's horrified crying could be heard in the background.

"Send the damn ambulance!" Father Ray ordered. He said in a calm, deep voice, "Vickie, get a blanket. We gotta keep her warm."

Aubrey allowed the rest of the recording to play but it contained nothing of interest to her. She returned to her scotch and drifted into deep contemplation.

"Archie's gonna love this," she said.

******

"Why, hello there, young man," said the quintessential "little old lady" as her voice echoed throughout the cavernous and empty Chapel. It was part of the Immaculate Heart of Mary Motherhouse in Monroe, Michigan, a university-like campus that housed 160 IHM sisters and provided numerous ministries and services to the community. One of those services was supportive care for aging nuns.

"Hi," Judas replied with forced politeness. The old woman, without invitation or the apparent need for one, struggled to sidestep her way down the pew aisle with her four-pronged cane. Judas tensed in irritation. Wishing to be alone with his self-doubt, he thought, "Not now."

The old woman, to Judas's dismay, eased herself onto the pew bench next to him. Wearing ill-fitting, beige pants, a white blouse buttoned up to her neck and a knitted, mint green sweater, she possessed copious wrinkles and dark, sunken eyes that unnerved him.

"Mind if I join you?" asked the woman despite acting like the matter was settled. Turning to her purse, she unzipped it and rummaged through its contents, saying, "I have something to show you."

"Okay," replied Judas in puzzlement, the teenager dreading whatever oddity was going to emerge from the woman's purse. His attention was drawn to the front of the chapel where a choir appeared from a side chamber and assembled around the altar.

"I make crosses, like the ones from the Crusades," announced the woman proudly as she continued to search through her purse. She found that for which she was looking and displayed it, explaining, "The soldiers used to sew crosses like this one onto their clothes as a sign of their commitment to the cause."

"Very nice," Judas commented with a feigned grin. The old woman was fast becoming a witness to his whereabouts and it concerned him. Standing up to depart, he said, "Well, I gotta go. It was nice to meet you."

"Oh, stay, stay," replied the woman as she grabbed his right arm and gently pulled on it. She looked to and pointed at the choir, stating, "They're very good. Very *inspirational*."

The manner in which the woman said "inspirational" caused Judas's spine to tingle. The chapel suddenly felt otherworldly as if God picked it up and removed it from the material realm. He hesitated but soon acquiesced to the old woman's request.

"Okay," Judas said uneasily while sitting down, "I'll stay."

"Good, good," the woman replied. She held onto his arm until he returned to the pew bench. They exchanged smiles - his anxious, hers reassuring – and then faced forward expectantly. Tempted to ask the woman's name, Judas decided against such a course as, if he did, she would most likely want to know his name. The woman stirred and said, "I think they're about to start."

The choir eased into the Samuel Barber's haunting Adiago for Strings. The beauty of the impeccably harmonized voices washed over him and bathed his heart in spirituality. Saturated in the presence of God, the chapel seemed, to Judas, to slip further into another realm. He failed to notice the woman again rummaging through her purse.

A series of tugs on Judas's right arm soon wrested him from his trance. Looking down, he noticed the old woman sewing her beloved cross onto the uppermost part of his right jacket sleeve. Judas flinched.

"Hold still," instructed the old woman. Minutes later, the choir reached its crescendo and, with every increase in volume, she completed another stitch in Judas's shirt. She added eerily, "Almost done."

The choir ceased singing. Judas, in the brief silence, accepted the revelation of God and saw the course of his future open before him. He recited what was to become the mantra of a rising tide: "'Vindicate the weak and fatherless; Do justice to the afflicted and destitute; Rescue the weak and needy; Deliver them out of the hand of the wicked.'" (Psalm 82:3-4).

The choir resumed its performance and the spirituality of the moment, though not subsiding, lessened and became elusive. There was no fanfare, no crowds clamoring for their own crosses of cloth, no ecclesiastical speeches. However, on that day, Judas Trent took the cross, the first such cross taken in commitment to the Millstone Crusade. Though Judas did not know it, it would not be the last.

The choir finished its song and, as if on cue, exited the chapel. The sound of the main chapel doors opening and footsteps approaching arose behind Judas.

"Sister Elsie, what are you doing in here?" asked a woman approaching in maroon scrubs. Noticing the cross on Judas's shoulder and Sister Elsie's sewing kit out, she griped, "You ruined his shirt."

"Leave me alone," insisted Sister Elsie. She waved her hands in a dismissive gesture and said in irritation, "Can't you see I'm talking to my son?"

"I'm so sorry," said the CNA with a sigh. Sister Elsie meticulously packed away her sewing kit as the CNA advised, "Sister Elsie's pretty good at escaping our Memory Care Unit. And she tries to sew crosses on everyone. You're the first person to actually let her do it."

"It's okay," Judas replied.

"C'mon, Sister Elsie," said the CNA. She glanced at the cross again and scolded Sister Elsie, "I should make you pay for his shirt."

"You pay for his shirt!" snarled Sister Elsie, her formerly sweet demeanor quickly souring. A scathing look from the CNA cowed her and she grumbled, "I'm coming."

Sister Elsie returned her sewing kit to her purse and zipped it up. Rising to her feet, she threw her purse straps over her shoulder.

"Goodbye, Judas," whispered Sister Elsie before pecking him on the top of his head. Astounded, he looked up to her as she winked at him, smiled and said, "You'll need more of those crosses. I'd better get some of the girls to help."

Grasping the handle of her cane, Sister Elsie scooted towards the main aisle. She complained the entire way about being returned to the Memory Care Unit though her protests seemed staged to distract the CNA from Judas.

"Your will be done," Judas said aloud as he fell to his knees and prayed a secret prayer in his heart.

******

Luna Pier, a small city nestled on the western banks of Lake Erie near the Michigan-Ohio border, lay hidden beneath a blanket of thick fog. The lightest of December breezes blew in from the east and produced ripples on the water. It failed, however, to disperse the mists.

Judas stood on the city's concrete pier, a short jetty created by a series of popsicle-stick-shaped sections dotted with benches and lined on its inner side with posts. It jutted out into the lake for a short distance before thrusting its arm northwestward along the fog-shrouded shoreline.

Judas heard footfalls long before he saw a person emerge from the mists. The scent of a cigar revealed the visitor's identity.

"Nice choice of venue, kid," said Father Ray as he walked towards Judas. Neither man looked at the other, the senior instead joining the junior in his observation of the nothingness. The cleric queried, "Got a copy of *Cloak & Dagger* for me?"

"A copy of what?" Judas inquired quizzically.

"*Cloak & Dagger*," answered Father Ray with a smirk. Gesticulating with his cigar in his right hand, he explained, "It's from an eighties movie with Dabney Coleman and that kid from E.T. Ya' know, the one where he finds the video game that's got secret files on it and spies are chasing him and . . . geez, what the hell am I saying? You weren't even born in the eighties. My God am I getting old. *Too old*."

The priest seemed to forget Judas and momentarily step out of the present. Snapping out of his trance fifteen seconds later, he rapidly shook his head and puffed on his soon-to-be-expended cigar.

"So, what's up?" asked Father Ray. The breeze grabbed a trail of cigar smoke and blew it over his left shoulder.

"I took the cross yesterday," Judas stated with conviction.

"You did what now?" inquired Father Ray as he cast a confused, sidelong glance at his protégé. He noticed the cross sewn into the fabric of Judas's sleeve.

"I took the cross yesterday," Judas repeated. Immediately recognizing what Judas intended to do but intent on quashing his plan, Father Ray sneered.

"You and your little gang of holy vigilantes harried a local human trafficking ring, and only twice at that," said Father Ray, the priest's ego tweaked by the young man's confidence and his successes. He continued with sharpness and skepticism, "They were just a ragtag band of drug addicts and lifetime criminals, Judas, with poor leadership, loose organization and little direction. I bet their masters are a little more formidable, and the only reason they've let this area slide is because it probably wasn't a significant moneymaker. Hell, you probably did 'em a favor by weeding out the underperformers."

"It's more than that," snarled Judas with a scowl. Father Ray turned towards him with a scowl of this own and waved a finger of warning at Judas.

"*You got lucky, kid,*" replied Father Ray. Agitated by what he considered foolishness, he said, "Lucky their masters didn't come after you. Lucky the FBI hasn't figured out who the hell you are. Lucky none of your friends got killed."

Father Ray paused and his eyes glazed over. The sound of a car accelerating in the distance roused him from his trance.

"Lucky your gift hasn't been revealed," muttered Father Ray as he turned his attention back to the fog.

"Why's that lucky?" Judas demanded angrily. Father Ray's wrathful eyes flashed back to him.

"Because if *that* gets out," answered Father Ray, "then *everyone* will be coming after you. Playing comic book hero in the shadows is risky. Doing it in the light of day? You'd better think that one over real damn careful, Batman."

"I have thought about it, and it's time to reveal myself to the world," Judas said. Father Ray laughed boisterously, the sound echoing throughout the tiny harbor.

"Is that so?" asked Father Ray in a tone of dubiousness. Kicking a small stone into the water, he asked, "How ya' gonna do that?"

"The establishment of a new Crusade, Father," Judas stated with a seriousness that rocked Father Ray's spiritual foundation. He recovered several seconds later with another uproarious laugh.

"A Crusade?" asked Father Ray, the mention of holy war tickling him. He chuckled and added, "You got balls, kid, I gotta give ya' that."

"A Crusade," Judas replied, "not against Muslims, but against the wicked, and not to deliver the Holy City, but to deliver the weak and fatherless, the afflicted and destitute, the weak and needy . . . every single girl like Courtney."

"I know her death was tough on you, kid, but the Crusades happened a *long* time ago in a time of kings and emperors, of swords and cavalry and archers," countered Father Ray. He walked to the city side of the pier and, with his back to Judas, expounded, "They occurred in a completely different era when the Church had far more power and influence over nations and their leaders than it does now. They were a creature of the past, of circumstances that just don't exist today."

Father Ray chuckled. He admired Judas's commitment and enthusiasm but loathed his delusions of grandeur. He returned to the young man's side.

"Besides, you can't just start a Crusade and, if someone is going to start one, it's the Pope in Rome, not some truant teenager in *Mon*-roe County, Michigan," continued Father Ray. Placing his cigar in his mouth, he said, "Sorry, Judas, but the Pope's gotta authorize it."

"He'll authorize it," Judas said with absolute certainty.

"Ha! The Pope of Peace call for a Crusade!" scoffed Father Ray. He laughed again. The gears of Father Ray's mind slowly turned and he looked at Judas with a peculiar, burgeoning gleam in his eyes. The idea of modern-day Crusades flickered in his mind on occasion, his contemplation of it stirred by the senseless violence towards and oppression of the weak and the innocent.

"I gotta admit, it's a tempting thought. There was an incredible power in the Crusades, in the armed expression of God's righteousness," explained Father Ray with a vigor that fueled Judas's passion, "yet it often degenerated into senseless, horrific violence and cruelty. The innocent inhabitants of Jerusalem were slaughtered by the thousands when the Holy City fell in 1099, Judas. Hell, the crusaders murdered thousands of Jews on their way there, too. *Pogroms* they were called. I just don't think mortals can be trusted with such endeavors. They always come off the rails."

Father Ray's face grew grim and drawn. He, though looking at Judas, seemed to stare through him. His gaze caused a chill to radiate down the young man's spine.

"A consideration for another time," said Father Ray with a weak, forced grin. Walking towards the other edge of the pier as if he intended to dive into the water, he tossed the nub of his cigar in the lake.

"God's calling me to do this, Father," insisted an undaunted Judas. His declaration of God's will caused the priest's blood to run cold.

"Look, kid, you can forget emancipation now, but you're not that far away from eighteen," Father Ray said as he pulled another cigar from his inner jacket pocket. He produced a matchbox, retrieved a match and then stowed it while reasoning, "No one knows you're involved with all this. You reappear, take your licks from Sister Genevieve, the judge and the State, and soon you'll be able to do whatever you want to do . . . go wherever you want go."

Igniting the match by striking it on his shoe, he then cupped his hand and held his cigar with his fingertips. Father Ray lit it and puffed on it in a plume of smoke.

"I'd like to see ya' go to college," said Father Ray, "maybe enter the seminary. The Church could use a strong, compassionate young man like you. What it needs – *what it really needs* – is good, moral priests whom children can trust in their day-to-day lives, not warriors."

"How many children will be raped and murdered while I become a priest?" Judas inquired with great angst. Father Ray sensed the disquiet in his spirit as he elaborated, "I hear every tear that falls and every cry that pierces the air. I will not abandon Tammy. I will not abandon any of them."

Father Ray held his cigar away from his face and observed his young charge in wonder. He felt a rising tide of righteousness within Judas, a tide which he could no longer control nor dissuade, and the eloquence of his words only underscored the work of the Holy Spirit within him.

"You'll pay a high price the second you step out of the shadows, and you'll continue to pay it for the rest of your life. Paying it might be exhilarating at times, but, mostly, it'll just be terrifying," advised Father Ray. He puffed on his cigar and said dourly, "Make no mistake, young man. Those who require that payment of you will not relent and they'll always come to collect. *Always.*"

"That's why I need your help," Judas said.

"*My help*," scoffed Father Ray. He stared into the whiteness again and exhaled before uttering, "A Crusade is far beyond what the Catholic Church has become or what the world will allow, Judas, and it's certainly beyond the abilities of a mediocre, middle-aged priest with a hankering for hooch and cigars and a fifteen-year-old, even as extraordinary as you are."

"I need you," said Judas in an angry, wavering tone. His insides burned in an inferno of rage, sadness and confusion while only his intense, watery eyes conveyed his emotion.

"No you don't, so back off," growled Father Ray with a threatening finger. Regretting his unjustified response, he recited in a low, tired voice, "'So I say to you, ask, and it will be given to you; seek, and you will find; knock, and it will be opened to you. For everyone who asks, receives; and he who seeks, finds; and to him who knocks, it will be opened.' You only need *Him*." (Luke 11:9-10).

Pausing only to glower at his mentor, Judas pushed past Father Ray and stormed away. The cleric watched him depart.

"The FBI'll flip those guys you busted," called out Father Ray, "and they'll get to Tammy before you do anyway."

Judas disappeared. Smoking his cigar while pondering the situation, Father Ray looked to the heavens.

"You can't seriously be considering this," said Father Ray. He received no answer, only silence and the chill of the strengthening wind.

******

Hurling sections of a tree trunk into an old, blue pickup truck as if they were children's blocks, Steve labored in one of the far corners of his parents' farm. A line of large, dormant trees loomed over him, their dark branches waving against the grey, cloudy sky. A heavily used chainsaw sat next to the truck along with a red gasoline container, gloves and safety goggles.

"Hey, Steve," Judas greeted his friend after the teenage giant tossed another huge piece of the tree into the truck with a clunk. Steve spun around and stumbled backward.

"Damn it, Judas!" exclaimed Steve, the fifteen-year-old regaining his balance after being startled by Judas's abrupt appearance. He lumbered up to Judas and yelled, "You scared the hell outta me!"

"We've gotta go again soon," Judas advised him coldly with a hard swallow. He already knew his companion's heart but held out hope that he was wrong. Standing with his hands tucked into his jacket pockets, Judas added, "I think I know where Tammy is."

Steve's countenance paled and he looked to Judas nervously. Despite his gunshot wound being healed by Ursula, the area where he was hit tingled.

"I'm out, Judas," declared an anxious Steve. He steeled his courage and stood up straight but spoke with a wavering voice nonetheless, saying, "And I-I-I talked to Mike, and, and . . . he's out, too."

A sudden right fist from Judas struck Steve in his jaw. Despite Judas's pulling of the punch, its force caused the young behemoth to crash to the ground. A stunned Steve remained down and massaged his sore mandible. Judas sighed.

"I shouldn't have brought you guys into this. *Any* of you," Judas said as he held out his hand. Steve, woozy from the punch, attempted to grasp it but his blurry vision prevented him from making contact. Judas grabbed his hand and hauled his large friend to his feet, saying, "I'm sorry about that. It's not your fight."

Steve's vision cleared. Judas pointed a quick finger at his own jaw.

"Now you take your best shot," Judas instructed Steve, "and we'll call everything even."

"Nah, I deserved it," replied Steve as he again massaged his aching jaw. Averting his eyes to the ground, he said, "I'm sorry, too, man. It's just so dangerous, ya' know, and I'm just not brave like you are."

"You are," Judas corrected him, "and you'll realize it someday."

Steve flinched as Judas lunged towards him but, instead of the attack he expected, he received a loving embrace. Several seconds later he returned the hug, the pair slapping each other twice on the back to express their affection.

"Where is she?" asked Steve as he and Judas released each other.

"It's best if you don't know," Judas answered.

"What about Charlotte . . . and Ursula, too?" asked Steve, his desire to see Charlotte betrayed by the structure of his question. Judas returned his hands to his pockets.

"It's not their fight, either," Judas replied. Steve offered his friend a guilty, sympathetic expression as he explained, "You guys did your part, and I'm thankful for that."

"Good luck, man," said Steve, his bottom lip quivering and his eyes watering. Judas felt the same emotions but repressed them. Steve added, "If you need anything-."

"I know," Judas interrupted him. Rendered inert by the gravity of the moment and his own fear, Steve stood motionless as Judas turned away and walked off across the cornfield and into an adjacent wooded parcel. He hung his head in shame when his best friend disappeared.

11 – For What Comes Next

Concealed within a stand of pine trees, Judas watched the old-yet-well-maintained farmhouse which it surrounded. There was no activity on the first or second floors and only a single light at the front of the house was visible. Light snow lazily drifted down from the night sky and through the cold air, the precipitation coating the grass in a thin layer of white. Judas shifted his weight and the ground debris beneath him crackled.

"Why don't ya' just blare an air horn? *Idiot*," Judas chastised himself. He breathed deeply though his ski mask and returned his attention to the farmhouse. A half-hour of Internet research revealed that it belonged to a ninety-three-year-old farmer and widower who resided in a nursing home due to a stroke. Judas also learned that one of its barns sat opposite the site of The Great Star Motel, the very barn that once housed vehicles connected to the human trafficking operation.

A huge community outcry led to the demolishing of The Great Star Motel a week prior to Judas's incursion. The barn, however, was spared and the farmhouse was ignored as its caretaker reported no unusual activity. The sudden reemergence of The Great Star Motel in the news brought Judas's attention back to the area and he had surveilled it for the last two weeks. The traffickers were using the basement of the residence as a safehouse but he had yet to see or sense any girls within it.

Judas's heart thumped in his chest as he stretched out his spiritual perception to scan the farmhouse for the first time in several days. It leapt when he sensed the presence of three guards and a girl in the basement. Her spirit was strong.

"Tammy," he whispered with great hope. Judas moved quickly through the trees but stopped upon clearing the last branch. He breathed deeply, the teenager taking what he believed to be his last peaceful breath for the foreseeable future. Committed to his plan and to the will of God, he squelched the presences of the three guards and ran towards the house.

******

171

Judas deftly used his bolt-cutters to sever the lock on the outer cellar door. He tossed it onto the grass, threw open the doors and descended the stairs. There was an unconscious guard at the bottom of the steps, his body lying on a tactical shotgun. Removing the firearm from beneath the man and setting it against the wall, Judas then slipped off his backpack and unzipped it.

"They were expecting me," Judas thought as he swiftly produced duct tape and zip ties. Moments later, the guard was tightly bound and Judas walked carefully to the foot of the stairs leading into the farmhouse. Another motionless guard lay there with a shotgun of his own. Repeating the process, Judas quickly zip-tied his wrists and legs and wrapped duct tape around his mouth and head.

The last guard stirred from his position in a closet beneath the staircase but Judas, acutely aware of his presence, let him stumble forward and fall with a thud. The guard's nine-millimeter pistol flew out of his hand and clattered across the floor. Judas stifled his lifeforce before he could reach it.

"I'm getting pretty good at this," he thought while zip-tying the third guard's wrists. He proceeded to his ankles and then finished his work by duct-taping the man's mouth. Satisfied that the guards were incapacitated and properly restrained, Judas stood up and moved to a door leading to another part of the cellar. He cautiously unlocked and opened it before stepping inside the room.

"Tammy?" Judas said as he recognized her face from the many pictures he had seen of her. A hasty application of makeup artificially brightened her countenance but her once-healthy, blondish-orangish hair was unwashed and stringy and her pale skin was smudged with dirt. Judas rushed to where she lay on a large cot, the teenager taking her chilled hand and beckoning, "Tammy? Tammy, wake up."

Tammy stirred in the nest of tattered blankets that were tangled around her, her heavy eyelids lazily raising, closing and then lazily raising again. Realizing that a male knelt next to her bed, she screamed and pummeled Judas. Tammy raged as she flailed at him, her consciousness wavering as she fought the last vestiges of the drug in her veins.

"No, no more!" mewled Tammy in a desperate tone that broke Judas's heart. Battering him with blows that he absorbed and blocked, she yelled defiantly, "*No more!*"

"I'm not one of them!" Judas shouted as he hugged Tammy to prevent her continued attack. She struggled against his embrace as he assured her, "I'm here to save you! I know Ursula!"

The mention of her friend's name halted Tammy's attack. Looking to Judas with blackish-brown eyes underscored with forlorn, dark circles, she pierced his spirit. Tammy grinned weakly.

"You're him, aren't you?" asked Tammy, the fourteen-year-old coming to life with relief and excitement. She continued with heightening spirits, "I've heard them talking about you. They're actually *afraid* of you, though the jerks won't admit it. Nice job making their lives so miserable."

Tammy wrapped her arms around Judas's torso and cuddled into his side. Feeling safe for the first time in months, she wallowed in his protection.

"You could've come a little sooner, though," complained Tammy, her body relaxing as she drifted into a light sleep. Despite their dingy surroundings and the presence of the guards, Judas maintained his hold on her and indulged in her affection.

"Let me see your face," said Tammy as she suddenly awoke. Judas recoiled, his first instinct being to shield his identity. Remembering his plan, however, he returned to his original position and offered himself to Tammy.

"Okay," Judas acquiesced with a sigh. Unabashedly grasping his ski mask with two hands, Tammy rolled it up over his head.

"Wow, you're cuter that I expected," remarked Tammy, the adolescent instantly smitten with her savior. Judas smirked in embarrassment. Giving him another hug and resting her head on his shoulder, Tammy asked thoughtfully, "So, how'd you get by the Three Stooges so fast?"

The smile vanished from Judas's face as Tammy's question brought him back to reality. He untangled himself from her and stood up.

"We've gotta get outta here before anyone else shows up," Judas warned. Removing his coat and gloves, he handed them to Tammy and said, "Here, put these on."

"Uh, Ursula may not have told you this, but I'm missing part of my foot," advised Tammy as she held it up to display it to him. Judas looked at her foot without reaction as she continued, "So I hope the car's not that far away 'cuz walking might be a little bit of a problem. Wait. You do have a car, right?"

Judas stifled a chortle. He admired Tammy's brave forthrightness regardless of her circumstances.

"Let's start with you putting on the coat and gloves," Judas instructed her with an amused smile.

******

Carrying Tammy piggyback style, Judas walked across the lawn of the farmhouse and passed through a narrow gap in the pine trees to the northeast. He then turned to the west and tromped across a dormant soybean field. Judas made no effort to hide his tracks.

"You're leaving a nice little trail of breadcrumbs for them to follow," said Tammy while glancing over her shoulder.

"It doesn't matter," Judas replied as he trudged forward.

"How come?" inquired Tammy. She thoroughly enjoyed her journey with Judas, the feel of her arms around his neck and his strong grip on the bottoms of her thighs. Tightening her grasp, she rested her chin on his broad shoulder.

"Because once I get you to the hospital," Judas answered matter-of-factly, "I'm turning myself in."

"That's the *dumbest* thing I've ever heard," stated Tammy bluntly, her dissatisfaction with Judas's plan evident in her tone. They arrived at a large drainage ditch and he paused.

"I know," Judas replied in a tone of resignation. He squeezed the bottoms of her thighs and instructed Tammy, "Wrap your legs around me for a minute and hold on."

"Not on a first date," countered Tammy with a playful grin.

"Just do it," insisted Judas with warming, reddening cheeks. Tammy snickered but complied and, without missing a beat, Judas descended into the ditch, leapt across the snow-covered ice and landed on the other bank. He climbed out of the ditch on all fours despite his lack of gloves.

"That was easy enough," Judas remarked. Standing up, he brushed the snow off his bare hands and again supported Tammy's thighs. Squeezing her legs once again, he said, "I got ya' now."

"You sure about that?" inquired Tammy softly in Judas's ear, the normally unimpressible teenager drawn to Judas's masculinity. He ignored her comment, turned to the north and entered a small, wooded area. Sensing his discomfort, Tammy changed the subject by asking, "So why're you turning yourself in?"

"It's what God wants," Judas cryptically responded. Exiting the trees, he marched up to a car. A film of snow covered the older model Chevy Malibu, the vehicle once belonging to the now-deceased aunt who raised Father Ray.

"It's a terrible idea, that's what it is," said Tammy with a dubious expression. Judas opened the car door in a light spray of snow. Moving with considerable ease and great care, he maneuvered Tammy into position and set her down in the passenger seat.

"That okay?" Judas asked her as he brushed the errant snow off the edges of the seat. Tammy touched his arm and their eyes met.

"They raped me," blurted Tammy. Her countenance hardened as if it were chiseled out of stone but her pain was palpable.

"I'm sorry," Judas apologized with a contorted expression. His bitter disappointment in himself and his rage towards his enemies boiled beneath his emotional surface. Seeing Courtney's lifeless face in his mind's eye, he uttered, "I'm always too late."

Judas checked to make sure Tammy was completely in the car and then shut the door. He hurried around the front of it, opened the driver's door and slid inside.

"I was just kidding about coming sooner," said Tammy as Judas pulled the door closed. Unable to look at her, he stuck the key in the ignition and turned it. The engine whined and rumbled but then died, its failure giving Tammy time to ponder her statement. Judas's second attempt succeeded after which she admitted, "Well, not really, but it's not your fault, either. *You saved me.*"

"I could've done better," Judas stated while fumbling with the heat controls. He clenched his jaw and grumbled, "I should've done better."

"You probably wouldn't date a crippled girl who's been raped, would you?" inquired Tammy, her bizarre question causing Judas to gaze at her in puzzlement.

"What?" Judas asked, the air between them crackling with romantic energy. Disregarding the consequences, Tammy lunged at Judas, grabbed the back of his head and pulled him into an ardent kiss. A flash of guilt and doubt paralyzed him but, after experiencing the emptiness caused by Courtney's death and Ursula's rejection, Tammy's warm attention quickly extinguished those emotions. Ending the kiss, she maintained her grip on him and said, "Saving the damsel in distress is a pretty epic 'how we met' story, though. It'd suck to waste it."

Judas smiled a smile of wonder. The burgeoning attraction between he and Tammy had become irresistible.

"Yeah, I guess it would," said Judas with a chuckle. He leaned toward Tammy for another kiss and she met him halfway. Falling into one another's arms, the unlikely paramours ignored the perils of the outside world and lost themselves in each other's affection.

******

"I can walk, ya' know," protested an annoyed Tammy as Judas rolled her into the Emergency Center at ProMedica Flower Hospital. He overruled her strident objections and demanded she use a wheelchair because he knew, as she did, that her legs were weakened by her harrowing ordeal and would not long support her.

"Yeah, I know, Tam," Judas replied. They passed a second set of sliding doors and entered the lobby.

"*Don't* call me that," snarled Tammy, ". . . *ever*."

Forgiving her complaints and her verbal jabs, Judas chose to simply absorb them. Tammy, irked by Judas's refusal to engage her, switched to a new line of attack.

"You need to get outta here before they call the cops," insisted Tammy while folding her arms in frustration.

"We already talked about this," Judas scolded her, his tone strong and convincing. A respect beyond infatuation arose in Tammy and she listened as he said, "I can't keep doing this outside the law. I did what I had to do to save you and to try to save Courtney. But that part's over. I need to accept the consequences of what I've done before I do anything else. It's important for what comes next."

"For what comes next?" queried Tammy. She simultaneously wanted Judas to flee and to stay but accepted the unlikelihood of both outcomes. Exasperated by her powerlessness, she grumbled, "What're you talking about?"

"Hi, how can I help you tonight?" asked the desk clerk at the Emergency Center's front desk. Concern spread across her face when she noticed Tammy's unkempt, disheveled appearance.

"I need a cane," demanded Tammy as she leaned forward and attempted to stand up. A disapproving glance from Judas caused her to desist. Satisfied that she would remain in the wheelchair, he leaned over the counter.

"She's a human trafficking victim and she's been raped," Judas explained firmly-yet-quietly. He directed the desk clerk, "She needs to see someone right away and you need to call the police."

"One moment," said the clerk as she nodded in agreement. Acting like a consummate professional, she stood up and set about her work.

"Take this," Judas advised Tammy while reaching into his jacket pocket and removing a phone. Handing it to her, he continued, "It's time."

"I don't want to," countered Tammy, the fourteen-year-old feeling a growing shame as she considered discussing the rapes with her parents. Judas crouched down to look her directly in the eyes. Tammy looked away.

"We talked about this, too," Judas said as he scooted over to again look Tammy in the eyes. They moistened as he expounded, "They're going to arrest me when they get here and I don't want you to be alone. *Call your parents.*"

"*All right,*" pouted Tammy. She perceived every second that passed, each one prickling her like a tiny electric shock as her time with Judas ran out.

"You can come right back," said the clerk as she appeared at the entry doors of the Emergency Department and waved them towards her. Judas placed his hand on Tammy's shoulder and she, in turn, grasped it. Communicating tactilely, the teenagers reassured each other and soon disappeared behind the automatic doors.

******

"Mom, *enough*, I'm fine," groaned Tammy as she endured her mother's swings from relieved blathering to frantic questions about her well-being. She listened for a few more seconds before saying, "I don't wanna talk anymore. Just get here, okay? *Bye!*"

Tammy groaned and tapped the screen with her thumb. Exhaling, she held out the phone and dramatically dropped it on the bed.

"C'mon, give her a break," Judas implored Tammy. He sat on the edge of her hospital bed and said, "She's just worried about you."

Tammy mercilessly eyed Judas. He crawled into the bed next to her and laid down, the move prompting her to rest her head on his shoulder and snuggle into him.

"I got in that stupid wheelchair for you and I'm allowing you to follow your stupid plan and get arrested like an idiot," sneered Tammy. Squeezing his arm punitively, she said, "That's all you're getting today."

Two Sylvania, Ohio police officers cautiously entered the room with their hands resting on their sidearms. Judas and Tammy sat up but she maintained a tight hold on him.

"Son, I'm gonna need you to step away from the bed and come with me," an older, white-haired officer directed Judas. Tammy shot icy daggers at him.

"It's all right, sir," said Judas calmly while raising his arms in surrender. He extricated himself from Tammy with some difficulty and stood up before advising the officers, "I'm giving myself up."

"Why don't you go arrest the guys who raped me instead of the guy who saved my life?" Tammy chastised the police officers. She wished she had her cane and thought vile thoughts.

"Tammy, they're just doing their jobs," interjected Judas with a glance over her shoulder.

"No, this is bullshit!" Tammy shouted. Gesturing furiously, she berated the officers, saying, "You're morons! I'd still be in the basement of that farmhouse if it wasn't for him and now you're gonna arrest him? *Stupid.*"

"Can I have a minute with her?" Judas requested. He lowered his arms slightly and pleaded, "*Please.*"

Tammy fumed as the older officer considered Judas's request. He narrowed his eyes and shook his head in the affirmative.

"Okay, son," said the officer, "but we need to pat ya' down first. We just wanna make sure she's protected. I'm sure you can understand."

"Yeah, I understand. Thank you," Judas replied. The second officer searched him for weapons and, finding none, nodded to the older officer. Rotating around carefully and moving to Tammy's side, Judas asked her, "Do you really want to help me?"

"I don't want *this*," Tammy whimpered with clenched fists and a reddening face. Judas said nothing and patiently waited for her answer. Faltering under his commanding aura, she fought angry tears and reluctantly admitted, "Yeah."

"Then let me do what He's asked me to do, and you . . .you be a good patient," said Judas. They clasped hands as he said, "Things are gonna get tough for me, and I gotta know you're okay."

Tammy's countenance grew terrible as she resisted the competing urges to break down and to explode in a rage. Managing to quell her conflicting emotions but unable to speak, she trembled. The young paramours kissed before hesitantly releasing one another. Judas turned to the police officers.

"Thanks," he said. Holding out his wrists, he said, "Can you read me my rights in the hall?"

"Let's just step outside and talk first," suggested the older officer. The officers led Judas out of the hospital room and, immediately after his departure, a doctor and two nurses hurried inside and closed the door. Tammy, too exhausted to cry or interact with the medical personnel, laid her head on her pillow, left her consciousness behind and found Judas in the world of her dreams.

******

"Father!" exclaimed Tammy's mother as she charged towards him in the middle of the waiting room. She crashed into his body with a powerful embrace that nearly knocked him prone.

"Whoa, Kate, easy," Father Ray pleaded. Shifting her to one side, he asked, "How's she doin'?

"She's been through a lot," replied Kate concernedly. The mere mention of Tammy's abduction caused her to break down but, infused with hope due to the return of her daughter, she soon composed herself and continued, "But she's alive, Father. *Thank God, she's alive*. We're letting her sleep right now, though. And she wanted everyone out of the room, of course. You know how she is."

"That I do," Father Ray said as he comforted Kate and extended a hand to her father. They shook hands and he greeted him, "Hey, Bill. I can't tell you how happy I am for you guys."

"All the prayers worked, Father," said Bill with a grin, the relief in his voice unmistakable. Kate moved to her husband and wrapped an arm around his waist.

"She wants to see you," said Kate, her voice tinged with jealousy. The priest offered her a quizzical expression. It was not his intention to remain at the hospital for more than a brief visit.

"Sure," Father Ray said, "I can hang out for a couple hours."

"Actually, she wanted to see you as soon as you got here," advised Kate gingerly. Grasping Father Ray's hand, she pulled him with her and said, "She was really adamant about it. I'll take you to her room."

"All righty, then," replied Father Ray. Kate hurriedly guided him to Tammy's room and ushered him inside. Tammy appeared to sleep soundly and, other than the dark, sunken circles underneath her eyes, she looked much like her old self. Father Ray thought, "They cleaned her up but the kid still looks burnt."

"Mucho tiempo, no veo, Padre," said Tammy. She opened her eyes.

"'How ya' feelin', kid?'" Father Ray asked with a smirk as he launched into Han Solo's lines from *The Empire Strikes Back*. He approached her and said, "'You don't look so bad to me. In fact, you look strong enough to pull the ears off a Gundark.'"

"You're so old and weird," complained Tammy with a disapproving glance. Kate gently smacked her thigh.

"Tammy, don't speak to Father Ray like that," scolded Kate.

"I love you, Mom, but get out," said Tammy bluntly. Using the remote control to raise her hospital bed, she added, "And close the door, too."

"Geez, Tammy," Father Ray admonished her.

"It's fine," said Kate, "whatever she wants is fine with me. At least for now, young lady."

Kate gave her daughter a pointed look and then stole a quick kiss of her daughter's forehead. Tammy unsuccessfully resisted it.

"Stop it, Mom," she griped. Grabbing the back of a chair as Kate exited the room, Father Ray slid it next to Tammy's bed and took a seat. She asked in a strengthening voice, "Can you hand me my cane?"

"I don't think the doctors would want you meandering around just yet," Father Ray said with a dubious look.

"I know," said Tammy. She shrugged and stated, "I just want my cane."

"Sure, kiddo, you got it," Father Ray said. He stood up, walked to a bank of drawers against which the cane was set and grasped it. Taking it to Tammy, he said, "Here ya' go."

Tammy grabbed the cane, flipped it around and smacked Father Ray's shoulder with its unweighted end. The teenager wanted to cause him temporary pain but no permanent damage.

"Damn it, Tammy!" Father Ray barked. Glancing around the room as he realized the volume of his voice, he lessened it and asked incredulously, "What the hell did you do that for?"

"That's what you get for abandoning him," growled Tammy, her revelation puzzling Father Ray.

"Abandoning who?" Father Ray queried.

"Judas," growled Tammy as she glowered at the cleric. Pointing her cane at Father Ray threateningly, she said, "He told me you wouldn't help him."

"Oh, he did, did he?" Father Ray inquired with healthy skepticism. His ire rising as his tolerance of teenage activism waned, he paced and gestured, ranting, "If you're referring to his imaginary *Crusade*, Tammy, there's not going to be one. It's ridiculous to even discuss it. You're *teenagers* and all he did was get lucky playing vigilante, and only *three times* at that."

"It's too late, Padre," warned an undaunted Tammy in an eerie tone. She lowered her bed and stared at the ceiling, saying, "It's already started, and you can't stop it. No one can."

"What's already started?" Father Ray inquired in a curmudgeonly tone. Flustered and frustrated by Tammy's cryptic words and doggedness, he continued, "And what do you mean no one can stop it? I swear, that kid's gonna be the death of me. By the way, where the hell is the car I lent him?"

"It's a few streets over at a bar called the Village Inn," said Tammy. She placed her folded hands on her stomach and explained, "The key's on the back passenger-side tire. Judas wants you to get it out of there ASAP."

"Is that so?" Father Ray queried in disbelief.

"Where did they take him?" inquired Tammy, her bravado cracking and revealing fissures of worry. Thrusting his hands into his pockets, Father Ray stopped in the center of the room.

"The Monroe County Youth Center, early this morning," Father Ray said, "but I don't know long he'll be there. The feds might want him. Ohio might want him. Who knows? But at any rate they're not letting anyone see him. I tried that already."

Tammy closed her eyes and remained silent for several minutes. Deeming her to be asleep, Father Ray sauntered to the window and looked out into the city. He desired a drink and a cigar, neither of which were at hand. Tammy opened her eyes and stirred.

"We've got to help him, Padre," said Tammy in a sad, tired voice. Feeling her energy draining away and true sleep creeping over her, she whimpered, "He can't do it alone."

"Well," Father Ray said, "it's real damn hard to start a crusade in custody."

He returned to his chair and slumped into it while watching Tammy slumber peacefully. Sifting her words and emotions, Father Ray discovered and assembled the clues she provided.

"Boy, Judas," Father Ray criticized his mentee in exasperation, "you sure know how to make one helluva mess."

12 - Youth Unleashed

Brilliant sunshine streamed through the window of the room to which Judas was confined. Interned in the Monroe County Youth Center hours after he surrendered to police, he now knelt on the floor next to his bed and prayed. The conviction of his heart warred with the logic of his mind as he spoke to his Master.

"How do I start a Crusade from here?" Judas asked God. Tammy's admonitions danced in his consciousness, her doubts as to the efficacy of fighting human trafficking while in custody becoming his own. The sound of her voice in his head, however, made him smile and he said softly, "I guess I should thank You for her. It's pretty cool to be wanted."

His smile faded when a vision of Ursula struggled its way into his mind. Her rejection still stung him and not even Tammy's forceful affection assuaged it. Judas's guilt burgeoned.

"Why did you even put us together in the first place?" Judas inquired. His attempts to expel Ursula from his thoughts failed and the competing images of Ursula and Tammy interrupted his prayers. Putting his faith in God, he climbed onto the bed and tried to clear his mind.

******

Father Ray's eyes followed the line of Tammy's IV as he contemplated the love triangle developing between she, Judas and Ursula. He visually traced the line back and forth several times before the door creaked open behind him. Father Ray sat up and listened intently.

"Father?" called out Ursula softly, her appearance seeming as if she stepped right out of the priest's thoughts. Peering into the room through the partially open door, she lingered and awaited permission to enter.

"Aw, geez," Father Ray whispered. He suspected that Tammy knew nothing of the trysts of Judas and Ursula and wished to avoid any conflict between the two fourteen-year-olds. Waving her forward over his shoulder after a brief hesitation, Father Ray said, "C'mon in, Urse."

"Is she awake?" asked Ursula as she carefully and quietly walked into the room. The sight of her best friend lying motionlessly in her hospital bed caused her heart to anxiously flutter. Father Ray heard Ursula's breath catch as she stopped next to him.

"No worries, kiddo," Father Ray assured Ursula, "she's very much alive."

"And I'd be asleep if everyone would stay out of my room," complained Tammy with feigned annoyance. Opening her eyes, she turned to Ursula and grinned impishly.

"*Tammy*," gushed Ursula. She hurried to her side and the two friends hugged each other exuberantly. Ursula, with Tammy's safety confirmed, immediately thought of Judas and asked sheepishly, "Was it Judas?"

Father Ray winced and clenched his teeth. Ursula squeezed Tammy's hand in anticipation of her answer.

"Yeah, he saved me," replied Tammy as her face lit up. Father Ray leapt to his feet and moved next to Ursula.

"They've got him at the Youth Center," Father Ray advised Ursula. Insinuating himself part-way between she and Tammy, he informed her, "They wouldn't let me see him but they did say his hearing will probably be tomorrow. We'll know more then."

"Is he okay?" inquired Ursula.

"He's fine," Father Ray replied, "or as fine as he can be while locked up in kiddie jail."

No one spoke for over a minute: Tammy stewed, Ursula worried and Father Ray brooded. The gears of Tammy's mind suddenly whirred to life.

"That gives us less than twenty-four hours to get his story out," declared Tammy as she stared ahead with narrowed eyes.

"Get his story out?" Father Ray queried, his disapprobation palpable.

"That's right," rejoined Tammy. She turned her head to the left to view Father Ray and explained, "You know, get him on the news and social media so everyone knows what he did. Force the cops to let him go."

"We could even, like, stage a protest," suggested Ursula. Her countenance brightened as she formulated her idea and continued, "And we could try to get all the kids from St. Judith to skip school tomorrow to attend. That'd get a lot of attention."

"That's awesome," replied Tammy with several pronounced nods and a smirk.

"Now wait just a minute," Father Ray objected, the cleric shielding himself from the ardent energy of his young parishioners.

"Padre, go tell my Mom I need her iPad," interjected Tammy, the teenager ordering him as if his compliance were assured.

"I've got my phone, too," said Ursula as she pulled it from the back pocket of her jeans.

"Tammy, you were locked up in a basement less than twelve hours ago," Father Ray argued. Ursula ignored him and typed feverishly with her thumbs.

"Yeah, and other girls still are," snarled Tammy with wild, passionate eyes. Irked by Father Ray's reluctance to join the cause, Tammy sneered, "Judas can save them, and we're gonna help him do it, *right*?"

Ursula ceased typing and set her phone aside. Grasping Father Ray by his forearms, she proceeded with a calmer, kinder approach and an appeal to his conscience.

"We both failed him when we let him go alone, but looked what he did, even without us," said Ursula. Releasing Father Ray's arms, she pleaded, "Father, imagine what he can do *with* us."

"And not *just* with us," added Tammy.

"I should've become a monk," Father Ray muttered. He fiddled with the cigar in his pocket.

"Please, Father," begged Ursula.

"C'mon, Padre, don't screw this up," urged Tammy. The priest contorted his face in an expression of resigned ire but, without saying a word, he shook his head in the affirmative. Father Ray headed towards the door while leaving two smiling teenage faces in his wake.

"I'll be damned," commented Father Ray as he exited Tammy's hospital room, "You actually *are* considering this."

******

Tammy, much to the chagrin of her mother and the medical staff, temporarily banned everyone save Ursula and Father Ray from her hospital room. Her persistence and Father Ray's intervention as her priest held them at bay, however, as the trio debated their next move.

"Are you really sure you want to do this?" asked Ursula, the doubts written all over her disfigured face. Her best friend had been free for less than a day and she worried about the implications of her plan.

"You'll be baring your heart and soul, Tammy," cautioned Father Ray. Standing at the foot of her bed with a sour expression, he continued, "You'll be opening yourself up to the entire world."

"I know," Tammy blurted. Her face contorted and trembled but, wrestling her fear into submission, she said, "But everyone has to know what I went through, how horrible it was . . . to be held prisoner, to be away from my family . . . to be raped . . . . "

Tammy trailed off and withdrew inside herself to ponder her ordeal. Father Ray and Ursula wished to dissuade her but could not find the words in the face of her inner turmoil.

"They have to know what all the other teens're going through," Tammy steadfastly declared, "and they have to know that Judas saved me, and he can save them, too. If I don't speak out now then I've failed them, all of them. And him. And I'll die before I fail him."

Deeming the matter settled, Father Ray brought up the video recorder on Tammy's mother's iPad. Ursula moved next to him as he positioned the iPad to capture Tammy and her hospital surroundings. Tapping the record button, Father Ray steadied the device and nodded to Tammy.

"Hi, I'm Tammy Parker," Tammy began without any sign of faltering. Ursula's palms grew sweaty with nervousness as her friend said, "I'm fourteen-years-old and I live in Whiteford Township, Michigan. Right now, though, I'm in Flower Hospital in Sylvania, Ohio. I'm here because, in October, I was kidnapped by human traffickers. I was just walking home from school. It wasn't that far and I felt safe in my own neighborhood. I didn't think anything would happen to me."

Tammy shrugged, frowned and bit her lip to stop it from quivering. A few tears rolled down Ursula's face.

"But something did happen to me, and I don't feel safe anymore," said Tammy. Sitting up straight, she grabbed a small, maize-and-blue Michigan pillow her mother brought her from home and expounded, "A guy in a van grabbed me, and I fought him, but he was too strong. He threw me in the van and kidnapped me. When I woke up, I was on a little cot and locked in a tiny, dirty room. The guys, the human traffickers, came in a little later, and held me down . . . they injected heroine into my arm and tried to force me to have sex with men. Adult men."

Ursula gently wept though Tammy's courage helped her remain calm. Father Ray battled nausea and an inner rage but continued to record her impassioned words.

"I kept fighting them, though," explained Tammy proudly, "and I fought the drugs, too. They moved me around to different houses, always at night, and I never knew where I was. Because I wouldn't have sex with the men who paid for it, they wouldn't let me shower, or brush my teeth, and sometimes they wouldn't let me go to the bathroom. That wasn't the worst part, though. Sometimes, they raped me. They raped me a lot."

Tammy, strong as she was, broke down and sobbed. Her anger at her captors gradually overcame her sorrow and embarrassment and she wiped away her tears. Ursula and Father Ray prayed for her as she calmed herself.

"I think I was raped ten times, maybe more, but I don't really remember," said Tammy with bleary eyes. Her demeanor leveled out and she continued, "It was hard to keep track of everything and fight them all the time. *But I kept fighting.* I thought I was gonna die, but I kept fighting. And praying. I prayed every day, begging God to help me."

Tammy paused. The storm clouds of negative emotion lifted and her countenance brightened. It appeared to Ursula and Father Ray as if her face glowed and they marveled at her strength.

"And then He did," said Tammy with a simultaneously heart-wrenching and heart-warming smile. Her love for Judas bubbling over, her smile burgeoned and she continued, "He sent me a hero. He sent me Judas."

Father Ray exhaled and his eyes darted to Ursula, who slowly grasped the extent of Tammy's feelings for Judas. Her countenance dimmed.

"Don't do this to her, *please*," prayed Father Ray in a plea for God to spare Ursula's heart.

"Judas Trent," stated Tammy with adoration. Setting aside the pillow in a clear sign she no longer needed it, she said, "He's not a police officer, or an FBI agent. He's not even an adult. But he rescued me from that farmhouse, and carried me on his back, in the cold and the snow, to get me to safety. And because of Judas, I'm here, in this hospital. I'm safe, and I get to see my Mom and Dad again."

Father Ray smiled softly as Tammy briefly paused her monologue. Ursula, however, remained emotionless. Looking directly into the camera as her surroundings blurred, Tammy grew grim and serious.

"But now someone needs to help Judas," advised Tammy. Speaking with the seriousness of a knife edge, she said, "He's in the Monroe County Youth Center in Michigan just because he took the law into his own hands. And that's not right. He saved six other girls like me and they're home with their families because of him. And he put eleven human traffickers out of business. *Eleven of them.* He's only fifteen and he did all of that."

Tammy paused to let the gravity of Judas's actions sink into the consciousness of her audience. Little did she know that Ursula also treasured Judas in her heart.

"That girl's something else," said Father Ray to himself.

"He has a hearing at 10:00 am tomorrow at the Youth Center, and we need to demand that the judge release him," explained Tammy. She implored her audience, "So, if you're watching this, especially if you're a teenager, and you wanna make a real difference in the world and in the lives of other teens, we're demonstrating tomorrow at 3600 South Custer Road in Monroe. Judas is the solution to human trafficking. He's special, and this is just the beginning of our fight. *Please come help us.*"

Tammy's easily readable emotions shocked Ursula. She never suspected that once she relinquished her grasp on Judas he would fall directly into the arms of her best friend.

"You're amazing, kiddo," gushed Father Ray with look of pride.

"Let me see it," Tammy demanded with an outstretched arm and an open hand. Ursula quickly exited the room. Tammy, worried for her friend, asked, "Is she okay?"

"That was pretty hard core, Tammy," replied Father Ray as he handed her the iPad. Knowing exactly why Ursula fled, he covered her tracks by saying, "And Urse's a pretty sensitive kid. She probably just needed to compose herself. I'll go check on her."

"Yeah, make sure she's okay," Tammy said as she accepted Father Ray's explanation and played the recording of her speech.

"She won't be okay for a long, long time," Father Ray thought. Turning over an idea in his mind, he halted in the doorway and said aloud, "You know what? I think I'll just leave her be for now."

******

The miles of Highway M-50 between Dundee and Monroe rushed past far too quickly for Ursula's liking as Aunt Vickie drove she, Tammy and Father Ray to Judas's hearing. Anxiousness prickled her: anxiousness over the risks they all took, anxiousness over Judas's confinement, anxiousness over seeing Tammy in his arms.

"I'm surprised your parents let you leave the hospital," said Aunt Vickie, Ursula's adoptive parent second-guessing her own decision to allow her niece to participate in the demonstration.

"I had to promise to stay with Father Ray at all times and go right back to the hospital afterwards," griped Tammy with a roll of her eyes. Despite sitting in the back seat, Tammy noticed Ursula's disquiet and prodded her with the end of her cane. She asked, "What's wrong with you?"

"Nothing," Ursula answered in a poorly feigned tone of composure. No one in the vehicle believed her assertion.

"There shouldn't be," countered Tammy. Brimming with energy and feistiness, she said, "This whole thing's about to go nova, girlfriend, and then Judas is gonna kick some serious bad-guy ass. It's gonna be epic."

Tammy mimicked an explosion with her hands. Father Ray shook his head and craved a cigar.

"That mouth," scolded Father Ray. Seated behind Aunt Vickie, he glanced at Ursula, who gave Tammy a dubious grin, and noticed her tenseness as she hesitated to speak. He waited patiently as she decided which of her fears to confess.

"We could get a lotta kids in trouble today," Ursula warned as she squirmed in her seat. Her comment disturbed Aunt Vickie who struggled with the urge to turn the car around.

"And a priest, too," muttered Father Ray.

"'Why don't you knock it off with those negative waves?'" Tammy said, the quote drawn from the tank-driving Oddball in *Kelly's Heroes*. Father Ray observed her incredulous expression and chuckled.

"You spend too much time with me, kid," replied Father Ray, the cleric amused that the fourteen-year-old quoted a movie made decades before her birth. He looked to Ursula and smiled, saying, "But you're right. Let's all show a little more faith."

"That's excellent advice, Father," Aunt Vickie agreed with a nod and glance in the rearview mirror.

"*Or* we could just look at the numbers," said Tammy. Producing her phone, she fiddled with it and then held it up to Father Ray. She announced proudly while displaying the YouTube page with her video appeal, "879,674 YouTube views since last night."

Aunt Vickie gasped. Ursula spun around in her seat.

"Really?" Ursula asked with wide eyes. She swiped the phone from Tammy and scanned the screen.

"Really," answered Father Ray. Leaning between the front seats, Tammy pointed to the sky.

"That's probably why the helicopter's flying around up there," she said.

Father Ray watched the helicopter circling ahead and then noticed cars parked along the shoulders of M-50. He swiftly came to the conclusion that the hand of God laid the path on which they were all to tread.

"I don't think you need to worry, Ursula," Father Ray said as his gaze moved along the line of cars reaching into the distance, "I think God's got this one."

******

The vicinity of the Youth Center was choked with a massive crowd of thousands, its ranks comprised primarily of teenagers. A relatively smaller contingent of college students were present as well; many of them had migrated north from Monroe County Community College while some came from as far away as Michigan and Michigan State Universities. Cars were parked everywhere: in local parking lots, all over the Monroe County

Fairgrounds and on the sides and in the medians of M-50. Ursula, Tammy and Father Ray, at Tammy's insistence, walked to the Youth Center.

"We don't have time to wait," grumbled Tammy, the teenager unwilling to brook the gridlocked traffic. She marched forward on her cane and replied resolutely, "After what Judas did for me, I'll walk my legs into bloody stumps for him."

Father Ray shook his head but Ursula said nothing. She bit her tongue and hoped the pain would keep her from crying over the loss of Judas. The trio soon joined the line of students and other protestors streaming towards the Youth Center.

"Hey, you're the girl from YouTube!" exclaimed a teenager standing amid a group of adolescents at the side of the road. Every face turned to gawk at Tammy as the lanky teen shouted, "Hey, it's her. It's Tammy Parker!"

The crowd surrounding them erupted into cheers and closed around Tammy to offer their support. Ursula initially felt self-conscious but, as it became evident that Tammy bore the full brunt of the crowd's attention, her apprehension eased. Feeling claustrophobic, Father Ray searched for a breach in the walls of humanity.

"Let's keep moving," he urged them despite the density of the crowd. Several small groups broke into political and religious debates over the purpose of the protest and hostility rippled throughout the sea of people. Chants ensued and makeshift signs were held up and thrust at opponents.

"This isn't about politics," declared Tammy angrily. The debates sputtered to a halt but were replaced by skeptical murmurs as she continued, "It's God's plan for us to save the victims of human trafficking. That's what we're here for."

"*Please* don't start that God stuff," scoffed a chubby emo teenager inappropriately dressed for the weather. Clearly hostile to religion, he said, "Where was God when you were kidnapped and raped? You should hate that asshole."

"Hey, Jesus freak, how many kids has your priest molested?" asked another teenager as she sneered and pointed at Father Ray. Tammy drew herself up to spew vitriol at the girl for attacking her beloved spiritual guide. An authoritative voice ascended above the din before she had the chance to speak.

"*Idiots*! God is neither the teachings of the misguided nor the criticisms of the misinformed," barked Father Ray with a withering glare at his detractors. The masses grew quiet as Father Ray shouted, "'But seek first His kingdom and His righteousness, and all these things will be added to you.' No one who has failed to follow that command has any standing to challenge God. *No one*! How many of you have picked up a Bible and read it for yourself instead of listening to the bullshit of others or just assuming what it says?" (Matthew 9:33).

The crowd remained silent with the exception of murmurings on its outskirts. Ursula took Father Ray's arm in her own and Tammy, inspired by his oratory, watched him with pride.

"*Wake up*! Tammy has invited you, as teens and young adults, to help other teens and young adults where we adults have failed you. And as far as Jesus, have any of you experts read the Gospel of Matthew, where He said: 'So it is not the will of your Father who is in heaven that one of these little ones perish . . . ,'" preached Father Ray. (Matthew 18:14). A few members of the crowd melted away but the majority of them drew closer to the priest as he spoke. "'. . . but whoever causes one of these little ones who believe in Me to stumble, it would be better for him to have a heavy millstone hung around his neck, and to be drowned in the depth of the sea.' So stop your bickering and feuding and faithlessness, join this Crusade, this Millstone Crusade, and save His little ones from those who cause them to stumble. Be the millstones that He hangs around their necks! Weigh them down and drown them in a sea of righteousness that none can withstand." (Matthew 18:6).

All that could be heard were the thuds of helicopter blades. Father Ray nudged Tammy forward and then stepped back, the priest ceding the spotlight to her. She readily accepted it.

"'Vindicate the weak and fatherless; Do justice to the afflicted and destitute; Rescue the weak and needy; Deliver them out of the hand of the wicked,'" recited Tammy. (Psalm 82:3-4).

Father Ray smiled as Tammy's own impassioned monologue unfolded. Seconds later, his phone buzzed. He moved away from her, retrieved his phone and read the text message waiting for him. Ursula, sensing something was amiss, followed on his heels.

"That was Sister Palladia," said Father Ray softly as leaned towards Ursula's ear. A concerned expression on his face, he explained, "She's back from the Vatican, and she wants to see you ASAP at St. Saturnin. I can't leave Tammy, though, not in all this. I promised her parents I'd stay with her."

"I'll be fine," Ursula assured him, "it's not that far."

"I'm not leaving you in all this, either," objected Father Ray. A young man bulled his way through the crowd just as the cleric said, "Your Aunt'd kill me."

"Steve!" Ursula cried out. Judas's best friend walked forward with Charlotte and Mike in tow. Ursula embraced Charlotte and said, "Thanks for coming."

"Thanks for making me babysit these two morons," replied Charlotte with a nod to Mike and Steve. Tammy's speech ended and she began the last leg of her journey to the Youth Center. Father Ray slapped Steve on the shoulder.

"I need your magic, big man," said Father Ray with urgency in his voice. Walking backward for a few steps, he met Steve's gaze and called out, "Get Ursula to her aunt, pronto."

"But I need to help Judas!" protested Steve.

"Then get her to her aunt!" Father Ray shouted before disappearing into the waves of people swirling around him. Steve turned to Ursula and offered her a conflicted, helpless look.

"I'm not gonna let him down again," insisted Steve. Ursula grabbed his forearms and looked into his eyes.

"I'm about to get him some serious help," Ursula assured Steve, "but I need yours to do it. I've gotta get to St. Saturnin."

Steve paused and contemplated Ursula's desperate request. Moving people like a bulldozer moves earth, he led his friends against the onslaught of protestors flowing towards the Youth Center.

******

The crowd parted and allowed Father Ray and Tammy to walk up to the Youth Center's main entrance. Anticipation crackled throughout the grounds as a group of Monroe County Sheriff deputies blocked the entrance and a familiar, scowling face appeared.

"At least the deputies can only shoot us," quipped Father Ray. Sister Genevieve detached from the gathering of deputies and approached him with firm, heavy footfalls. Tammy defiantly stepped between them but Father Ray said softly, "Easy, Tammy. Let me handle this."

"The Court has adjourned the hearing indefinitely until they have your little uprising under control and further assess the situation," advised Sister Genevieve with disapprobation. Father Ray displayed his open palms in a sign of innocence while Tammy bristled.

"Hey, don't look at me, Sister," Father Ray said. The crowd remained subdued and observed the servants of God with great interest.

"So you're saying you had nothing to do with it?" inquired Sister Genevieve sharply. Father Ray could not contain his guilt and thrust his hands in his pockets.

"Not exactly," Father Ray confessed. Tammy thumped her cane on the cement walkway.

"Why don't you back off?" growled Tammy.

"Why don't you show a little respect, young lady, and a little more faith in Judas?" countered Sister Genevieve. Drawing herself up to loom over Tammy, she said, "He told me everything."

"Everything?" Father Ray queried uneasily. His right hand inveterately slipped into his jacket pocket to search for a cigar but, much to his chagrin, he forgot them in his truck.

"That is correct, Father," answered Sister Genevieve with a stinging glance. Looking to Tammy with a softening countenance, she continued, "And his foremost concern, other than this ill-advised youth movement, is your well-being, Ms. Parker. He's requested that you return to the hospital."

Tammy wanted to debate the efficacy of the Crusade with Sister Genevieve but, touched by Judas's concern for her, she stood mute. Studying the Youth Center building, she wondered where Judas was and desired to see him.

"I must admit, Father," said Sister Genevieve grudgingly, "that though I have misgivings about all of this, I, too, believe it just may be the work of God."

"Great," Father Ray said sarcastically.

"Why do you say that?" asked Sister Genevieve, the nun surprised by Father Ray's response.

"Because if the kid managed to convince *you*," Father Ray answered with a smirk, "then this *is* for real."

13 – Three Times Rejected

"Sister Palladia!" Ursula exclaimed as she ran to her and embraced her. The nun wore the full maroon robes of her order but the small, wooden shield charm no longer hung from her leather necklace; in its stead was a round, metal circle bearing a calligraphic "C" set on a field of lilies. Noticing the change, Ursula asked, "Where's your shield charm?"

Sister Palladia hesitated as St. Saturnin's Marian shrine silently towered over her. Ursula patiently waited in the January cold yet the fourteen-year-old, as if constructed of the same metal as the statue, failed to register it. Her anticipation of the Pope's sanction of a Crusade rendered her impervious to the icy air: his blessings would give her an excuse to stand by Judas's side.

"I . . . ," began Sister Palladia, after which she hesitated again and then continued, "*decided* it was time to honor the Blessed Mother. Lilies are one of her symbolic representations."

"What's wrong?" Ursula inquired with concern, the teenager puzzled by Sister Palladia's odd demeanor. Unable to meet the child's gaze, she bowed her head.

"I spoke with His Holiness, Ursula," replied Sister Palladia grimly. She turned her eyes to the soothing countenance of The Blessed Mother and prayed for the strength to fulfill her duties to the Church.

"What did he say?" Ursula asked. Sister Palladia's grave expression revealed the answer.

"There will be no Crusade," answered Sister Palladia, her disappointment palpable. Offering the youth a look of pity, she explained, "The Pope is reorganizing the Emerian Order and eliminating its martial functions. Permanently. Henceforth, it will be renamed The Order of Celsa, Servant of the Blessed Mother and Sister of Emerias."

"Why?!" Ursula cried as she plummeted from the height of her expectation. She demanded desperately, "Why would he do that?!"

Sister Palladia closed her eyes and bowed her head. Her hands trembling as she exhaled, she glanced sidelong at Ursula.

"He's doing it in the name of peace, and we must obey him," said Sister Palladia. Turning her back to Ursula, she explicated, "You see, during his election to the papacy, he said he thought of all the wars in the world and chose the name Francis after St. Francis of Assisi, a man of peace. We Emerians always hoped and worked and prayed for peace, but when peace was threatened by evil, we worked in a way that was not peaceful. The Holy Father does not want us *fighting* for peace any longer, and he most certainly does not want a holy war, even against the evil of human trafficking."

"What about all the girls like Tammy?" Ursula inquired acerbically, her ire surprising Sister Palladia as the nun turned to face her protégé. Astounded by the Pope's refusal and driven by the courageousness of her friends, Ursula declared, "Judas and I want to relieve their suffering and bring them peace. And we're going to do it."

"The Holy Father is our superior as sisters and as Catholics," argued Sister Palladia. Gesturing to underscore her point, she reasoned, "We may disagree with his commands but we must obey them. He has rendered his decision on this. There will be no Crusade."

"I'm not a sister," Ursula snapped, the fire in her tone giving Sister Palladia pause. Moving shoulder-to-shoulder with her, Ursula gazed on the statue and said, "Maybe it's time for the youth of the Church to change his mind."

"He will not change his mind, Ursula," advised Sister Palladia. Placing her hands on Ursula's shoulders, she said, "But he sincerely wishes for you to join us. He has pledged his total support in sharing your gift with the world in a peaceful, loving manner."

Ursula's anger cooled and her eyes became hazy. Watching her ponder the Pope's wishes, Sister Palladia felt her spirits rise.

"She may just agree," thought Sister Palladia with an intense eagerness and a barely perceptible shiver. Ursula grasped her hands, moved them off her shoulders and brought them together between their bodies.

"Tell him thanks, but no thanks," Ursula said as she demonstratively dropped Sister Palladia's hands, "and sorry, not sorry."

The teenager whirled around and left a dumbfounded Sister Palladia standing with mouth agape. Confident that she followed God's will, Ursula strode down the cobblestone path.

"You can do nothing without Papal approval, Ursula," shouted Sister Palladia in a last-ditch effort to dissuade her. Charlotte appeared from the evergreens ringing the shrine and, as her friend turned to face the nun, she loomed behind her.

"She already has," snarled Charlotte with fiery eyes and little regard for Sister Palladia's station. The two adolescents glared at her briefly before departing.

"What have I unleashed?" asked Sister Palladia aloud.

******

Watching the news coverage of the rally at the Youth Center, Father Ray indulged in, at least what he believed to be, well-earned cigars and whiskey. He propped up his feet on his desk and enjoyed the solitude of his office after his whirlwind day. A knock at the door ruined his mood.

"Damn it," Father Ray complained. The last confrontation of the day, a confrontation he wished to avoid but was inevitable, beckoned at his threshold. Ashing his cigar and taking a drink, he called out, "Enter!"

Appearing in her full sisterly garb, Sister Palladia stepped into the office and quickly shut the door. Father Ray gave her a dubious look when she locked it.

"You here to assassinate me?" Father Ray inquired half-jokingly. Sister Palladia moved to the front of his desk and displayed her haggard face beneath the glow of the track lighting. Father Ray's mirth disappeared and he asked, "What the hell happened to you?"

"The Pope denied Ursula's request," advised Sister Palladia without the usual strength of tone.

"Yeah, I know," Father Ray replied. He studied her countenance meticulously.

"Then you know you must divert their energies elsewhere," pleaded Sister Palladia. Managing to muster a hidden reserve of strength into her voice, she implored Father Ray, "And very soon at that. It is the year 2019. Crusading belongs to a bygone era and has no place in our times, and that includes the atrocities and senseless violence committed during them. Do you not remember the Children's Crusade of 1212 and how many of those youth simply disappeared? Some were rumored to have been sold into slavery, which is the very evil this 'Crusade' seeks to eradicate."

"Trust me, I once thought like you do," Father Ray said while pointing with the two fingers that held his cigar, "but those three teenagers are special and blessed by God. I couldn't stop them if I tried and I'm not sure the Holy Father can either."

"The Pope made his wishes perfectly clear on this matter," warned Sister Palladia, "and threatened excommunications for those who encourage it."

"Yeah? Well he might wanna check with his boss on that," Father Ray countered. He and Sister Palladia engaged in an optical battle as he shamelessly smoked his cigar and imbibed his whiskey. Father Ray finally said, "You know, I'm glad you came here tonight, Marybeth."

Father Ray's use of Sister Palladia's birth name struck a chord with each of them. Its pronunciation made the priest realize his longing for the nun and caused the nun considerable alarm over the priest's desire.

"My name is Palladia," scolded Sister Palladia. She retreated behind a chair, placed her hands on its backing and said, "*Sister* Palladia."

"These crazy kids won't need me for much longer, Marybeth," Father Ray reasoned. He stood up with cigar in hand and continued, "Once they're on their way, which could be any day now, I'm leaving the priesthood."

"Reynald, no!" objected Sister Palladia with palpable distress.

"The decision's already been made, sweetheart," Father Ray replied. Moving out from behind the desk, he approached her while saying, "I'm leaving . . . either with you or with Aubrey, and I'd much rather it be you, but – and of this I'm very certain – I'm not leaving alone."

"She's an ungodly woman," countered Sister Palladia. Utter astonishment washed over her comely face as she used the chair to shield herself from Father Ray's advance.

"And you're a godly one," Father Ray said with an outstretched hand and a smile. He added pointedly, "We can both leave this mess behind. Come with me."

"Reynald," mewled Sister Palladia, "with all my heart, *no*."

Absorbing the rejection he fully expected, Father Ray crossed off Sister Palladia in his mind and in his plans. He set his cigar in the crystal ash tray on his desk.

"The billionaire it is, then," Father Ray said with a sigh. Swallowing his emotions, Father Ray drained his glass and sauntered to the door. He unlocked and opened it, coldly uttering, "See ya' on the other side, Sister Palladia."

"Goodbye, Reynald," said Sister Palladia. She lingered for a few seconds but the stony gaze of Father Ray drove her from the room. Hurrying past him, she exited his office. The sound of the door slamming caused her to shudder and she sighed through tears, "God be with you."

14 – Not Anymore

Aubrey walked down the main aisle of the Cathedral of the Most Blessed Sacrament and admired its high ceilings and arches. Her heels clacked the entire way but she made no effort to muffle their sound.

"This is a little risky for you, inviting me here," Aubrey remarked as she ascended the steps of the apse. Passing two wooden candle stands, she sauntered up to the altar as if it were a bar and grabbed its edges with outstretched arms.

"The situation has changed," Archbishop Wunderlich replied. He did not venture even a quick glance at Aubrey but kept his hawkish gray eyes on the floor. Sitting in the celebrant's chair and dressed in complete archbishop regalia, he held his crosier in his left hand and let his right hand rest on his thigh.

"You have no idea," Aubrey said with sinister delight.

"I am not referring to the protests and those ignorant children's absurd calls for a crusade," grumbled Archbishop Wunderlich with disdain. He muttered with a grimace, "A crusade. *Fools.*"

"Neither was I," Aubrey said while folding her arms. Confused by the Archbishop's melancholy mood, she tilted her head and inquired with mock concern, "Why ya' so down there, Archie?"

"Because an exceptional opportunity may be arising. One, however, of which I cannot take advantage," explained Archbishop Wunderlich, the old cleric bereft of his usual ability to grasp the neck of serendipity. He ruminated for over thirty seconds before turning his gaze to Aubrey in a predatory manner and saying in jest, "Unless you've brought me a miracle."

"I take it you've got the defrocking plan in place," Aubrey replied, the billionaire forever concerned with her profit on any deal.

"Yes, yes," answered Archbishop Wunderlich despite having no such plan. He knew of Father Ray's intention to resign but kept it from Aubrey.

"So what's this opportunity?" Aubrey inquired, her interest and her intuition piqued by the Archbishop's secret.

"It is none of your concern," snarled Archbishop Wunderlich with a blistering gaze. His anger failed to daunt Aubrey.

"You know what, I think I forgot that 9-1-1 recording," Aubrey said as she feigned forgetfulness and threw up her arms in fake exasperation. The Archbishop sneered but, despite his better judgment, he decided on a desperate gamble.

"My seventy-ninth birthday is in two weeks and, when I reach age eighty, I can no longer be elevated to the office of Cardinal," explained Archbishop Wunderlich. He twice tapped his staff on the floor and waved his other hand dismissively, saying, "Even now the chances are miniscule."

"The fact that you're old is not a secret," Aubrey said. The Archbishop seethed but resolved to continue his revelation.

"It has come to my attention that the Pope is very ill, perhaps terminally," stated Archbishop Wunderlich without remorse or sorrow. Aubrey's smile faded as she pondered his words. The Archbishop added, "One does not need to be a cardinal to become Pope, but it would take an occurrence of miraculous character to elevate anyone but a cardinal to the Holy See. It may be my last chance at promotion."

"You must have someone buried pretty deep in the Vatican," commented Aubrey. She stalled for time as her devious genius, which was not attached in any way to scruples, whirred to life and she formulated a new course of action.

"I've been employed by the church since my twenties," said Archbishop Wunderlich. Bent with the gravity of the moment, he rose to his feet, hobbled to the altar and stated proudly, "I know personally and command the respect of holy men and women in every corner of the world."

"Except here where it counts, in your own backyard," Aubrey said, her words drawing the rapt attention of Archbishop Wunderlich. Gesticulating in a demonstrative and mesmerizing manner, she expounded, "Let me paint a picture for you, Archie. A spiritual leader lends his support to a fledgling movement in his own archdiocese and backs an army of teenagers in their daring quest to end the sexual exploitation of children. Their efforts, at least in the minds of the faithful, wash away the stains left on the Church by pedophiliac priests and elevate Catholicism back to respectability in the world. To advise his child crusaders, he appoints the priest whom they trust and who's served as their spiritual guide for years. He finds a financial backer, a gorgeous, philanthropic billionaire with boatloads of cash, which she pours into the crusade as she works closely with the priest and develops a very special relationship with him."

"It's not enough," argued Archbishop Wunderlich although Aubrey's spell already wrapped its slimy tentacles around his brain and bolstered his ego.

"It is if one of the child crusaders can heal the sick," stated Aubrey with a seriousness that struck the old man's heart. Stunned by her revelation, the Archbishop dropped his staff and it clattered on the floor. Aubrey waited for the echoes to subside and, with a smug grin, said, "Admit it, Archie. I'm amazing."

******

Two Youth Center staff escorted Judas to the after-hours entrance on the east side of the building. He thanked God for his first taste of freedom in days as he emerged from the door wearing his cross-bearing jacket. Waiting outside for him was Father Ray with his arms folded but no cigar.

"Come, Simon Barjona!" beckoned Father Ray with a demonstrative wave to Judas, "We are to become fishers of men!"

The Youth Center staff shot Father Ray weird looks and then disappeared into the building. Judas, however, grinned at the priest.

"How did you do it?" Judas inquired after a long pause, the youth bewildered by his unexpected release. Father Ray smirked.

"I didn't," admitted Father Ray. Judas chuckled and approached the priest, mentor and mentee embracing while patting each other on the back. Proceeding to Father Ray's truck, Judas listened as he explained, "Tammy and Ursula saved your bacon by staging that demonstration. Those girls are something else, and you'll have to see Tammy's video. She put a hell of a lot on the line for you."

"How is she?" Judas interjected though even he was not sure if he asked about Tammy or Ursula.

"I take it you mean Tammy? She's fine and safely tucked away in a hospital bed like you asked," answered Father Ray, "but I wouldn't expect her to listen like that again . . . it could be years."

Judas smiled. He loved Tammy's ferocious, independent spirit but even her sacrifice could not drive Ursula from his mind. Father Ray and Judas stopped at the tailgate of Father Ray's truck.

"As for the legal end of things," continued Father Ray, "after the social media turmoil and news frenzy those two caused, the County Prosecutor decided your case was too hot to handle and dropped the charges, and the other jurisdictions don't want anything to do with you, either. Prosecuting you brings bad mojo in this age of mob rule by public opinion. Of course, your probate judge wants to see you now and I doubt she'll be as forgiving. She's never liked your tendency to AWOL whenever you feel like it."

Judas barely perceived Father Ray's words, the teenager distracted by conflicting thoughts of Tammy and Ursula. He missed them both, Tammy more urgently and Ursula more deeply. Father Ray read his mind.

"You'd better figure out how to handle those two," suggested Father Ray.

"There's nothing to handle. Ursula's giving her life to God," Judas replied. The issue clearly unnerved and saddened him, however, and his face showed it. Cramming his emotions deep into the pits of his spirit, he added, "Besides, I'm with Tammy now."

"That's true," said Father Ray as he patted the edge of the truck, "and Tammy's a great kid, but I wouldn't give up on Ursula. Not yet."

"Why?" Judas inquired with a puzzled look. Father Ray and Judas walked along opposite sides of the truck bed and stopped just before its cab.

"Very few things last, Judas," advised Father Ray with the image of a younger Sister Palladia haunting him. Offering his mentee a pointed look, he said, "Most are only temporary . . . and they can fade away in an instant."

******

Father Ray sat on the first step of St. Saturnin's altar dais with his elbows on his knees. He held a lit cigar in his right hand and a small, half-empty bottle of whiskey in the other. The Church was dim as only the nighttime security lights shone through the darkness.

"What would God say about smoking and drinking in His house, Father?" asked Ursula without any judgment in her tone.

"He hasn't said one damn word so I think he's giving me a pass tonight," Father Ray answered, the priest unperturbed by Ursula's question. She heard the sloshing of alcohol as he drank from the cap-less bottle. Puffing on his cigar and staring into the floor, Father Ray said, "Times are a' changin' Ursula."

"They're getting better, Father," replied Ursula with a serious-yet-hopeful mien.

"I knew God was going to spare you the night you were attacked," Father Ray mused, his reference to the incident causing Ursula's skin to crawl. She replaced her hopeful expression with a pained one as he explained, "What I didn't know was *why* he was going to spare you. And I asked him that night. Why would he mar your pretty face like that and leave you alive? It just didn't make sense to me . . . and he waited a long time to let it finally sink in."

"Like you said, it's my cross," advised Ursula without doubt or hesitation despite being unnerved by the memory of the attack, "and a permanent reminder to stay humble even though I've been given a great gift."

"Yeah, maybe," Father Ray said with a shrug of his shoulders and an ugly look. The sourness of his face gave way to sternness and, while waving the two fingers which held his cigar at Ursula, he uttered, "But it was also for the two of you to be together. That boy needs you and he always will. All it would take would be for you to leave his side and he could stumble onto the wrong path, wunderkind though he is."

Ursula's suddenly watery eyes widened in astonishment. Two tears escaped and rolled down her cheeks.

"He's with Tammy now," scoffed Ursula, "and I've taken a vow of celibacy."

Father Ray smiled evilly and swigged from the whiskey bottle. Ursula shivered in response to the deviousness oozing from her spiritual guide.

"A *temporary* vow of celibacy," Father Ray corrected her.

"It'll be permanent soon," countered Ursula, the teenager growing indignant.

"Well, before that happens, you might wanna take a look at this," Father Ray said ominously while rummaging around in his jacket pockets. He, after a protracted search, produced a photograph and held it out in his hand. Ursula was reluctant to accept it and watched it warily.

"What is it?" asked Ursula.

"It's not gonna bite ya," Father Ray said with a chuckle. He intentionally let the moment hang and then added with feigned innocence, "It's just a picture."

"Of who?" demanded Ursula. A small flame of curiosity ignited in her spirit and burned away the edges of her fear.

"Someone very special to Judas," Father Ray stated with particular relish. He thrust it closer to her and urged, "Take it."

Ursula hesitated but then cagily stepped forward and plucked the photograph from Father Ray's hand. Her eyes lingered on him for several second before she lifted the photograph and allowed herself to look at it. Horrible scarring marred a woman's face, her disfigurement evidently caused by severe burns. Her sparse, stringy hair and mannequin-like appearance disturbed Ursula.

"Who is this?" asked a distressed Ursula.

"Judas's mother," Father Ray answered slowly. Tears streamed down Ursula's face though she made no sound. Father Ray stood up and, doused in a wave of sorrow and pity, explained, "She was caught in housefire when he was six. Died of complications a few years later. His Dad bolted early on so she was all he had. It's amazing that kid's as well-adjusted as he is."

"Why did you show me this?" mewled Ursula, her heart breaking for Judas.

"To prove to you that Judas was designed by God especially for you," Father Ray said as he stifled his emotions. Overwhelmed by the revelation, Ursula's tears dried and she gazed on him with piercing eyes. Father Ray added cynically, "He needs you, you need him, ya' know, all that wonderful, storybook garbage."

"What about Tammy?" inquired Ursula.

"His mother didn't lose part of her foot, kid," Father Ray replied. He lifted the bottle to his lips, took several gulps and then said, "Tammy's tied up in his story but she's not his answer."

"Can I keep this?" asked Ursula as an eerie calm settled over her. She studied the photograph intensely.

"Sure, kid," Father Ray said, the priest taking his turn at being unnerved. Ursula's eyes fell to the floor and, with a slow, dramatic rotation, she faced towards the exit of the church and languidly departed. Watching her every step, Father Ray observed her pass the doors and disappear into the darkness.

"How dare you interfere like that," Sister Palladia chastised Father Ray as she emerged from the shadows. Father Ray felt her glower but did not meet it.

"You know what, *Marybeth*?" asked Father Ray acerbically. Walking away from her in a trail of cigar smoke, he growled, "*Get the hell outta my church.*"

"It's God's will that she head the Order someday, and I don't believe that day to be far off," said Sister Palladia bitterly. Towering over Father Ray on the altar dais, she continued, "Besides, they're just children, Reynald."

"Not anymore," Father Ray replied as he took a final swig of whiskey and departed.

"*Not anymore.*"

THE END

NOVELS BY JOSHUA R. FIELDS

A Dog Among Thorns. Descending on the post-apocalyptic city of Kaiser in a flurry of vulgarity and vitriol, the towheaded demon Miriam hunts the weak in spirit and the unlucky in love. Men mired in turbulent romantic relationships lose more than their faith in God as she manipulates them into taking their own lives. None of Miriam's victims survive her wily ways. Her latest mark, the brooding and sinful Jacob Gottschalk, seems easy prey until she discovers the Holy Spirit wards him from her very touch. Miriam's devious webs fail to ensnare him and she, instead of causing his downfall, becomes his reluctant-yet-loving protector. That impassioned defense, however, raises the ire of the most powerful person in Kaiser: Elizabeth Nicks, Jacob's wife and the city's Constable. The resulting war between the two women threatens to destroy them all as Miriam's penchant for carnage flourishes and Elizabeth confronts the dangers of the demonic world. Hurtling towards their intertwined destinies, the three troubled lovers enter a tempest of gory violence, romantic intrigue, shifting political alliances and the evil schemes of conniving spiritual beings.

Girls Without Gods. Emerging from the fog of her war with Elizabeth for Jacob's heart, a victorious Miriam departs Kaiser with her prize. The demon and her unlikely paramour travel to the fantastical skyscraper of Chinese Peak, an opulent casino that flourishes in the post-apocalyptic world. Miriam's evil nature and savage jealousy, however, clash with Jacob's spiritual growth and reluctance to abandon his marriage. The resultant emotional conflict threatens to tear their fledgling relationship apart at the seams. Elizabeth, meanwhile, remains in Kaiser, the Constable refusing to pursue her husband and his "demon whore." Yet the spiritual world forces her hand when Miriam's former handler, the demon Marcion, possesses her teenage daughter and absconds with her. Desperate to rescue her oldest child, Elizabeth travels to Chinese Peak seeking the aid of Jacob and Miriam in hunting down her child's abductor. Thrust together once again in sea of unbridled decadence, Jacob, Elizabeth and Miriam encounter a constantly evolving kaleidoscope of nefarious schemes, political intrigues, old lovers, new threats and alluring temptations. The deadly demonic gauntlet through which they tread promises but one simple truth: loss is inevitable.

A Dog Returns to its Own. Months after banishing his demonic lover, Miriam, to the Abyss, Jacob Gottschalk travels into the frigid Canadian wilderness to rescue the corpses of his possessed stepdaughters and properly lay them to rest. The violent and insatiable Sophie lures him from the narrow way, however, and, blinded by his waning faith, he fails to detect the terrible secret she hides. His fortunes seemingly improve upon his arrival at New Oneida, an esoteric Christian settlement located in a pristine river valley. Its leader, Dr. Irinushka Zhukova, tempts Jacob with many beautiful vessels of spiritual purity and seeks to create in him a wellspring of the Holy Spirit.

Hundreds of miles to the south, Miriam - newly paroled from the Abyss by an unexpectedly merciful God - searches Kaiser for Jacob. She discovers her paramour has fled the City but encounters Sarah, the nun hiding a precious secret of her own, and Darby, who teeters on the edge of sanity due to the brutal loss of her family. Together, in an unlikely and tenuous alliance, they flee Kaiser and its vicissitudes and journey north with a powerful new ally to find Jacob.

Unbeknownst to them all, a greater spiritual storm stains the skies of their future and threatens all those who dwell upon the face of the earth. Facing a terrible new evil and the destruction of everyone he loves, a stoic Jacob holds on desperately to the words of Christ: "But the one who endures to the end, he shall be saved."

'85 Love Affair. Ten years after the unexpected and tragic deaths of their parents, siblings Elliott Warden and Emma Hastings enter 1985 in very different places. Emma, as matriarch of a loving family and owner of the successful club Johnny Dubs, prospers but Elliott, lost in a meaningless career and a sea of shallow relationships, flounders.

The return to Michigan of his high school sweetheart and her best friend, Donna, provides Emma the perfect excuse to intervene in her brother's love life. Her machinations quickly go awry after the arrival of a pretty, young waitress with a heart of gold and a vivacious, talented and beautiful musician with a soon-to-be fiancée. Believing Elliott to be courting romantic disaster with the younger women, Emma makes several risky plays to finally set him on the path to wedded bliss with Donna. Elliott has other ideas, however, and seems destined to make 1985 one hell of a year.

'86 Love Affair. New Year's Day 1986 dawns with Elliott holding his glittering prize, the young and pretty Nora, while his former best friend, the effervescent and beautiful Toni, celebrates her engagement to Bobby on a fantastical cruise ship in the Caribbean. Even Emma, Elliott's sister and indefatigable architect of his love life, surrenders her dream of Elliott's reunion with her best friend and his high school sweetheart, Donna. The ties that bind prove unexpectedly fragile, however, and, as they unravel and snap, seemingly unbreakable romances are thrown into doubt and turmoil. Beset by shocking secrets and fateful surprises, new ties form and all hearts soon learn that 1986 will be a year like no other.